HAITI, LOVE AND MURDER... IN THE SEASON OF SOUP JOUMOU

D1713324

Michael Matza

Cover painting:
Clairvius Narcisse (Lo Zombie Haitiano) by Fabrizio Inglese
Book Design: Fanlight Books

"Yo pa voye wòch sou mango vèt"

You don't throw rocks at a green mango;
you wait until it's ripe to knock it down.

Creole Proverb

For Linda, who inspires my everything.

Mole Saint-Nicolas

Baie de Henne

Ile de la Gonave

La Ca

Grande Cayemite

Jeremie

Dame-Marie

Anse d'Hainault

Pestel

Petite Trou de Nippes

Miragoan

Les Anglais

Aquin

Les Cayes

Cote

Port-Salut

Ile a Vache

CHAPTER ONE
Charlie, years before

No water. No electricity. No ambulances. Tanks charging by with machine guns blazing. After two weeks under siege in the ravaged West Bank, everything, everywhere, wore a coat of dust as fine as talc. Deserted streets swarmed with flies where blood pools curdled. On the ground amid the turmoil, Charlie Carter was in his element.

A temporary ceasefire had brought out the press corps. Charlie and a Brit who writes for The Telegraph had teamed up and headed straight for the home of an Arab doctor who worked for Save the Children but couldn't save one of his own – a baby girl born prematurely during the height of the fighting.

Charlie and the Brit, who speaks a little Arabic, were chasing that story in Charlie's silver Isuzu Trooper, plastered with red adhesive tape to identify them as media, as if being non-combatants would somehow protect them. Charlie poked fun at such magical thinking but put his faith in it anyway.

They had set out cautiously then froze before a mammoth Merkava tank, 70 tons of killing machine positioned diagonally across a deserted intersection.

Charlie waited anxiously, not knowing if it was safe to proceed.

Ballsy and unflappable, the Brit, Alan, hopped out,

leaving his cell phone cradled in the charger. "I'll find out."

Charlie watched him tiptoe up to the tank, hands in the air, and disappear behind it.

A minute went by. Nothing … Another minute. Still nothing. Charlie was scoping out the landscape to his left when suddenly, *pfft … pfft … pfft*, three bursts of automatic weapons fire that appeared to come from the hillside he was looking at.

Oh shit, where's Alan? What's happening? Why the fuck didn't he take his phone? Who's shooting? From where exactly?

The tank barked back … a thunderous blast that wobbled the Trooper's suspension, denuded a part of the hillside and left a puff of smoke.

It's the hill, it's coming from the hill.

Charlie frantically processed the scene, trying to widen his peripheral vision, to get the big picture, to make sense of it. Too late. Another round of auto-fire, and another gut-shaking retort from the tank.

Now Charlie was panicking. Pull back? Go forward? His sphincter spasmed. His heart thrummed in his ears. Dear God, where is safety?

His mind swam. Every instinct said retreat. Okay, now! It's ride or die.

He slammed the car into reverse, twisted his body, threw his right arm over the seat back and swerved backwards 100 yards to the lee side of an abandoned warehouse that he hoped would shield him from the hillside sniper.

Exhaling, he knew it was his best move. But in his rush to hide, he drew the attention of the tank, whose cannon turned in the mechanical slow-motion way of a

Velociraptor. Staring into the muzzle of the cannon, realizing he was in the tank's crosshairs, his blood ran cold. He raised his open hands above the dashboard in a gesture of surrender.

Oh fuck, fuck, fuck, fuck fuck! He pinned his eyes to the pivoting cannon. Don't sneeze, don't move a fucking muscle. Pray to God that nobody in that tank sneezes either.

The cannon stared Charlie down for an eternal minute then slowly swung away. Lethal one minute. Disinterested the next. The exchange of fire between sniper and tank ended as unexpectedly as it had begun. The lanky Brit emerged from behind the Merkava and speed-walked back to the Trooper. "They're not letting us through."

CHAPTER TWO
Corinne, on the warpath

The griping began in the nurses' break room and carried on outside the Truro hospital when Corinne's night shift ended. It was 8 a.m. The sidewalk teemed with office workers balancing take-out cups and shoulder bags. A corner newsstand hyped a headline: "Dead in their beds."

Scandalous under-staffing had contributed to hundreds of unnecessary hospital deaths. Britain's National Health Service responded with new guidelines, setting a limit of eight patients per nurse per shift. Corinne was accustomed to difficult working conditions. Everything about Haiti after the 2010 earthquake, where she had volunteered, was dire in every way. But she expected better from her native England.

Passionate and fulminating, Corinne Martin was in her element too.

"One-to-eight, that buys us what? Seven and a half minutes per patient per hour?" she grumbled. "What can we do in seven and a half minutes? Make a cup of tea? Strip and make two beds? Start CPR, knowing that three minutes without oxygen leaves our patient dead or brain dead? It's not just dangerous. It's *bloody unconscionable*."

Medical-surgical nursing is a cornerstone of the profession. Corinne had a knack for it, with the personality to cajole cooperation from even the most non-compliant patients. But the new NHS guidelines left her aching for a change. Humanitarian field work, providing direct medical assistance to vulnerable people, held enormous appeal. The more she read about "The Jungle," the infamous refugee camp in Calais, France, the more she wanted to go there and help. Thousands of desperate families from all over the war-torn world were barely surviving in the old, damp camp while they hoped for asylum on continental Europe or in the U.K. if they could stow away on a train or lorry through the Channel Tunnel.

Online at home that night and still angry about the nurse-patient ratio, she poured herself a glass of white wine. She opened her laptop and contacted the charity Care4Calais to offer herself as a Jungle volunteer during her upcoming week of vacation. Accepted by the charity, she prepped by discreetly pillaging her hospital's store-room for a thermometer, otoscope, pulse oximeter, surgical shears and strips for testing blood and urine.

Situated in a patchy forest beside a highway, the Jungle was a springboard to freedom for some refugees, or the dead end of their desperate journeys, where all hope died. On her first day, Corinne's eyes fell upon heaps of ruined clothing and shoes, blue tarps on off-kilter wooden frames made of cannibalized shipping palettes. At the edge of the camp, she saw six fresh graves for people who died trying to break into lorries or hop aboard moving trains. A putrid queue of 20 mobile lavatories overflowed with waste. In a shack labeled Infirmerie, she examined her first patients, a Syrian couple and their six-year-old son. An interpreter explained that they had walked for weeks from Daraa, the Syrian town outside of Damascus where the uprising against Bashar Assad began.

Early in their journey the father had stepped on a nail, which went straight through his right shoe and foot. Unwilling to sidetrack their escape, he removed the nail himself, bound the wound with a strip of fabric torn from a towel, jammed the oozing mess inside his boot, and limped on. By the time he arrived at the Jungle, a virtual cement of coagulated blood, sweat and mud had fused the boot to his foot. The first nurse he saw at the reception center was unable to free the foot.

Then Corinne tried. She gently heated a liter of bottled water over a backpacking stove, filled a bucket she found lying around and plunged the man's foot in. "Tell him to stay like that for at least an hour," she told the interpreter.

While the husband's foot was stewing, Corinne treated the wife for a respiratory infection and the son for scabies.

The warm water softened the leather of the boot and Corinne attacked it with her surgical shears. The man howled. The eye-watering stench of the wound was overpowering. Corinne moved in for a better look, holding her breath behind her surgical mask.

Ugh … blackening … gangrene.

Working through the chain of command, she arranged to have the man transferred to the nearby Medecins Sans Frontieres clinic, a critical move, which she later learned had arrested the infection and saved the foot.

In the squalor of the Jungle camp, she felt a rush of renewed purpose, and thought again about her time in Haiti.

She returned to her job at the Truro hospital, but not for long.

CHAPTER THREE
Desire at Haiti's Hotel Le Désir

"Could I be obnoxious for a minute?" That was Charlie, playing peek-a-boo behind a fat brown bottle of Prestige.

"Could you not be obnoxious, even for a minute?" That was Corinne.

And that's the way it was with them.

Long-time friends, chummy but never fully intimate, snarky and swinging at every straight line with the gallows humor of first responders.

He had been instantly intoxicated by her incandescent smile on the night they met 10 years ago. She had loved the way his hazel eyes cut furtive glances at her. Both had enjoyed flirting as edgy young professionals, mainlining adrenalin, avoiding commitment.

Seeing her now, a decade on, and hearing her husky chuckle, he was smitten again.

They had met in the fractured aftermath of Haiti's 2010 earthquake, with 230,000 people dead, bodies ferried in dump trucks to the mass burial pits at Titanyen, scared survivors panicked by the aftershocks, hobbled amputees wrapped in blood-tinged gauze and a country that barely stands upright on its best days, cut off at the knees once again.

Corinne Martin, 27 at the time of the quake, was a nurse-midwife who came over from England a month before the terrible *tremblemant de terre* with the goal of providing maternity care at a clinic where she volunteered. Smart and committed, she began learning Creole. Since her earliest days in school, she was a dry sponge for language and culture.

A wiry brunette with curls that danced above dark brows, she was a MacGuyver in the clinic, making do with whatever meager resources she could scrounge in her shabby hospital 70 miles north of Port-au-Prince. Getting there from the capital meant traveling on a treacherous mountain road that lacked guardrails and was dotted with lashed-stick crosses and Vodou talismans to mark the places where people had died.

Set back from a rutted-dirt road that turned to ochre slop whenever it rained, the 100-bed hospital in Hinche lacked everything, including running water in the wards and screens on the windows. It was the kind of place where pregnant women delivered on bare gurneys – unless they brought their own bed sheets. Bedside buckets were their only toilets. Electricity was sporadic; defibrillators were non-existent. Once, a patient went into cardiac arrest as Corinne was passing through the intensive care unit. As its poorly-trained staff stood by nervously, unsure of what to do, she leapt onto the gurney – to the staff's astonishment - and began administering powerful chest compressions, but too late to save the patient.

"Intensive care?" she'd scoff. "Bollocks! There is no care. It's Death's doorstep. No defibrillator? Well, improvise! Do what you can, with whatever you have."

After the earth stopped shaking on that calamitous day, Corinne had taken personal leave from the clinic. Located in Hinche, a long way from the epicenter, it was unscathed, so she decamped to Port-au-Prince to do triage under an immense white tent erected for medical relief teams. The Cubans, Haiti's Caribbean neighbors, were among the first foreign doctors on the scene. They and the Israelis. Eventually, the U.S. Navy's hospital ship, USNS Comfort, anchored in the harbor off the ruptured capital. Its fully equipped operating suites took on the most severe cases.

Charlie Carter - Charles III on his dog-eared passport - was born in Paris to a French magazine writer and her husband, an American exporter of wine, who still lived in France. He was the third in the family's line of Charlies and they called him Trey. Foxhole buddies from the conflict zones where he had reported nicknamed him C-squared. If you wanted to piss him off you called him CeeCee.

Fluent in English and French – but struggling in Creole - he had worked for the New York Daily News after graduating from Columbia Journalism School and eventually landed as a staff writer at the Boston Globe. Thirty-three years old at the time of the quake, he had the energy, good looks and savoir faire to land plum foreign assignments. He was cocky, but with battlefield experience to back it up. Although he was born too late to have crossed paths with Edward R. Murrow, he liked to think of himself as in the mold of "Murrow's boys," living an updated version of the dashing foreign correspondent cliché - with a black leather jacket instead of a trench coat, and a featherweight Surface Pro instead of a heavy, battered Corona 3.

Charlie was passionate about covering the news, so much so that his wife, Molly, a freelance graphic artist whom he married two years after the quake, felt she often played second fiddle to the world's *crise du jour*. Whenever a breaking story beckoned, Charlie could become mindless of birthdays, anniversaries, holidays, parties with friends. Their apartment in Somerville, never a real home to him, was more like a way station where he parked his "go bag" en route to the next terrorist attack, military incursion, or tsunami. In the end, it wasn't another woman that broke them up. It was another story - the 2015 Charlie Hebdo massacre in Paris. In the two weeks that Charlie had spent covering that gore and its aftermath he managed to miss their anniversary, Molly's birthday, and her sister's wedding. A perfect trifecta of personal irresponsibility. Twelve people were murdered by Islamic terrorists in that horrifying incident, but for Molly it marked the death of their marriage. "You are a selfish man," she said when she left him. "But you're not in control. You let the newspaper rule your life."

Among journalists, Charlie was a bit player in the "bang-bang club," the veteran "hacks" who ran around in conflict zones, dodged bullets, managed to survive, smoked nargilas in the Middle East, chewed coca leaves in Central America, brought back Russian nesting dolls after covering the war in Chechnya, and somehow lived to witness another day.

That was it. You weren't living unless you were on or near the front lines somewhere, witnessing, running from one story to the next, fueled by coffee, cigarettes, camaraderie, adrenaline and the occasional "attaboy" email from an editor back home. Even then Charlie knew it was a rash way to live, high wiring above catastrophe after catastrophe on the dangerous line between bravery and bravado.

The death of his marriage was just one part of the price he paid for all the witnessing – trying to be present for all the mayhem, and at the same time stand apart from the perilous events.

Courting danger over and over was a game of chance with diminishing odds, Charlie knew, recalling the great ones like Marie Colvin, Anthony Shadid, Tim Hetherington and Chris Hondros, all killed covering stupid wars. Deeply committed as writers and photojournalists, they perished in the line of duty, prompting an industry-wide gut check: Is any story worth dying for? That's the question that sometimes came up when the bang-bang boys, and the women among them, were down in their cups, drinking hard after deadline during what they liked to call a "cease-file." The consensus, drunk or sober: Every story seems worth it, and when something goes horribly wrong they are reminded of the stakes.

"Keep your head down over there," a top editor once advised Charlie, with a been-there-done-that bravado.

"I keep my head up," said a cocky Charlie. "It's how I see things."

At times he could be too cocky for his own good, like the night rushing to the scene of a suicide bombing in Jerusalem, when he tried to bull his way past an Israeli soldier at a military checkpoint and had his shirt nearly ripped off his back, stretching the buttonholes to the size of quarters.

Now, 10 years after the quake, Corrine, the impatient healer, and Charlie, the headstrong professional witness, were seated at the Hotel Le Désir patio bar in Port-au-Prince, having a reunion in the place where their friendship began. Personally and professionally Haiti had gotten under their skin. It was almost inevitable that they would be drawn there again, though neither could have predicted that they would overlap, or that the vibe between them would be so fraught in a different way.

In the days following the earthquake, the Désir, on a hilltop overlooking the blue-gray sea of Cité Soleil Harbor, had been the base for arriving international media. Charlie had been lucky to snag a coral-colored bungalow before they all were occupied. The less lucky writers and TV crews who arrived late paid a lesser rate to sleep outdoors on deck chairs around the trapezoidal pool.

Within hours of the quake's eruption, the hotel was invaded by sat-phone-toting guests in tactical shirts, pants with endless hidden-zipper pockets and bouquets of press credentials dangling from lanyards. Weary cameramen, just back from documenting the rubble-strewn streets, grabbed catnaps on the chaise lounges and cuddled their video cameras like they were teddy bears. When the motel's supply of Prestige, Haiti's best-selling beer, was exhausted, drinkers dug deeper into expense accounts for Heinekens, which soon ran out too. Barbancourt, Haiti's premier rum, was everyone's go-to nightcap.

The Désir compound, surrounded by a concrete wall topped with embedded shards of broken glass, was the sort of place where business travelers found relative security, clean food, and a bed in a room with its own toilet and shower. In Haiti, that equaled lavish living. The earthquake transformed this *gens d'affaires* hotel into Media Central. Satellite dishes were positioned on the lawns beneath the palms and among the hedges of bougainvillea dripping with sprays of purple blossoms. Extension cords snaked everywhere.

Government officials in sport coats and ties sometimes held luncheon meetings there, escorted by armed men in camouflage pants tucked deep into their military boots. On many nights, an attractive Haitian couple, speaking Creole and passable English, sat on stools at the small bar, watching English football on TV and nursing their drinks. They'd ingratiate themselves with any Americans or Europeans who happened to be present. Then, months later, in a sob-story email, they'd plead for money. Who knows how often it worked? Even once would have been a bonanza.

The Désir also became the watering hole where relief workers, "disaster tourists" and NGO staffers had mingled and decompressed at night. That's what brought Corrine there, a week after the quake, along with another triage nurse and a doctor from the hospital where they volunteered. Seeing a chance to amplify his reporting, Charlie, Prestige in hand, had introduced himself and broke the ice by asking about the injuries they were treating.

"Lacerations and broken bones, all day. Plaster casts and endless stitches," said the doctor, slumped wearily over his beer.

"Compartment syndrome. It's the worst," Corinne had said, explaining that it occurs when a limb is so badly crushed that the veins, arteries and capillaries can't carry blood. Gangrene sets in, infection spreads, and unless the limb is amputated the patient very likely dies of septicemia.

"Awful," said Charlie.

"Bloody beastly," she said. "A miserable choice. Lose a limb or lose your life."

Over the next few days, Corinne worked at the hospital, Charlie reported from the streets, and each night they met at the Désir to debrief and drown their stress in alcohol in an atmosphere of ruin that somehow heightened the libido. Charlie had an extra bed in his room and on some nights Corinne crashed there. One night they fell asleep interlaced. She, still in her scrubs; he in a salty, sweat-stained tech shirt after a day of reporting that included watching a 30-year-old domestic worker, a victim of compartment syndrome, have her left arm amputated above the elbow by a U.S. medical relief team.

The poor woman got first-rate medical attention in one of Haiti's best hospitals, and still, Charlie noted as he related the story to Corinne, a flyswatter was standard equipment in the operating room.

Exhausted and emotionally drained one night, she and Charlie lay diagonally atop the bedspread on a beat-down mattress and listened to a sultry mix of Nina Simone and Sade on Charlie's MP-3 player - an essential bit of kit in the "go-bag" of veteran correspondents in those days. In the rare downtimes, it was nice to have soothing music.

Talked out and craving sleep, they clung to each other, fully clothed, and passed out. Hours later, Charlie stirred first. He felt her sleeping breath on his forearm. He heard the thud of her heart; the rush of her blood. His arm, tucked under her head, tingled with pins and needles but he hadn't moved it. He savored the closeness.

That was nearly a decade ago. They had kept in touch with the occasional flirtatious email. Privately they each wondered if their relationship could have ever been more than a friendship. She had heard about his divorce, although they had never spoken about it. He had stalked her on Facebook, "liking" the pictures that she posted from Haiti, where she was working full time now.

He had returned to Haiti once again to write about a medical clinic in Cité Soleil, the sprawling slum of tin-roofed shanties visible in the distance from the Désir patio. The clinic, a converted cinder block house, had been used by a notorious gang to hold hostages for ransom. How it came to be transformed into a health center supported by an American NGO was the heart of the story.

Out of habit he holed up at the Désir. He checked in, threw on a clean white tee shirt and khaki cargo shorts and called Corinne. She came down from Hinche on her next day off.

He was accustomed to seeing her in scrubs, but she arrived in jeans, an embroidered blue tunic and pink Crocs. "Ther-ere she is," Charlie crooned, spoofing the Miss America anthem.

Corinne looked uncomfortable being the center of attention and Charlie immediately sensed something was wrong. His normally intrepid friend seemed nervous. She chose a table behind a breeze-block divider where the wall pocketed into a private alcove. Charlie grabbed two Prestiges from the bartender - *Mesi, mesye*, that much Creole he knew - and joined her.

He told her how good it was to see her. He asked about her job and if she had kept up with some of the people they knew in common.

"You remember Chris, right? Hondros? Killed in Libya. Tim too. Hetherington. A Brit like you. Such talented sweet guys."

"I heard," said Corinne. "Gutting."

They spent more time catching up on what the other had been doing the last few years.

Charlie reminded her about his reporting from the Middle East during the Second Intifada. Back then, as she knew from their previous conversations, he had covered many suicide bombings, airstrikes in Gaza and failed peace negotiations.

He spoke about the intervening years, during which he returned to cover the growing Israeli settler movement, the election that brought Hamas to power in Gaza, and the political maneuvers by Prime Minister Benjamin Netanyahu to cling to power.

"Don't let anyone in the Middle East tell you they want balanced reporting of the Israeli-Palestinian conflict," he said. "They want unrelentingly sympathetic coverage of their side."

She told him about the impoverished villages in the Haitian countryside where she traveled to meet women who walked all night for the chance to have a prenatal check-up. She talked about the pregnancy complication called eclampsia, a perfect storm of high blood pressure, nausea and abdominal pain, which can lead to life-threatening seizures. "In America or England, it is usually treatable," she said. "In Haiti, too often it's a killer."

With a few sips left in his Prestige, Charlie noticed that every time someone entered the bar area, Corinne's eyes darted fearfully toward the portal.

"Expecting someone?"

"Don't be a twat," she said, rhyming it with "cat" in the British way.

"How are you, really? The person I'm looking at doesn't seem like the Corinne I know. What happened?"

Corinne propped a hand against her forehead. She swallowed and lowered her eyes.

"I don't know. … I never felt scared here before. Now I do."

Concerned about his friend, Mr. Can-I-be-Obnoxious toned it down.

"Of all people, you know that Haiti is a constant challenge. It is the beauty of "mountains beyond mountains," and a daily horror show. You've always known that. So what's got someone like you so spooked?"

Mountains Beyond Mountains, by Tracy Kidder, was the book about Dr. Paul Farmer, founder of the highly-regarded NGO, Partners in Health, which Charlie had read and had loaned to Corinne. She in turn had loaned him Herbert Gold's Haiti memoir, *Best Nightmare on Earth*.

Each respected Haiti's culture and history as the world's first free Black Republic.

But Haiti also was the place where foreign troops stationed as United Nations peacekeepers - known by the French acronym MINUSTAH - had coerced hungry 10-year-olds to perform oral sex for the promise of a candy bar. It was the place where those same troops left behind thousands of children conceived in one-night stands, and where the U.N.'s failure to properly dispose of the troops' human waste had triggered a devastating cholera epidemic.

"Okay," Corinne finally blurted. "Someone I know was murdered last month. … "

"Whoa … What? … Murdered? Who?"

"A doctor I worked with."

"Why?"

"I'm not sure, but I have some pretty strong suspicions. Can't get into it. Not here. If they knew what I think I know …" She shook her head.

"If who knew?"

"The people who had him killed."

"Was your friend mixed up with bad people?"

"He wasn't mixed up. But they are bad. Very bad."

"I said you look good. I lied. You look tired. Terribly tired. What's going on?"

"I'm not sleeping." Corinne's eyes flooded. She bit her bottom lip. "I can't get the horrible image of Sanctis' face out of my head."

"Sanctis?"

"That's his name. They killed him, Charlie. They murdered him and cut out his eyes!"

CHAPTER FOUR
Liberty in a Soup

Haiti was still in shambles as the first anniversary of the quake approached. The gleaming presidential palace in Port-au-Prince lay in ruins, a broken-back white whale bleaching in the sun. Across the street on the Champs de Mars, people made homeless by the devastation expanded and embellished the tent city that had taken hold there just hours after the rumbling ended.

Blue plastic tarps strung between broom handles and the trunks of scattered palm trees were beefed up with makeshift walls made of cardboard, tin scraps, scavenged plywood, and wooden pallets. Clotheslines groaned with wet shirts drying in the sun. A water-filled bladder the size of a school bus lying on its side served the needs of drinking and washing up.

It was as if everything these survivors knew about the world had to be forgotten and relearned.

Amid all the uncertainty, there were signs that life would go on. Under one tent a woman provided manicures for a few Haitian gourdes – about 10 cents - using nail polish that she had scrounged from the rubble of a collapsed pharmacy. Under a nearby tent, a barber cut hair. The quake had pancaked buildings and left an estimated 15 million cubic yards of rubble in Port-au-Prince, enough to fill 5,000 Olympic-sized swimming pools. A year later, less than a fifth of it had been cleared away, and across the country, mostly in the southern and western parts, more than one million people still lived in ramshackle shelters and temporary encampments. Adding to Haiti's misery was a continuing cholera epidemic that in its first year alone killed 3,000 people.

Dr. Sanctis Beauvoir was born in Miami in 1980, trained in medicine at Tulane University and was a resident in general medicine at a Tulane Hospital when the earthquake struck. Two days later his family got the devastating news that his Aunt Lorette, who lived in Leogane, the country's worst affected region, had been killed by a falling wall when the cathedral on the town's main square collapsed.

Beauvoir wanted to go to Haiti to help with the relief effort but his mother and father were in Miami, where the old man was fighting colon cancer, so their dutiful only child didn't go. For a few years he worked as a general practitioner at hospitals in Florida. After his father's death in 2016, an opportunity to work in Haiti presented itself and he accept the offer to work at Notre Dame des Miracles - snidely nicknamed Notre Dame des Douleurs - the dilapidated hospital in Hinche where Corinne worked too. They met on Beauvoir's first day and eventually shared long walks through rolling fields on their days off. One of their landmarks was a stand of trees that muscular sawyers used as a makeshift sawmill. Their last walk together was in 2020, on the tenth Christmas following the quake. Sanctis had confessed that he was homesick for the pace and ease of life in America - the comfort of warm beignets in New Orleans, the happy buzz around the student center at the University of Miami where his mother was a housekeeper, the serenity of breezy bike rides beside Biscayne Bay.

"Sometimes I really miss those things," he told Corinne. "But in Haiti I know I can do the most good."

The approach of January 1st for Haitians brought the season of soup joumou, a New Year's Day tradition. The squash-stock-based soup is said to date back to January 1, 1804, the day that enslaved revolutionary leader Jean-Jacques Dessalines declared Haiti's independence from its French colonizers. Legend has it that Haitian slaves were forbidden from eating soup joumou because it was a delicacy reserved for their white masters. Eating it after independence became symbolic of liberation, with each spoonful a reminder of the 12-year revolt that established the world's first black republic. "Liberty in a soup," a Haitian filmmaker had called it.

For Beauvoir, the soup was a comfort food that he enjoyed annually, even when he lived in America. He planned to prepare it and invite Corinne and a few other colleagues to his mustard-colored stucco bungalow on the edge of Hinche to share it on New Year's Day. The night before, on New Year's Eve, weather permitting, they would gaze at the glittery stars and winter constellations through his fancy tripod-mounted, computer-controlled telescope. An astronomy buff, he loved turning on his friends to the stark beauty of the pitch-black sky lit with planets and stars. "When you see Mercury or the rings of Saturn for the first time," he said, "it's visceral. You'll never forget it."

To prepare for the get-together, Sanctis went to the covered market in the heart of town to shop for the soup's ingredients. The place was a jumble of repurposed café umbrellas, droopy blue tarps, shadowy light and sun-wrinkled women balancing produce-filled baskets on their heads. It teemed with shoppers. Its ambient soundtrack was a thousand voices speaking at once. The merchants were mainly older women who sat crossed-legged on tatty blankets strewn with the produce they sold. Some sat on overturned crates. Almost all had kicked off their cheap rubber slides, which lay loose at their dusty bare feet. The little bits of raw meat and fish that were available in the market were not on ice. At times it seemed like the merchants' main job was shooing away flies, which they did with fans made of folded cardboard.

Corinne joined Sanctis for the shopping but was brought up short in front of a public-service poster that gave the address of a cholera clinic an hour south in Mirebalais. She had been inside such clinics, where each patient is on a wooden palette with a hole cut in the middle so their involuntary defecations could drop into a bucket below. In her native England, where hospitals are stocked with sterile IV fluids, patients could be rehydrated and expect to recuperate. In Haiti many died of uncontrolled diarrhea.

"They literally shit themselves to death," she told Sanctis. "It's wrong."

"The U.N. needs to fix this," he said. "You break it, you own it. MINUSTAH troops caused this. The U.N. needs to step up."

Squeezing past a man pushing a hand truck, Sanctis began looking for the ingredients on his shopping list: cabbage, carrots, turnips, scotch bonnet peppers and kabocha, a local cross between a pumpkin and a butternut squash -

fleshy orange on the inside - to be pureed for the base of the soup.

"*Konbyen?*" - How much? - he asked, pointing at a kabocha.

The merchant's head swiveled from Sanctis to Corinne and back to Sanctis.

"Hundred dollah," he said, stone-faced.

Sanctis was used to the hazing. He was obviously so much better off than the other shoppers that his transactions usually started off with a verbal affront in broken English.

He responded in perfectly accented Creole, lingering on the two syllables: *Ki-sa?* What's that?

When Sanctis began walking away, the merchant called after him, "*Trant gourdes,*" about 30 cents. Sanctis paid him and said nothing.

And so it went until the list was complete, down to the purchase of a dusty, dented can of beef stock. Buying the actual beef that would be cut into chunks and added to the pot was a challenge. He chose the piece with the fewest flies.

Sanctis had learned to cook soup joumou from his maternal grandmother, who had lived with him and his mother in Florida when he was a boy.

Step one in her recipe called for an overnight marinade for the meat by pureeing garlic, scallions, parsley, thyme, shallots and the scotch bonnets. After removing the meat from the marinade, he browned it in oil in a saucepan.

He brought the stock to a boil, tossed in the meat, reduced the heat and let it cook for 90 minutes.

The annual ritual meant more to him since the pass of his beloved *grann*.

He leaned over the saucepan, keeping his distance from the heat, and took a deep drag of its aroma.

He turned up the Kompa coming from his boombox, cracked open a Prestige and took a swig. He boiled the cut pieces of kabocha and mashed them. He added the vegetables to the stock and let them simmer for 20 minutes. Marrying the ingredients in one pot, he stirred until the soup thickened. Then he remembered that he wanted to serve it with citrus wedges. He called Corrine.

"Corinne *cherie, c'est Sanctis*. On your way over here will you please pick up some limes if you can find them?"

"*Tan lacho. Dako. Na we tale*," said Corinne, practicing her Creole. "Lime time. Okay. See ya soon."

While awaiting the arrival of his guests, Sanctis heard what sounded like the propane tank that fueled his stove fall off its concrete base. He went outside to have a look.

Dinner was called for 8. Around 8:15, Corinne and the others began showing up. Her knock at the door brought no response. She waited a minute and knocked harder. She called Sanctis' cell phone. No answer. She dialed again and thought she heard it ringing somewhere out behind the house. The guests trooped around back in the dark, guided by their cell phone flashlights.

There, half covered in weeds, lay Sanctis. It appeared he had been strangled with the rubber tubing of a stethoscope that was knotted around his neck.

Corinne shrieked. It looked like his eyes had been

replaced with jet black coals. Rivulets of coagulating blood rimmed the orbits and ran down his cheeks.

There was no sign of a break-in. No sign of a struggle. Peering through the half-open door Corinne noticed that Sanctis' prized, computerized telescope, a $1,200 gift to himself after he graduated medical school, was missing, although its tripod was set up outside.

Corinne knew Sanctis had wanted to stargaze that night with his friends. But what the hell had happened?

"Why? Who would do such a horrible thing?"

Corinne stared at Sanctis's mutilated face. A sour taste flooded her mouth. She ran to the edge of the dirt driveway and retched bile into the tall weeds.

In a country where police often fail to show up without seeking a bribe, saying they need "gas money" for their squad cars or some such pretense, no one held out much hope that the homicide of Sanctis Beauvoir would be solved any time soon.

Likewise, no one familiar with Haiti's culture of sorcery and superstition needed police to tell them the significance of the scooped-out eyes.

It is a belief among practitioners of witchcraft that the killer's image would have been the last thing that Sanctis saw and so the image would have been engraved on his retina for eternity. Looking into his lifeless eyes would reveal his killer. When hitmen steeped in superstition take a life, they take the eyes to cover their tracks.

CHAPTER FIVE
A secret side hustle

From the window of his office in the gray-stone administration building at Notre Dame des Douleurs, Dr. Reynard Pinay could see the morning-shift nurses arriving for work. Dressed in sea-green scrubs, some dismounted from the backs of rumbling motorbike-taxis – Haiti's ubiquitous motos. Others arrived in a crowded, garishly painted "tap-tap" bus emblazoned with red letters above the windshield, *Sang de Jesus*, Blood of Jesus.

They started work at 7 a.m., but it would be hours before Pinay, who walked with a pronounced limp, left his dimly lit office to make rounds. His awkward gait was due to fibular hemimelia, a birth defect that occurs when one shinbone is dramatically shorter than the other. Some days he skipped rounds altogether. As head of obstetrics, he was also on the board that ran the hospital. His office, shrouded behind heavy drapes and off-limits to everyone, held the locked filing cabinet that contained the hospital's inventory, calendar of deliveries and other business records. The donated supplies came from a variety of sources - the World Health Organization, the United Nations, the U.S. Agency for International Development, and private NGOs in America, China, Japan, and France. The boxed donations all were prominently marked "Not for Sale or Exchange."

On days when the shipments arrived, Pinay went to

the sheds behind the hospital's main building to oversee their storage. He wore a white shirt and tie snugged up to his prominent Adam's apple, even on the hottest days. His filthy, three-quarter-length white lab coat looked like it had never been washed. Like him, it smelled of Comme Il Faut cigarettes, Haiti's top-selling brand.

The shipments to the hospital included alcohol disinfectant wipes, bandages, surgical gloves, gauze compresses and surgical shears. Among the donated pharmaceuticals were amoxicillin, ciprofloxacin, ibuprofen, paracetamol and anti-fungal medications.

"Not there! Put them here!" Pinay barked, ordering the hospital's lanky porters to stack the boxes of drugs furthest from the loading dock door, away from the outdoor heat and humidity. "How many times do I have to tell you idiots?"

Pinay's grandfather had been a lieutenant in the Tontons Macoutes, the machete-wielding paramilitary goon squad formed during the regime of President Francois "Papa Doc" Duvalier in 1959.

Fearful that Haiti's military would overthrow him, Duvalier had cultivated the volunteer group of torturers, kidnappers and extortionists who went on to murder some 60,000 dissidents and hung many from lampposts to scare and destroy the opposition. Their name derives from a Creole myth about an uncle (Tonton) who punished naughty children by snaring them in a burlap sack (a Macoute) and hauled them off to be eaten.

In a country where so few people have a formal education, Pinay had graduated from Louverture Cleary, a prestigious Catholic boarding school, and went on to medical school at l'Universite d'Etat d'Haiti. In training he did a rotation at a well-regarded clinic treating people whose disabilities and psychic pain had touched him personally. He became skilled in the taping-and-bracing procedure used to treat clubfoot, a deformity caused when a too-short Achilles tendon forces a foot to rotate and turn under. Above the entrance to the clinic he hung a felt banner with a Haitian proverb: "*Avan ou ri moun bwete, gade jan ou mache,*" before you laugh at those who limp, check out the way you walk.

After a residency in obstetrics, he joined the public hospital in Hinche, eventually moving into management, which seemed to change him. He began to carry himself imperiously, as someone much smarter and more deserving than his patients. Much of the staff, including Corinne, found him difficult to deal with.

Choosing to be seen as someone who is intimidating was also part of his private revenge against the now-grownup classmates who had bullied him because of his deformity when he was growing up in Petionville.

The tormentors had left him on the sidelines whenever they had chosen teams for pick-up soccer games. They had called him *defo*, meaning defective, and shooed him away with the hands-flapping movement farmers use to chase off chickens. Since his first name, Reynard, means fox, they had called him *kase rena*, "broken fox," and roared with stupid laughter.

They had mimicked the wobble of his gait, which caused even his shoulders to roll and shake. They had pointed at his strange, high-laced shoes, with one heel-and-sole nearly five inches higher than the other.

They had put their shoes on the wrong feet, and had staggered around mocking him. It was their little game, and they were awful. The sting of the mistreatment lingered.

But now here he was, Doctor Reynard Pinay, hospital administrator, with power and financial security.

And where were they? Unemployed? Humping a delivery truck somewhere? Carrying a load of bricks up a scaffolding, or desperate for work? Scratching at some no-money job, hoping to inch up in status another block higher in the Delmas neighborhood of Port-au-Prince if they had even gotten that far?

Well, fuck them! thought Pinay. Fuck. Them.

CHAPTER SIX
Red-handed

It took three beers and a rum and Coke at the Desir before Corinne calmed down enough to make herself understood. Charlie had convinced her to stay a while and she was more comfortable speaking after the bar had thinned out. The setting sun bruised the sky over the distant water with a purplish light. When it appeared that they were the only ones left in the bar, she told Charlie about the general workings of the hospital and her dislike of the peevish Pinay.

"I don't trust him. I think he had Sanctis killed because Sanctis caught him embezzling,"

"And you know this, how?"

That was Charlie the journalist, for whom the sourcing always mattered.

"He told me. Sanctis told me."

It was during one of their early morning walks in the hills around Hinche, she said, that Sanctis had confided in her. He said he was on a break, alone and getting some fresh air behind the hospital's main building one day when he saw Pinay stamp out a cigarette, steal into the storage shed and emerge with the pockets of his filthy lab coat bulging with blister packs of pills. Seeing Sanctis eyeball him, Pinay scampered away, ambling like a fox, and haphazardly had dropped two packets before vanishing under a covered walkway. Examining the fallen packets, Sanctis saw they were from the inventory of donated anti-inflammatories.

"Not exactly Schedule I narcotics," said Charlie. "What are we talking about? Advil and Tylenol?"

Yeah, generics and other stuff, said Corinne, but by "cooking the books" - under-reporting deliveries in the hospital's records that he alone controlled - Pinay was able to pilfer thousands of pills, diverting hundreds of pounds of the donated medicines marked "not for sale or exchange" onto the street market of roaming pill vendors and profiting from the theft. "It's why he had Sanctis killed."

In Haiti, where any resourceful person with a plastic bucket and access to a cache of pills can be a "street pharmacist," purchasing medicines from these roaming street vendors is the norm. Pills are peddled just like candy or the ubiquitous palm-sized packets of clean drinking water that sell for pennies a packet. Most of the vendors use the same distinctive set-up: a colorful array of pill packets strapped with rubber bands around a cardboard cylinder that stands up inside of the bucket. Attached atop the cylinder is a pair of surgical shears which are used to snip off as many pills as a client wants from the blister packs. Selling medicines this way is technically illegal, but the laws are rarely enforced by the Ministry of Public Health and Population.

In fact, many customers prefer the informal street trade because government health services are unreliable and private clinics too expensive. Actual pharmacies sell medicines by the box. On the street it's possible to buy individual pills.

"Pinay, as a middleman-supplier, was cashing in," said

Corinne. "I'm sure what Sanctis saw was just the tip of the iceberg."

"Was Sanctis threatened?"

"He never said."

"You told me his fancy telescope was stolen. Sounds like a robbery that turned deadly."

"It's more. It's the pills."

"Maybe. But why take the risk and trouble to kill him?" said Charlie. "Corruption is endemic here. Everyone has a side hustle. Why would someone with Pinay's power fear Sanctis? What could he do to him?"

"I don't know. Ruin his sweet deal, for starters. And there must be other people involved. People in P-a-P. Middlemen. I don't know. People for whom taking a life might just be the cost of cleaning up after their dirty business."

"Have you told the authorities any of this?"

"No. When Sanctis told me I thought it sounded like Pinay being Pinay. Smarmy bastard. Stinking of tobacco, swanning around, helping himself to the hospital's stash for his own greedy purposes. Then, when Sanctis was murdered …"

"You thought Pinay was capable of more?"

"Yes. I was scared and angry that my friend was killed."

Charlie was skeptical. How could she be so sure? He hadn't heard anything that sounded like proof, just conjecture from an admittedly biased source. Corinne just didn't like Pinay, she had said as much, so she imagined the worst about him. But Charlie also had to leave open the possibility that she was right, and he wasn't about to repudiate the vehement suspicion of a distraught old friend, especially one who had triggered old passions in him that went beyond all reason. She was vulnerable, angry and beautiful in her outrage about her dead friend. He wanted to help her.

In reporting on the former hostage house turned health clinic in Cité Soleil, Charlie was assisted by a street-smart fixer named Maffi, who had good contacts in the slum where she had once worked with a humanitarian food-distribution program and came to know the rival gangs. He asked Corinne if he could discreetly run some of what she told him past Maffi to get her thoughts.

Corinne looked away. Then her head came back around to stare at Charlie, reading the lines of his bushy-browed face to see if the seriousness of her allegation was sinking in.

"Go ahead," she said. "But be so careful. I don't need these people coming after me."

CHAPTER SEVEN
Slavery's legacy

Maffi Frantz, aka "Maffi Tattoo," was among Haiti's most sought-after fixers. Charlie felt lucky to have her guide his reporting for $150 a day, plus $75 for Junior, her rough-looking driver in his greasy overalls and worn-out engineer's cap. His beat-up red Chevy pickup, covered in dents and splotches of gray primer paint, was as old and ragged as Haiti's hills. Working for foreign media at the rate of their per-diems, Junior and Maffi made more in a day than most Haitians make in a month.

Maffi was born in Haiti and was 16 when she slipped into Brooklyn without immigration papers in 1996, two months before her daughter was born. A year after that, the baby's father took off. Maffi had worked as a bookkeeper at an auto repair shop. To supplement her salary, she sold small amounts of weed to friends. A law enforcement sting against her supplier put her in legal jeopardy. Other than a short pre-trial detention, she had never served time in prison. But her guilty plea, on top of her "illegal presence" in the United States, triggered her deportation back to Haiti.

Not long after she returned to Port-au-Prince, she got a tattoo on her right shoulder, which gave rise to her nickname. The ink, which looked iridescent against her dark brown skin, depicted Le Marron Inconnu, the runaway "unknown slave," holding a conch shell to his lips in 1791 and trumpeting a call to rebellion against French slaveholders in what was then the colony called Saint-Dominique. It is Haiti's most famous icon.

A larger-than-life-size bronze sculpture of the runaway was installed on the Champs de Mars in 1967 to commemorate Haiti's abolition of slavery. Designed by the Haitian sculptor and architect Albert Mangones, it became an instant symbol of black liberation. It showed a muscular man, wearing just a loincloth and kneeling on one knee. His back is arched. His left leg is stretched back. The severed links of a broken chain are still shackled to his ankle. With his head tilted upward, he blows into the shell. His right-hand grips a machete.

In 1989, the United Nations adopted the statue as a central image on postage stamps commemorating Article 4 of the Universal Declaration of Human Rights: "No one shall be held in slavery or servitude; slavery and the slave trade shall be prohibited in all their forms."

Maffi liked that sentiment just fine, so one night, prompted by an ocean of Barbancourt, she had the icon etched onto her skin for posterity.

"Slavery's legacy is on my back with or without the ink," she told people.

Also on every Haitian's back, she said, is the bitter legacy of the crushing debt imposed on the country in its infancy. After the revolution in 1804, France demanded an "indemnity" comparable to $21 billion today. The payment secured Haiti from future French aggression but left a permanent hole in its economy.

"Add a coupla decades as a puppet under U.S. occupation, and *Manman!*" – Mother of God, said Maffi. "Haiti never had a chance."

In Junior's car heading to Cité Soleil one day, they had rolled slowly past shops with hand-painted signs in Crayola colors. They passed the "Jesus Saves" bakery; "God is Good" barbershop, *"Anglais Rapide"* language school, and *"Bon Jean"* supermarket.

Charlie thought of telling Maffi about Corinne's suspicion but decided to wait for the car to arrive at Cité Soleil and for a private setting. He was alone with her on a narrow lane that led to the medical clinic when they passed the rain-flooded sunken courtyard of an abandoned building. Its fetid pool was the neighborhood's latrine. Knotted blue plastic bags filled with excrement stuck up here and there like foul lily pads. Barefoot children stood around the pool's edge and threw stones into the muck. The stench watered their eyes.

A low stone wall, upwind of the stink, provided a place for Charlie and Maffi to sit and talk. They weren't due to begin reporting at the clinic for another half hour.

"Can I confide in you? Charlie asked.

"You're paying me, right?"

"No, really, this is sensitive, and not directly related to our assignment."

"Oh-kayyy." Her inflection made the affirmation sound more like a question.

"You've met Corinne, my nurse-midwife friend. Someone she knew was murdered recently in a way that evoked superstition and possibly Vodou. She thinks she knows why he was killed. She is very scared, but wants the killers brought to justice."

"Haitian justice?"

"Justice justice."

"Good luck with that. Why are you telling me?"

"You know everything about this country, and certainly this city. I thought you might have some ideas."

"Ideas about how to name the killer and get myself into the kind of trouble that got your friend's friend killed?"

"No. No. Of course not. Nothing like that. Not to involve you in any danger. I just thought you know a lot of people. You hear a lot of things."

"You're paying my bill, right? You want to add murder-investigation to our to-do list? We can, but that doesn't seem too smart. Sounds like playing with fire. What if I do hear something? How exactly does your sweet little *blan* girlfriend from England plan to get justice?"

Charlie knew it was best not to push Maffi when that sarcastic edge crept into her voice. She had agreed to help. For now, that would have to be enough.

He opened his hands - palms up - in the universal gesture that said he really didn't know what more to say.

CHAPTER EIGHT
Le Village Artistique

Corinne had mentioned that Vodou, black magic and most certainly superstition, might be involved, so Charlie and Maffi on one of their forays made a stop at the Village Artistique de Noailles, not far from her house in Croix des Bouquets. The village was a collection of hundreds of open-air ateliers where artists wielding hammers, chisels and nailsets tapped out intriguing designs onto sheets of metal recycled from flattened steel drums. The skill, which began in Haiti in the late 1950s, was passed from fathers to sons and masters to apprentices, who learned to hold a flat piece of metal in place, usually with the toes of a bare foot, as they struck it endlessly to bring forth primitive designs in bas-relief. The themes were naturalistic and biblical, Adam and Eve in the Garden of Eden being tempted by the serpent, for example. But the religion most often represented was Vodou, with its pantheon of fantastic demons and spirits, who in Vodou hold the real power over lives and fortunes. With close links to nature, many Vodou deities lurk in rivers, streams and mountains. Everything that happens, for better or worse, is because of their intervention.

Exiting Junior's truck with a *blan* man trailing her, Maffi gave the appearance of a Haitian guide leading a foreign tourist. The shops' touts came running.

"*Gade isit la*," look here, look here, they shouted,

pointing to their ateliers.

"*Arret!*" Maffi barked, squaring her shoulders and narrowing her eyes to drive them away.

The ateliers all looked the same; their walls displayed similar wares. Many featured the Vodou deity, La Sirene, the beautiful mermaid with Medusa-like tresses, goddess of music, whose kingdom is at the bottom of the sea, but who, legend has it, walks on water when she wants to. In Vodou lore, she can be as fierce as a tempest and as gentle as the Caribbean's lapping waves.

Hardly waiting for Charlie to catch up, Maffi headed straight for a shop run by a man named Baron, who wore a top hat in the style of Baron Samedi, the Vodou intermediary between mortality and the hereafter, usually depicted in a black tuxedo, with dark glasses and cotton plugs in his nostrils, the way a corpse is prepared for burial, Haitian style.

"*Koman ou ye, Baron?*" she said.

"*Maffi, ma fille! Koman ou ye, Maffi Tattoo?*" His wide smile said he was delighted to see her.

Maffi knew she would make more headway in her quest for information if she promised to make a purchase. She told Charlie to browse inside the shop and pick out something. Then she and Baron went behind the shop to talk privately.

She told Baron about the murder, the missing telescope, the gouged-out eyes, and the embezzled pills destined for the street market.

He listened with no reaction, his top hat perfectly still.

"To anyone else I'd have nothing to say, but for you Maffi Tattoo …" He was flirting with her. Although at this stage of her life Maffi preferred women to men, she wasn't above leading him on to believe that he just might get lucky if he produced information.

"I'm not saying he is your man, and you didn't hear this from me," he said, "but all of the pills on the street are controlled by Evans."

A notorious gang leader in Cité Soleil, Maffi knew the name from her days distributing food relief.

Back inside the shop, Charlie had chosen a foot-square image of La Sirene, bare-chested, rising out of the sea, with a leaping fish aiming to suckle at her breast.

"One hundred dollars," said Baron.

"Fifty," an impatient Maffi said before Charlie could utter a word.

Baron looked chagrined but dutifully accepted Charlie's fifty U.S. dollars.

Maffi steered Charlie to a corner of the shop. "I've got something, maybe a lead," she mumbled. "Go to the car."

Before they left, Maffi blew a slow, suggestive kiss at Baron. The smile on his face, and the theatrical tipping of his hat, said he dearly hoped she would be back.

CHAPTER NINE
One more!

A week later on a shopping spree in Port-au-Prince, Corinne picked up some essentials that her colleagues had asked for - ink for the office printer, black castor oil for hair and skin treatments, and coconut *cremas*, Haiti's answer to eggnog. A commuting hospital handyman with a car had driven her down to the city. She splurged on a taxi for the three-hour ride back to Hinche.

As her cab passed a dump truck-turned-tap-tap straining to climb the steep highway out of Port-au-Prince, the crowded vehicle, with its passengers all standing in the truck's bed and packed in as tightly as sardines, reminded Corinne of a favorite joke in Haiti. It had taken her a moment to grasp the punch line the first time she heard it, but when she did, she felt like she was finally beginning to understand Haitian humor, equal parts fatalism and whimsy.

The question at the heart of the joke: How many people fit in a tap-tap?

The invariable answer: One more!

She had heard that joke just hours before the quake as a first-time volunteer at Saj Fanm, which in Creole means both midwife and wise woman. She had returned to England post-quake, divided her time between hospital assignments and humanitarian aid missions, and later jumped at the chance to return to Saj Fanm as an employee. She hadn't expected to stay on beyond a year, but Haiti's enormous medical needs took hold of her. Then she met others who also felt the metal-to-magnet pull of duty. One was Sanctis, for whom a deep connection with Haiti was coded in his DNA.

For Corinne, Haiti's resilience against long odds only enhanced her affinity for its people and culture, an allure made manifest by events like the outdoor church service she had attended next to a quake-pancaked school where children had died, or the makeshift beauty parlor inside a crowded displacement camp. A few months later, in an article for an American women's magazine about the impact of the quake, author Edwige Danticat spoke to Corinne's heart, citing the camps where "one destitute woman gives another destitute woman a manicure and pedicure, or sets her hair in rollers, bypassing the silenced hair-dryer because there is no electricity." Looking pretty, indeed, "looking beautiful in a disaster zone," Danticat observed, "might be one more way of exclaiming to the world that you are doing more than breathing, that you are surviving, that you matter."

As Corinne's taxi slowed and came to a stop on the crest of the next rise, she gazed left, across a dun-colored plain. Her eyes fell upon the pointillist panorama of Port-au-Prince, a mosaic of drab shanties, which shimmered mirage-like in the hot haze.

"Why are we stopping?"

The words had barely escaped Corinne's mouth when she noticed that several other cars and a tap-tap were parked on the uphill side of the highway near three makeshift leantos selling food, drinks and cigarettes. The crudely built, three-sided lean-tos made of scrap wood, tar paper and rusty corrugated metal looked like it wouldn't take an earthquake to topple them - the first high wind would do it.

Inside the center structure was a woman who looked 60 but was probably 40, poking a sharp stick at scrawny chicken legs cooking on a fire-blackened grill made from scrounged rebar and an oil drum cut in half. Its fire was fueled by twigs, which she pulled from a pile at her feet. She used a scrap of cardboard to fan the coals. Skinny chickens clucked and ducked in and out behind a yellow plastic jerry can that was filled with cooking oil.

Having just returned from behind a tree where he had gone to pee, Corinne's driver eyed the sad-looking drumsticks as they barely sizzled under the weak heat of the mostly spent charred twigs.

"Oh god, if he orders I'll have to order something too," she thought, "but it won't be the chicken." Even after years of living in Haiti, her English constitution was no match for underdone road food.

The driver chose a piece, shelled out a few gourdes, took a paper towel and started eating. Corinne ordered a Cola Couronne, Haiti's favorite soda, in a flavor called Fruit Champagne. She dripped sips into her mouth without touching the bottle top to her lips.

She was anxious to move on, but her now greasy-lipped driver was taking a cigarette break with another for-hire driver. This was their regular roadside rest, every bit as important to them as an M25 motorway stop for London lorry drivers. They savored every minute. Corinne looked over at the tap-tap, which was preparing to leave. A man boarded carrying a small, live goat, hog-tied and writhing.

He grabbed the clustered hoofs like a handle and lifted the hapless animal like it was a suitcase. All in a Haiti day's commute, she thought.

When she finally arrived back at the walled compound where she and the clinic staff lived in a two-story house surrounded by an untended garden, the road outside was pitch black and tropical rain was pouring down in buckets. Periodic power cuts were common in this rural area, which was electrified just a few decades ago. Seated in the back of the taxi, amid the splatter of fat drops making a racket on its roof, Corinne used her cell phone to call the compound's security guard. A moment later the compound's heavy blue steel sliding door began rolling on its rain-slicked tracks, dragged open by the guard who had a rifle slung over one shoulder and water running off the brim of his New York Yankees cap.

Corinne dashed inside. The guard quickly retracted the door. Her brunette bangs were plastered to her forehead. Her tunic had turned see-through, revealing the lacy bra she'd worn to see Charlie. She was drenched to the bone.

Being back in Hinche, less than half a mile from Sanctis' house, refreshed the horror of his death. Her fellow nurses were shocked by the murder, of course. After hearing about the missing telescope, they chalked up the death to a robbery gone wrong. Corinne had not shared with them what Sanctis had told her about Pinay on their walk through the hills. It didn't seem safe to share her suspicion. As she headed to her room to get cleaned up, she had a flashback of Sanctis' hollow-eyed stare. She found herself wishing that Charlie was around.

The house, which was large by Haitian standards, was

built by a prosperous maize farmer during the Papa Doc regime. For a time, it was a dormitory for Catholic missionaries. Then the California-based NGO that runs Saj Fanm bought it to use as a base for its program, which provides certified birth attendant training for Haitian nurses, and hands-on examinations of mothers-to-be by a rotating cast of Haitian nurse-midwives and volunteers from the U.S. and Europe who stay for stints of two to four weeks. Changed out of their work clothes and into sundresses with flip flops after work, they look like ordinary women, ages 30 to 60. Suited up in their scrubs, with their game faces on and hair tied back with bandannas, they were a bad-ass brigade.

The program's in-country director, Annabelle, had her own room, and a cuddly stray kitten that she named Jean-Claude, which she carried everywhere, often tucked into the space of her ample cleavage. Everyone else shared a dormitory outfitted with bunk beds and webs of indoor clotheslines. The shared bathrooms, one on each floor, were tiled but spare. A bucket of water had to be poured into the toilet's tank to make it flush. The showers, which trickled like they do in prison movies, were just pipe ends without showerheads that jutted out from the wall.

After three years with the program, Corinne had grown accustomed to these daily discomforts. But now, in the cold-water shower, with not enough pressure to rinse the shampoo from her hair, she felt sorry for herself. Miserable. Dejected. She dwelled on the death of Sanctis and how randomly a life could be cut short. If Sanctis had not witnessed Pinay skulking away red-handed with the stolen pills, would he be alive? Was robbery the motive? Corinne felt sure Pinay was behind the murder, but where was her proof? Was she right to suspect the worst of Pinay? Was her judgment sound, or clouded by grief and anger? She hated feeling so uncertain.

The compound's sleeping quarters were upstairs, divided east from west by a parlor that served as the Saj Fanm administration office. Downstairs was the kitchen, a dining area and clinical training rooms. A bookshelf in one corner held dog-eared medical texts and guidebooks about the history and geography of Haiti to orient each new cohort of volunteers. The refrigerator, in chronic need of defrosting, growled incessantly. On one side of the kitchen's island were the sink and soot-stained propane stove; on the other, an oilcloth-covered dining table with benches and mismatched chairs able to seat 10 people.

Breakfast was catch-as-catch-can. Toast slathered with *manba*, Haiti's spicy, chili-infused peanut butter, was a favorite. Corinne, who was always the first to rise, generally made herself two fried eggs and was the first out the door to the hospital.

Lunch and dinner were prepared by Roseline and Eveline, identical twins from Hinche, who laid out the meals on the island's countertop. People served themselves.

Dinner on the night that Corinne arrived back in Hinche was dirty rice, scrawny chicken legs and plantains, which the twins had cut into half-dollar-size discs, pounded flat and deep fried. Yellow and crispy brown, they looked like Ninja throwing stars.

Dinner conversation centered on patient updates and hospital gossip.

In the short time that Corinne had been away, one expectant mother and her newborn had been lost to the ravages of hard labor and eclampsia, a sadly common scenario in Haiti, where midwives liken the rigors and risks of childbirth to "women's war."

"Tragic," said Jackie, a short-haired American volunteer in a red bandanna. "First the baby, then a couple of hours later the mom. Her family waiting outside the *salle* howled - didn't know what hit 'em."

Another nurse, Marie, changed the subject: "The porters came to Sanctis' locker and boxed up his stuff. Same at his house. They took them to Pinay's office for safekeeping."

Safekeeping? More like seizing control of Sanctis' possessions, Corinne thought. She felt sure Pinay wanted to go through all of Sanctis' belongings secretly to make sure there was nothing incriminating in there. This was more than a robbery, she thought again. Much more. But she kept the thought to herself. After all, she had no proof of Pinay's role in Sanctis' murder. Even if she had proof, then what? After responding initially to the scene, the police didn't seem to be investigating at all. A missing telescope worth more than their annual salary, which only a spoiled American doctor could afford? Yeah sure, they'll get right on it. Other than Corinne, who cared?

As the dinner plates were cleared away, Annabelle cuddled her kitten and went over the schedule for the next day. Corinne was assigned to the mobile clinic.

Saj Fanm played two roles: It staffed the maternity ward at Notre Dame des Douleurs, using it as an instructional clinic for certifying the birth-attendant trainees.

Separately, it ran a mobile clinic, which used a beat-up Land Rover laden with a fold-out examination table, pregnancy tests, urine-test strips and prenatal vitamins to bring obstetric care to Haiti's most remote villages. With supplies strapped to its roof rack, and the nurse-midwives swaying shoulder to shoulder in its seats, the SUV bumped along on rutted roads and took advantage of its high-clearance chassis to drive right across shallow streams. The first time Corinne had been aboard when the Rover plunged in, she'd yelped, thinking it would sink, and held her breath for an anxious moment until it charged up the bank on the other side. On this morning she was so lost in her dark thoughts about Sanctis and Pinay that she didn't even notice as the Rover churned through the water.

"We're here," said the driver as he pulled over next to a winding dirt track that sloped down into thick forest.

The staff and volunteers piled out. They lugged the folded-up examination table and other equipment for a quarter mile on the narrow goat path to a clearing where a dozen pregnant women, some of them teenagers, awaited. Often on these remote-clinic days, more than 100 were waiting. Some were from families that grew sugar cane in the small hamlets high in the mountains. It was not unusual for them to begin the hours-long trek to the clinic the night before.

"Looks like a small turnout today," said Corinne.

"There'll be more. It's still early," said Yves, a Haitian colleague.

Yves led the assembled women in the recitation of the Lord's Prayer, and lectured them about maternal nutrition and the warning signs of problem pregnancies.

Then one by one they came forward, kicked off their muddy sandals and stepped barefoot inside a concrete block house that had been built in the woods. Each had her heart rate, blood pressure, and weight measured. To provide urine samples they squatted behind the blockhouse and peed into black plastic trays about the size of a pack of cigarettes, which they carried back carefully. They were tested for venereal diseases.

"*Koman ou ye?*" Corinne asked each woman in turn

All answered the same way: "*M'ap boule*" … I'm pressing on.

Delphine Desir, 23, had brought her one-month-old daughter, Lovelie, to the clinic to get her checked for a small rash on her right forearm. Back in Desir's village, an elderly matron who'd been her birth attendant had treated the rash with a traditional remedy - a small, white plastic shirt button tied with thread around the baby's wrist.

The midwives were unconcerned about the classic, splotchy newborn's rash. It would likely clear up on its own, they told Desir. Being sensitive to the new mother's cultural traditions, however, they left the button tied to the baby's wrist.

"I don't want to sound like a bloody-clueless, ethnocentric First Worlder," Corinne said to Yves as the mother walked away. "But if that baby breaks that button loose and swallows it, she'll have much more than a rash to worry about. At what point do we say, 'Okay, enough with these home remedies?'"

CHAPTER TEN
Bois Neuf

"*Sa'k pase?*" - Whassup? – Maffi asked a boy no taller than her belt buckle a few days later as they were out reporting. He ran forward to greet her and Charlie after they'd jumped from Junior's pickup into the Bois Neuf section of Cité Soleil.

In this place where toys are a rare luxury, this child had one – a plastic juice bottle cut into the shape of a car, with four bottle caps attached for wheels and a string to pull it. Within seconds more small curious children swarmed. They trailed Charlie, chattering in Creole and constantly reaching for his hands. Sometimes, a child would grab and hold just one finger.

"*Tanpri, tanpri*" - please, please, they exhorted. And in English they begged for money, which they pronounced *moh-nay*.

Maffi led Charlie into an alley lined with houses made of bare concrete blocks. A shallow ditch trickled streaky gray water down the middle of the alley. Seated on the house thresholds, women with flat, woven-grass baskets on their laps picked bits of dirt out of dried beans and seeds. Every so often they popped a seed or two into their mouths and nibbled.

Maffi and Charlie had come looking for Evans, the reputed kingpin of the pill peddlers.

First, they stopped by the clinic that was the focus of

Charlie's story assignment. It included a level patio surrounded by a 10-foot wall and the luxury of four tall shady palm trees. For patients waiting to see the volunteer doctor, it was an oasis of calm amid the squalor. The patients presented with a variety of ailments. Most wanted treatment for hookworms, tuberculosis, and malnutrition.

He took out his notebook and wrote that the pale-green, peaked roof building is more substantial than most of the others in this slum, which a donor from the United States had once described as "the sorry place where Capitalism's toilet flushes out."

Charlie kept on taking notes in his personal shorthand: "1 doc; 2 nurses; 6 assist. Donations: 50K/year. Mon., Wed., Fri. 200 pts./week."

In the clinic's mostly bare examination room, the doctor lowered the top of a 6-year-old girl's sun dress and thumped lightly on her chest and stomach, listening for blockages as her mother stood by. He weighed her on a simple bathroom scale - a mere 35 pounds - severely underweight but all too common here - and wrote her a prescription for antibiotics. After a brief wait outside in the courtyard, an assistant handed the pills to the mother through a barred window.

"The challenge now," said Maffi, "is for them to find enough clean water to swallow them down."

Because many patients are unable to read, staff members drew circles on the prescription envelopes to indicate how many tablets they should take. Next to the circles, they made a drawing of the sun if the tablets were to be taken during the day, and a moon if taken at night.

An assistant explained to Charlie the importance of

tuberculosis patients completing their full course of treatment, which can involve taking pills for more than a month. If they stop when they begin to feel better, they can develop a drug-resistant strain of tuberculosis. To keep them on their medications, the clinics staff watched as they consumed their first doses and then handed them small packets of rice and beans. Clients were told to come back in a day for another pill and to receive another ration of food. In Cité Soleil, that was a mighty incentive.

While Charlie observed the examinations, Maffi stepped outside with one of the clinic's maintenance men whom she knew to be savvy.

"Evans," she asked. "You know him?"

The man said nothing. Savvy, yes. And wary of speaking about any gangster in this place where, years earlier, the maintenance man's family had been caught in the crossfire of a militarized raid to provide security after the rebellion that ousted Haitian President Jean-Bertrand Aristide. The raids, by MINUSTAH, were designed to dislodge the gangs, including the one that agitated for Aristide's return to power.

On one of those pre-dawn raids the blue-helmeted soldiers of MINUSTAH had killed the pro-Aristide gang leader Emmanuel "Dread" Wilme and six of his followers. Wilme's supporters fought for hours amid Bois Neuf's cramped dwellings, using sniper fire, heavy guns and Molotov cocktails. The MINUSTAH troops, in the operation they called "Iron Fist," had responded with tens of thousands of rifle rounds, scores of grenades and five mortars.

Also killed in the 12-hour siege were two dozen innocent residents of Bois Neuf. Survivors said some of the victims were struck inside their homes when rounds sprayed from a U.N. helicopter gunship pierced their corrugated metal roofs and flimsy walls. The maintenance man's 10-year-old niece had been inside her family's scrap-steel shack when she was hit by a stray bullet and later died. The deaths were never fully investigated. A U.N. commander asserted to the U.N. Special Rapporteur on Civil and Political Rights that the gang, after the fighting ended, had systematically murdered people they suspected of having collaborated with MINUSTAH. Survivors said that wasn't true. If the maintenance man was being wary, he had good reason to be.

Maffi tried again.

"Evans?"

This time the man was prepared to answer after looking left and right.

"There is Evans Legros. Sometimes he brings medicine to the clinic. Pills he donates. We never know when he will come. If he will come? But we are grateful."

"How do I find him?"

"*Sa k konnen*" – who knows, he said.

"What does he look like?"

He looked around again. This time he whispered.

"My height. My build. With a raised scar from ear to throat where someone cut him."

"Thank you, my friend. *Na wè pwochen fwa*" – until next time.

"*Pa dekwa.*"

###

Maffi filled Charlie in as Junior drove them back to the Désir.

"It sounds like Evans is our guy," said Charlie.

"*Nou pral* we – we'll see," said Maffi. "Are you ready for this? You know, Evans don't play."

Charlie pictured Corinne's face and anticipated her happiness on hearing that they were making progress.

He nodded. "I'm ready." Maffi sighed, raised her eyebrows, and turned away.

A few minutes later, Junior pulled into the Désir parking lot and Charlie hopped out.

"*Na we demen*," see you tomorrow, said Maffi.

Charlie raced up the stairs, past reception to his room.

CHAPTER ELEVEN
"Shut your mouth, old man"

No one had ever heard Sanctis raise his voice in anger before. But now, on a late fall day before his murder, he was deep into a full-blown screaming match at the hospital, getting louder and closer to violence with each verbal exchange.

"Despicable. Sinful. You should be fired. I should report you," he said.

"See where that gets you, *estipid Ameriken!*"

Sanctis had caught a young porter, barely 20 years old, helping himself to the cubed jackfruit griot that a patient's family had left at his bedside to sustain him.

"You can't be serious. Without this food, this man will starve."

"Shut up, old man. He'll be dead in days no matter what and you know it."

Old man? Sanctis was 39, hardly ancient, but to the hotheaded cleaner half his age, he was a relic.

The defiance of the porter, a troublemaker who was always getting into arguments, inflamed Sanctis. A vein bulged on his forehead. The confrontation drew bystanders expecting fists to fly. The surprising explosiveness of the argument was memorable.

"I should report you."

"See where that gets you, *estipid Ameriken.*"

"Let it go," a bystander said to Sanctis. "Everyone

knows that man is not right in the head, *malad mantal*. Sick. Belligerent. Unstable. Don't argue with him."

"So why do we employ him?"

The man shrugged, mumbled something about nepotism and *koripsyon*, and began leading Sanctis away.

Turning back to speak over his shoulder Sanctis wouldn't let it go. "These are our patients. We should take care of them, not steal from them!"

His trembling voice echoed under the covered walkway, as did the porter's threatening reply, "Shut your mouth, old man, before I shut it for you."

CHAPTER TWELVE
Granola and guilt

Being back in Haiti, seeing Corinne again, Charlie felt nostalgia for the time of their first meeting in 2010, when the urgent plight of the country was the biggest news story in the world. Reporting from quake-stricken Haiti with the whole world watching fed Charlie's passion to take the pulse of crisis-affected people and convey their ground truth wherever big, international stories broke.

From Corinne's place on the front line of the medical response, she'd taken Haiti's pulse, too. It resonated daily in her stethoscope.

They were two young professionals, living the exciting, demanding lives they had trained for, in an atmosphere made more intense and erotic by the nearness of sudden, senseless death.

When Charlie had introduced himself that night at the bar, he saw a vivacious woman, compact and confident. Her athletic physique, dark curls, verbal quickness and deep commitment to comforting the afflicted appealed to him immediately. He was a sucker for her pearly smile.

Back in London after her stint with Care4Calais, she had worked for Medicins du Monde because of its commitment to the founding principle of *temoignage*, (witnessing), which meant MdM aid workers didn't just treat the afflicted, they made the atrocities they witnessed known to the world.

Bear witness? Comfort the afflicted? Charlie thought he had met his soul mate.

By day, in the company of a fixer and driver, he struggled to get from place to place on damaged, often impassable roads. As a writer on assignment for the Globe, he worked hard to convey Haiti's culture and explain how nature's brute force had so easily upended the country's fragile infrastructure.

At night, hunched over his laptop, he wrote and filed his stories. He was laser focused. The work was all-consuming. He loved it.

Corinne loved her work too, using her special set of skills to identify the severity of traumatic injuries and putting broken people on track for treatment and recovery. While Charlie imagined the compassion and professionalism she exuded at patients' bedsides, he left room in his head for other thoughts – fantasies really - about her when she was off the clock. He dreamed about her in bed. Thought about her in the shower. He was enchanted.

Thinking back on those heady days, he wished he could turn back time, to live it all again but more mindfully. If he and Corinne hadn't been so personally driven, so deeply committed to their individual work, they might have noticed that they could have had something more, something like a future together. Instead, he had missed his chance with Corinne, and two years later back in the States had entered into a less passionate love and marriage with the woman who would become his ex-wife.

When Charlie had arrived four days after the quake, Port-au-Prince appeared before him in shades of ochre and gray. Dust from the streets smoked up around his shoes with every step. Desperate men and women lacking shelter foraged for food in the rubble of collapsed markets. Sensationalist news accounts characterized them as looters, when in fact they were ordinary people forced to scavenge to survive.

The destitute slept outdoors on buckled ground. They washed in muddy drainage ditches and defecated in the street, leaving behind the distinctive smell of human waste. At one site, exhausted men working by hand formed a chain gang to remove chunks of concrete and pull a dead colleague from the wreckage of a pancaked government building. Drowned in a sea of sand, stone and twisted rebar, all of her that was visible was a hand reaching for the sky. Around the edges of almost every recovery operation was the stench of decaying bodies and dazed, dust-covered people, plaintive zombies, holding out upturned palms to every foreign stranger.

Because the control tower of the Port-au-Prince airport had been instantly crippled, Charlie had to move quickly and pitch persuasively to score the last seat on a humanitarian-aid flight out of Boston, headed for Santo Domingo in the Dominican Republic, Haiti's neighbor on the Caribbean island of Hispaniola.

From the DR's capital, Charlie rode with a team of U.S. doctors to the border town of Jimani, where the local hospital spilled over with incoming Haitian amputees needing follow-up care and wound dressing changes. Mattresses covered every square inch of the hospital's floors, including its hallways. The scene was sheer bedlam, a Hieronymus Bosch hell-scape.

On one bed, nurses struggled to unwrap the gauze that

covered the stump of a teen whose right leg had been amputated above the knee. She shot upright in bed, her twist braids standing on end as the team of nurses restrained her. She threw back her head, eyes wide, and howled with animal ferocity. She rocked and keened, mourning not only the loss of her leg, but also the mobility and quality of life now gone forever. This was the sort of immersive reporting Charlie lived for, but it came with his gnawing shame at having been privy to the poor woman's agony in her darkest hour.

From Jimani, Charlie and David, the photographer the newspaper had sent to work with him, hitched a ride into Haiti with a busload of Christian missionaries who wore identical yellow tee shirts and ball caps emblazoned "Honey in the Rock." When the bus finally pulled up outside the closed gates of the stricken airport in Port-au-Prince, Charlie and David hopped out and began the reporting for what would be their first in-country dateline. As night fell, they made their way to the makeshift satellite city taking shape at the Désir.

Before catching the humanitarian-aid flight into the DR, and not knowing what he would find in a shattered Haiti, Charlie had added last-minute essentials to his go bag: A package of wet wipes; two freeze-dried meals he bought at REI; a dozen granola bars and a thousand U.S. dollars in small bills. The meals came in handy late one night after the Desir's kitchen was closed, the wet wipes were a blessing in the sweaty field, but the money was soon gone, eventually having to be supplemented by the newspaper via Western Union.

A month after he completed his first reports about the

quake and its aftermath, Charlie was back in the United States. That's when a friend who was an adjunct professor at Northeastern University asked him to speak to a class on journalism.

Charlie had done this sort of lecturing before and thought he knew what to expect. He usually began by explaining why reporting from abroad appealed to him as opposed to, say, being a reporter on the domestic politics beat, or working exclusively as an investigative reporter.

"As an investigative reporter, you research and research. You pick the strongest thing that you can say, and you say it most strongly. You can do a lot of good with that. It's a public service. It can bring about change. But the pace can be plodding.

"The pinnacle of political reporting is getting to be a White House correspondent, right? You get to travel with the President of the United States, tracking his every move and utterance. Tracking the same person, day after day, after day. I never saw the excitement in that."

Speaking to his friend's class, Charlie gave that familiar introduction. He spoke for 15 minutes about the adrenaline-fueled intensity of reporting from a place like Haiti.

"Hey," a student in the back row raised his hand. His shaved head was covered with a beat-up tweed flat cap. He had a bushy swath of red beard. Over his black tee shirt, he wore a green vee neck sweater with holes at the elbows.

"You make being a foreign correspondent sound exhilarating, invigorating. Gee whiz! Maybe it is for you. You get to come home safely to America when you're done. But isn't it, in the end, all just very exploitative? These people are suffering in the worst ways possible. And you want to interview them? Photograph them? Seriously? In places like Haiti after the earthquake, what's the difference between what you do and disaster porn? I don't have the stomach for that kind of reporting. I don't want to have that stomach. Handing out those granola bars to the starving people is the first thing I would do."

Charlie said nothing. An image flashed in his mind of a heavily bandaged woman with two broken legs. He had interviewed her at the hospital in Jimani. When he told her that he was from America, she raised her hands like claws, tearing at the invisible wall of objectivity that separates journalists from their subjects. Tearfully she pleaded with him to save her life by taking her with him back to the United States. "Please! Please! Take me with you! *Tanpri!!! Tanpri!!"*

Not knowing what to say, Charlie told her that it wasn't his choice, his government would not allow it. That was true, but still it felt like a dodge.

Charlie shut his eyes. He halted the flashback with a cleansing blink, and with another brought himself back into the classroom.

"I've felt the feelings you've expressed," he told Flat Cap. Instead of pushing back at the snark in the student's question, Charlie embraced it.

"You are right. You've gone right to the heart of this kind of work. But try thinking about it this way," he said, reaching for a local example. "I could walk the length of Blue Hill Avenue from Mattapan to Seaver Street and probably get panhandled a dozen times. Every one of those poor people might deserve my help. Each and every one. If I gave a handout to each, I'd be out of money in no time.

And the people I would have helped would still be hungry and poor the next day. I could have given away all those granola bars and been done with that in a minute. Instead, I used them to sustain me so that I could try to illuminate the urgent reality on the ground.

"Everyone decides what to believe in, where to put their faith. My faith is in journalism, in bearing witness, with the hope that the spotlight I cast with my reporting is bright and focused enough to draw wider attention and bring some good."

In the back row, Flat Cap shrugged. Charlie could see he wasn't convinced.

CHAPTER THIRTEEN
Mood of the mob

"They're going to kill him!" Corinne shrieked as she ran into the Saj Fanm compound's courtyard early one evening. "They're going to kill him!!"

She was frantic. Breathless. Waving her arms. Losing her flip-flops. "We have to stop them."

Her fellow nurses, some freshly showered and in street clothes, were unwinding after a long day at work. No one knew what Corinne was shouting about but she was so distressed they had to follow her outside the compound's walls. That sent them straight into the whirling scrum of a lynch mob - 40 angry townspeople, pursuing a bloodied man who stumbled, tried to run, and fell again as they lashed his back and legs with sticks.

There was shouting. Men on motorbikes gunned their engines and tore dangerously around the edges of the crowd, popping wheelies. Some carried machetes. Someone splashed the fallen man with lighter fluid.

"*Sispann li, sispann li!*" Corinne shouted, imploring the attackers to "Stop It."

Five-feet-three, in a spaghetti strap sundress, she fearlessly grabbed at the sticks the men were wielding to torment their prey. They didn't know what to make of this crazy *blan* berating them, but they didn't dare strike her.

There was a police station about a kilometer up the road. The mob was moving slowly in that direction. Maybe they were going to deliver the man there. But it wasn't clear if he would arrive alive.

Unable to halt the assault, Corinne finally stepped back and was nearly run down by a bucking moto.

"Come inside now, please," said the clinic's nervous security guard standing by the gate. "Please come now."

The sun slipped behind the hills of Hinche, giving way to rusty twilight as the grumbling mob moved on in a cloud of dust and moto exhaust - still beating on the guy.

Before she returned to the compound, Corinne asked a bystander what had triggered them. The bystander said the man being beaten was a horse thief. He denied stealing another man's mare, but the animal was found grazing behind a fence in the beaten man's pasture, which was all the evidence the lynch mob needed.

At dinner, the nurses talked about the vigilante justice they had just witnessed.

One said the alleged thief was no more than a suspect really and was being punished undeservedly if he was innocent.

Another said the mare found in his pasture, behind a fence, seemed like proof of his guilt.

Corinne didn't offer an opinion. Her effort to stop the assault spoke for itself. Privately, she thought about the difference between the rough justice she had just witnessed and the evidence she would need to bring down Pinay, who was not just some upcountry peasant. She would need more than what a court would call "hearsay" from Sanctis. In her gut Sanctis' murder felt more like a targeted hit than a random robbery. But what hard proof could she muster? And how?

The disturbing episode was also unsettling on another level. These villagers with their blood up were not waiting for all the evidence to come in before meting out rough justice. Was she doing that very thing in her head to Pinay? Didn't he deserve the same benefit of t h e doubt she was willing to extend to the alleged horse thief?

After they rinsed off the dinner plates, Corinne's colleagues stayed up late gossiping, teasing, and playing gin rummy. Aisha, a volunteer who worked as a lactation consultant at a Florida clinic, won every hand and sassily crowed about it. "We're playing to 100 points, right?"

Corinne stepped behind Aisha, stole a look at her cards and pulled a long face. "The rest of you are going down," she teased. "Me? Knackered. Off to Bedfordshire."

"I think that means she's going to bed," Aisha deadpanned, eyes on her cards. The other players laughed.

The next morning, Corinne rose before the sun.

It was Saturday. She could have slept in. But she felt drawn to walk the path she used to hike with Sanctis. It would be muddy. It always was. Probably worse now after the recent rain. She set off wearing the Wellingtons she'd owned since university.

Roosters crowed. Goats gamboled. Mules brayed. The chilly morning air smelled of wood smoke. The rising sun was burning off the ground fog. As she pushed on, avoiding puddles in the rutted dirt road, she passed the modest shacks of Haitian families living deep off the grid. No electricity. No running water. No plumbing. All cooking outdoors over soot-caked braziers and charcoal.

First light brought out the children, none older than 10. It seemed each house sheltered half a dozen of them. A few silently fell in step with Corinne, not sure where she was going, but enjoying the novelty of marching along with this *blan* they had seen before, but never walking alone.

In front of her was a series of rolling hills. At the bottom of the deep valley to her right ran a tributary of the Artibonite, Haiti's longest river. In the distance, she saw women squatting on the river's banks, scrubbing clothes over washboards, or slapping them hard against flat rocks. Some men, probably drivers for better-off families, drove their cars axle-deep into the water and washed them with soapy sponges. Despite all the lathering and suds, people downstream drank untreated water from the river, which also was the vector for the cholera outbreak. At Saj Fanm, the nurses drank purified water, delivered in five-gallon jugs.

Ten minutes into her hike, she came to a grassy mound rising 200 feet from the landscape like a massive camel's hump, with an array of wooden poles planted at the top. According to legend, it is a holy site, where worshippers go to be closer to the heavens when they beseech God in this country often described as "80 percent Catholic, 20 percent Protestant and 100 percent Vodou."

She climbed the mound, leaning forward, her Wellies seeking traction on the grass slick with dew.

At the top she looked across the valley, exhaled and said a silent prayer, asking for strength and guidance in her quest to bring Sanctis' killers to justice. She didn't really know how to pray, knew no formal prayers by heart. With her it always came out: Please, please God, oh please! I'll be a better person, just grant me this wish.

Every time she prayed like that she felt like a hypocrite, like flattering the butcher you ignore most of the year but give a great greeting at holiday time when you desperately need his last crown roast of lamb. God, she knew, owed her nothing. Frustrated, she picked up a stone and threw it as far as she could. The pack of children in her wake watched from a distance. They must think I'm crazy, she thought.

The turn-around point for her hike was an area the size of a classroom covered in sawdust and wood chips. She and Sanctis had always called it "the old sawmill," but in truth it was just a spot with two large, forked trees capable of supporting a huge log placed horizontally between them about seven feet off the ground.

Turning logs into flat boards was a two-man operation involving a long, double-handled crosscut saw. One man stood atop the log with his vulnerable bare toes gripping its slippery surface. The other stood below, getting showered with sawdust as they pushed and pulled the saw back and forth, perpendicular to the grain, along the length of the log, taking half an hour to produce a single board. If they came upon a hidden knot, they worked that much harder or started over. It was back-breaking work.

Sanctis had marveled at the setup.

In Haiti, if you need boards to build your chicken coop, he said, there's no running to Home Depot on Saturday morning to get some smooth, perfectly planed lumber. No, you come to these muscular sawyers, who sweat for hours to slice you what you need from a whole tree.

"Resourceful. Hard working. Stuck with century-old tools. That's Haiti at every level," he'd said to Corinne. Recalling Sanctis' words, she re-experienced the horror of losing her friend so suddenly and savagely. Her heart raced. Palpitations. Staccato beats. As a nurse, she knew the physiological reactions to trauma. Sanctis wasn't just a good guy. He had an uncanny ability to notice things and draw out lessons, like the time he remarked on the significance of crossed fingers.

"Cross your fingers for luck, people say. ... At the same time, holding crossed fingers behind your back means you're lying. What does that tell us about luck and cunning? Maybe they're related. Maybe not. But they can get you to the same place," Corinne remembered him saying, with an air of discovery.

Saturday also was the day that some of the nurse-midwives dropped in at the local orphanage, a facility for 100 children, run by Sisters of Charity, the order founded by Mother Teresa. For Corinne, who'd brought countless babies into the world but seemed destined never to give birth, it was a chance to share affection and fantasize about "what-if." A chance to indulge the softer side of her tough-nurse nature.

As was true for many of the orphanages in Haiti, these children generally had living parents who simply lacked the means to care for them. The orphanage in Hinche was really a feeding center where undernourished, sickly children received three meals a day and medicine to nurse them back to health. The nuns who ran the center, several of them from the Philippines, could not have been more dedicated and loving. But they did not have enough hands to feed or arms to hold all of the children, who were as hungry for affection as they were for the corn porridge they got for breakfast.

Late morning when Corinne had arrived, the children, most of them younger than four, were seated silently and dressed identically in a narrow hallway lined with tiny chairs. No noise. No horseplay. They didn't seem like children at all, more like miniature old people, the boys in navy pants and pale-blue, short-sleeve button-downs; the girls in floral-print sack dresses fashioned from pillowcases and made size-adjustable with spaghetti straps and bows that tied at their shoulders.

They came alive when the nuns dismissed them into an open portico with a tiled floor, a large crucifix on one wall and folding chairs around the perimeter. They scampered. They grabbed the hands of the visiting volunteers and clung to their legs like koalas hugging trees. Each child wore a hospital-style plastic bracelet with their first name and the date they had arrived. Many just wanted to be held and comforted.

On this Saturday, a tiny girl named Fabilene grabbed Corinne's hand, pulled her to a chair and jumped onto her lap.

"*Alo*, Fabi," said Corinne, cribbing her name from the bracelet.

Cradled in Corinne's arms, the child leaned into her chest. She was probably four but looked no older than two. Her hair was dry, reddish, dusty and brittle. On the back of her neck was a small birthmark that resembled a five-pointed star. Her stomach was hard and distended, a symptom of kwashiorkor, the severe form of malnutrition associated with a lack of dietary protein. Corinne had learned about the condition in nursing school but had never encountered it in the field until she came to Haiti.

She spoke softly and stroked the back of Fabi's neck, tracing the birthmark. The child nuzzled deeper into Corinne's shoulder.

All around them joyful chaos reigned. Little boys ran and stagger-stepped from one end of the portico to the other.

One swarmed volunteer looked like a female Gulliver, pinned to the floor with a Lilliputian child wrapped tightly around each of her limbs. In an adjacent room, children too young or too sickly to participate lay in steel-barred cribs.

Corinne felt guilty about not spreading her affection around to more of the children, but Fabi was so deeply content in her arms that she didn't dare move.

Just then a little boy with a runny nose ran up to Corinne and tried to wriggle his way onto her lap next to Fabi.

Summoning strength that she didn't appear to have, Fabi swatted the boy, hard, several times on the top of his head. He struck back once, tiny fist flying, and ran off.

"*Non, Fabi,*" said Corinne. "*Pa fè sa*" - don't do that.

Corinne fantasized about what it would be like to have Fabi as her own, to be responsible for her care, safety, and life lessons like how to get along with other children and keep her hands to herself.

In the survival-of-the-fittest world that Fabi was born into, it was natural that she would fiercely protect her new, comforting relationship with Corinne and run off any usurpers.

If Fabi were hers to rear, Corinne thought, could she ever give the child so much love and protection that Fabi would relax and not feel the constant need to be on defense?

Corinne held Fabi tighter and toyed with her plastic bracelet as the child melted into her.

She looked across the portico and saw that several children had hung back near the raised threshold, afraid to enter. One had a pronounced limp. For a second, Corinne flashed onto Pinay, and squeezed her eyes shut tight to banish the image. Two of the other children looked developmentally disabled. No volunteers were holding them.

The two-hour visit was coming to an end. Corinne would have to disengage – physically and emotionally - from Fabi.

Sensing the coming disconnection, Fabi clung tighter to Corinne. This was the part that Corinne hated about these visits. She had to stand up and peel away a child's hungry little hands.

She summoned the words in Creole to tell Fabi that she would see her next time. "*Na we pwochen fwa.*" She set the child down on her feet and began to walk away. She told herself not to look back, but she knew she would.

Fabi's face was contorted and streaked with tears. Her mouth was wide open. Instead of sobs, no sound came out.

CHAPTER FOURTEEN
What bad did I do?

The ring of Maffi's cell phone trumpeted the open bars of Goldfinger and pulled her from a deep sleep into the swelter of another Croix des Bouquets morning. The sun was barely up and already the air shimmered with heat waves worthy of a blast furnace.

She reached for a packet of water, tore off a corner with her teeth, wet her parched throat and croaked.

"*Alo?*"

"*Maman, c'est Tatianna. Koman ou ye?*"

"*Bonjou, Ti Tati.*" Maffi's ordinarily deep voice was thick with the aftereffects of sleep … and a trill of concern. "*Tati?*"

Maffi usually liked hearing from her daughter, her grown-up "baby girl," who telephoned from the United States every month or so. This time, though, Maffi knew what Tatianna was calling about and wasn't eager to engage.

"So, Mommy? Have you decided?"

"So nothing," said Maffi. "Nothing. There's nothing to decide. Nothing to talk about."

Maffi had been 16, pregnant and unmarried 24 years earlier when she snuck across the U.S.-Mexico border guided by a Spanish-speaking coyote who demanded payment in U.S. dollars. Tatianna's father had gone on ahead to New York City to set things up, leaving Maffi to make her way there alone. They got together at the studio apartment he rented in Flatbush, the city's largest enclave of Haitian immigrants. Two months later, Tatianna, a pretty baby with long eyelashes and coffee-bean irises, was born. Maffi found work as a domestic. Tati's father did odd jobs.

On some days Maffi left Tati with an informal, unlicensed daycare in the neighborhood. Other times she strapped the infant into a backpack carrier, which she wore while she cleaned houses and hummed the lullaby *Dodo Dodo Titit* – sleep, sleep, little-little one.

It was a hard life, made harder when Tatianna's father took what was supposed to be a one-off job as a furniture mover with a long-haul trucker and started being away for a week or two at a time. Eventually, their union broke under the strain. That's when Maffi dug deeper and started earning more money running the front desk of an auto body repair shop where, behind the counter, she kept hotplates bubbling all day with exotic stews she sold to the mechanics. When she needed more money, she began a side hustle dealing weed. Then came the bust.

Maffi's deportation at 28 years old meant she was barred for at least 10 years from seeking a visa to re-enter the United States. Her return to Haiti was a hard adjustment. To everyday Haitians desperate to leave the beleaguered country, it seemed that Maffi had what everyone's heart desired, a golden ticket to live in America, and had managed to mess it up. People kept their distance.

Tatianna, American-born, and thus automatically a U.S. citizen, was 12 and stayed in Brooklyn with a paternal aunt to finish school after her mother was forced to leave.

Maffi was 39 now, not a shoe-in for readmission to America, but eligible to try. Tatianna, 23, a private in the Army, had been lobbying in those monthly telephone calls for her mother to come back, even if only for a little while.

"You're finally eligible. Come!" she said. "Why won't you?"

"You watch the news, right? America is deporting plane-load after plane-load of Haitians."

"Your situation is different."

"America had me, Tati. They had my heart. They had all of me. Then they decided they didn't want me. They threw me out. For what? What bad did I do? Who did I hurt? Threw me out. *Piman bouk!* I don't need that stinking shit." Maffi's wounded pride was ferocious, a volatile mix of heartache, anger and repressed regret.

"I was a good person. I worked. I paid my taxes. I worked even harder after your father left. …"

Tatianna hung on the line, silent as a falling leaf.

"A good person," Maffi repeated. "And they threw me out. That's your America, *ti cheri*. You can have it. I'm staying here. It's where I belong."

Later that day, a jagged bolt of chain lightning sizzled over the Caribbean, casting light like shards from a disco ball over Cité Soleil.

Charlie looked up.

"Heat lightning," Maffi scoffed. "Not gonna rain."

Charlie's return to Cité Soleil revived decade-old memories of his first time in the sprawling slum. He went there in the aftermath of the quake and found, ironically, that these flimsy, one-story shanties with their rusted tin roofs proved less lethal to the occupants than the heavy concrete government buildings, which pancaked, floor upon floor, squeezing the life out of trapped victims.

The depth of the hunger in Cité Soleil was vividly etched in Charlie's brain one day when he was out reporting, riding in the back of Junior's pickup. They came upon a burlap sack of foreign-aid rice that had fallen from a truck and split open onto Route 9, puddling loose rice on the highway. Cars sped by the sack, narrowly missing it. Then a woman in a tattered dress ran out and squatted beside it, risking certain death as she used her bony fingers to desperately sweep up as many grains as she could gather, along with random bits of gravel, into a black patent leather evening bag.

"That's raw hunger" like none he had seen before, thought Charlie, "even in Gaza." And the shiny leather bag added to the surreality.

Kathy, the Globe's deputy foreign editor who had sent Charlie back to Haiti to report on the gang house-turned-clinic, had edited his first earthquake dispatches. Since then, they had become close colleagues.

Deeply cynical, usually right on the money with her harsh criticism of the paper's senior management, she shared with Charlie a dedication to spell-it-all-perfectly perfectionism, and copy that was vivid, true and reliably sourced. She bristled if a higher-up, reading a yet-to-be-published story behind her, said or implied she had missed a hole in it.

She was a curmudgeon, who clashed routinely with

higher-ups, particularly male top editors, but was beloved by many reporters. It is a truism in journalism and other fields that many ultra-ambitious middle managers kiss up to management and kick down at the rank and file. Kathy did the opposite. She wasn't a careerist willing to do whatever it took to climb the masthead. Rather, she was an old-school great, who used a dog-eared dictionary instead of spell-checking and took the time to learn what makes a reporter tick as a person and a writer. Then she relentlessly pitched stories into their particular wheelhouse.

The resulting journalism was superb. Because she was frequently crosswise with top management, though, the stories didn't always get prominent display, the proverbial "good ride" that writers lusted after. Other "backfielders," as the editors who worked directly with writers were known in newsroom parlance, would do a charming fan dance to nudge a story past a top editor's quibbles. That wasn't Kathy's style. She didn't dance. She butted heads and did so with the stubbornness of a Rocky Mountain Bighorn sheep.

Charlie took a selfie in front of the Cité Soleil clinic and texted it to her.

"J-u-s-t c-h-e-c-k-i-n-g i-n!" he one-finger typed into his phone. It was his way of letting her know that he was on the ground and on the case.

Charlie had done his research for the clinic story's B matter, the context and background for the article:

The eight square miles of Cité Soleil, home to half a million people, are the most densely populated and marginalized part of Haiti. It was settled in the 1950s by government employees assigned to the then-burgeoning sugar industry. At the time it was called Cité Simone, named for Simone Duvalier, the wife of the despotic "president for life," Francois "Papa Doc" Duvalier.

In the decades that followed, job shortages, deforestation and political instability forced hundreds of thousands of rural Haitian families to leave the countryside. Many went to Port-au-Prince to search for work and settled in Cité Soleil for its easy access to cheap housing and factory jobs. When the government-sponsored housing projects failed to keep up with the demand, people began building informally on any piece of land they could grab, much of it on vulnerable flood plains by the sea. The development sprawled and blossomed with makeshift shanties.

After the fall of the regimes of Papa Doc and his son, Jean-Claude, aka "Baby Doc," there was an effort to erase anything associated with the Duvaliers. Cité Simone became Cité Soleil in homage to Radio Soleil, the populist, anti-Duvalier station. The re-christened Cité was initially organized as a suburb of Port-au-Prince. In 2002, a decree by President Jean Bertrand Aristide made Cité Soleil its own municipality.

Moving deeper into Bois Neuf, Maffi and Charlie came face to face with a muscular man in his twenties. He wore a red rolled bandanna as a headband and a black sweatshirt with white lettering in two decks of type, two words per line: "Love Life … Give Blood." Probably just a blood drive slogan on a give-away shirt, thought Charlie, but on this guy it looked sinister. They could see he had a pistol tucked into his waistband near the small of his back. He eyed the pair suspiciously but said nothing and let them pass.

"*Bandi*," Maffi whispered to Charlie, using the Creole word for thugs. "Gangs. They're running Haiti again."

"Evans' crew? Can you ask him?"

Maffi was impatient.

"You can't just walk up to any gangbanger and ask about Evans. That's a good way to get your feelings hurt."

Maffi explained the only safe way to proceed. She would let a few of her trusted contacts know that they want to meet Evans, letting them believe that it was about his donations to the clinic.

"If he's game, he'll find us. That's the way it works."

She explained that gang protocol is serious business in Haiti, with inter-neighborhood warfare over turf, contraband and shake-down rackets as common as the sunrise. Gangs play a complex role in this place virtually abandoned by the government. They fill the void by providing protection, a rough-justice system and money for community projects - mob rule masquerading as government.

"*Pep la* - the people - flinch at the gangs' fists, but still come running for their open hands," she said.

Bandi also do the bidding of prominent politicians, who use them like local militias to crush opposition neighborhoods, where the men are often killed and the women gang-raped.

From what Maffi already knew and could piece together, Evans fit the gang-leader profile. In his early thirties, he was a Haitian football fanatic and frequently dressed in the pec-hugging royal blue-and-white jersey of Haiti's national team. From time to time he donated new soccer balls to the local league, a gesture deeply appreciated by the children who ordinarily played their games with a plastic bag stuffed with dozens of other bags, and wrapped tightly with duct tape.

"He's seen by some as a benefactor," said Maffi, "but cross him and he'll make you piss yourself." Everyone assumed the long scar on his face was from some long-ago fight, but no one dared ask him about it. Once, to scare a rival gang member, he strapped the man's hand to a kitchen cutting board and approached with a barber's straight razor, angling it to catch the light. But instead of wielding it, he bent low and suddenly bit off the tip of the man's pinky, and added to the horror by swallowing it. Another time, to punish a stool pigeon who ratted him out to U.N. troops, said Maffi, he bound the man's arms, crucifixion-style to the bumper of a parked car and used needle-nose pliers to grab and extend his tongue. With a box cutter, he sliced it lengthwise from the back of the throat to the tip of the tongue.

"He wants to be a lousy rat bastard? *Youn zandolit zozo santi?*" a stinky-dick lizard, Evans had said. "A forked tongue will make it easier for him."

"That's Evans," said Maffi. "You still in?"

CHAPTER FIFTEEN
She snores!

Back in his room at the Désir, Charlie stood under the shower, rinsing off the sweat of the day's reporting and the dust from Junior's pickup. It took only a minute for the shower's hot water to run cold. The Désir was comfortable, provided you graded on a curve. Drying off, he plugged a phone charger into the short-cabled power strip that he carried in his go bag because rooms on the road never have enough outlets. He tried to connect to the hotel's WIFI to check for messages, but the WIFI was down.

If Kathy needed to reach him in a hurry, and his cell was out of range, she could call the hotel's landline. He opened his laptop and began distilling his notes. For the moment, at least, his room had electricity. He wouldn't need to reach for his headlamp as he had so many nights in a blacked-out Gaza.

Charlie was happy with the progress of the reporting. Poverty, gang violence and misery abound in Cité Soleil - no news in that. But the success of the clinic is a sign of change since the night of the quake, when thousands of Soleyans from rival blocks slept together in *Plas Fyete*, the main public square, because they feared sleeping indoors due to the aftershocks. Humbled by the awesome force of nature, they shared blankets, water, and a camaraderie previously unknown because of their inter-neighborhood rivalries.

The residents he interviewed also described the quake as a call to conscience, as God shaking Haiti out of its sad status quo. People spared by the devastation felt they had a new lease on life. People who had never been involved in community activities began to volunteer, tamping down the divisions that had kept them apart.

Those would be the themes of his article, but he needed more details about how precisely a former hostage house had become a house of healing.

At the clinic, a mother whose five-year-old daughter was being treated for tapeworms had allowed Charlie to follow them home to the walk-in-closet-sized shanty they shared with three adult relatives. There was only one bed - reserved for the mother and child. The others, two aunts and a teenage nephew, slept on mats on the floor. Empty fruit crates turned sideways served as shelves for their folded clothes, of which they had few. A wire hanger, holding a threadbare blouse, dangled from a line above the bed. A fire pit for cooking was outside. Amid the grim tableau was a clutch of waxy artificial flowers - brilliant reds and yellows in a cheap vase.

These are the patients the clinic serves, resilient people with dire needs at every level. No doubt the newspaper's secondary headline on his story - the "subhed" - would say something cliched about the clinic's volunteers "doing God's work," thought Charlie, but he wanted to delve deeper.

The sun was sliding below the horizon when he closed his laptop and left his room. The Désir's patio was filling up with guests wanting dinner. Tables were arranged with their square red cloths set at an angle over round white ones, and ladderback chairs painted blue - forming the three colors of Haiti's flag. Charlie, wearing a light sweater, sat alone near the pool and ordered a hamburger and fries.

Crickets hummed. The distant mountains stretched out like lazy dogs.

An hour later, after he had cluttered his table with three empty bottles of Prestige, Charlie switched to Barbancourt and tipsily daydreamed about Corinne, flashing back again to how they met.

He recalled her confidence and sass, moon face and sexy smile below brown curls that reminded him of the actress Maria Schneider in Last Tango in Paris.

Corinne and a fellow nurse had spent a night in a backpacking tent at the Port-au-Prince hospital triage center. Decompressing at the Désir they had teased about that night while standing at the bar.

"She snores," said Corinne's friend. "Horribly."

"Not me. You!" Corinne parried, chuckling.

"We are such a sight! You should see us sleeping together."

Charlie, ever the wise-ass, waited a beat, then said, "I'd pay tall money for that."

"Get in line!" a grinning Corinne shot back, tossing the comment over her shoulder with a teasing grin.

Was she just being clever? Or was she saying that his snarky joke was way out of line, and he should rein it in? The exchange was the beginning of what would become his tendency to over-analyze the things she said. He didn't like that about himself, but he couldn't help it.

They had developed a friendship that was close but chaste. Could it be more? Seeing her now, years later, but unexpectedly off balance, Charlie had thought of admitting his infatuation. She was single. Since his divorce in 2015, he was too. If he spoke up, confessed his feelings, would they be reciprocated? Or would the admission fall flat? It might not ruin their friendship, he thought, but if unrequited it would make things awkward. Fuck awkward. Charlie hated awkward. He even hated the sound of the word. At some point, he would have to be honest with her.

"Another Barbancourt, *tanpri,*" he said to the waiter. Charlie took one swig and was careful not to spill the rest as he wobbled with it back to his room.

The next morning, he heard from Maffi, calling from a noisy street in Croix des Bouquets.

"Can you hear me?"

"Maffi? Maffi? I hear you. Where are you?"

He could hear car horns blaring and pushcart vendors hollering.

Maffi spoke again, but the transmission was garbled.

Charlie tried: "Where? …" and suddenly Maffi's voice came through, smothering his.

"Doesn't matter. … Still no contact from Evans," she said. "But I got something. Two *bandi* in his crew went up north to do a job."

"When?"

"I don't have the date. But they are gang … ers." Another garble.

"What? You're breaking up."

"Gangbangers."

"What about them?"

"Evans' crew. Two of 'em. Went north. Hired by a limping, well-dressed Haitian man. Said he needed them for a security job."

"You're still breaking up. I can't understand. Ask Junior to drive you to the Désir. Lunch is on me."

Almost two hours later, frazzled by the bumper-to-bumper gridlock of Port-au-Prince, Maffi finally arrived. Her clothes smelled like burnt tires.

It's less than 10 miles from Croix des Bouquets to the Désir. But massive street protests had tied the city in knots. Cast initially as protests about gasoline shortages, these demonstrations had morphed over time into a broad campaign against government corruption and the feckless leadership of Haiti's President Jovenal Moise. Protesters wanted him out. Flaming-tire barricades on the main roads, along with rock throwing and some gunfire, added new levels of insecurity to the country's everyday woes, which included 70 percent unemployment. Exploiting the chaos, gangs were barricading streets, highjacking commercial vehicles, holding foreigners and prominent businessmen for ransom.

"You like this place?" Maffi said, wrinkling her nose as she looked around the Désir's patio. "Not me. *Two boujwa*" - too bourgeois.

"If you'd rather not eat …," said Charlie.

"No, I'll eat."

She signaled the waiter, who wore a white jacket, black bow tie and black pants. "Bring me two Coca-Colas. Two, for me. *Tanpri*. Send another one outside to the guy in the parking lot with the red truck. Also," – she looked over at Charlie's plate to see what he was eating – "yeah, bring me a hamburger."

Aggravated by the slow ride through the blocked

streets, Maffi had started out snappish but settled down after the first Coke slaked her thirst.

"I got nothing on how we get to Evans. But *tripotay* - the gossip - is that the gangbangers that I told you about are his soldiers."

"I couldn't hear you on the phone. Tell me again."

"A Haitian man, well dressed, wearing a tie, hired them for some kind of security operation up north. I doubt that they'd do a job like that without Evans' blessing. Are you sure you want to follow wherever this leads?"

Charlie nodded.

He never asked. Maffi never said. But he had the feeling that her source on this information was the metal-art merchant Baron. Having downed the burger and the second Coke, she left the Désir trailing attitude and the sour scent of burnt Goodyears.

CHAPTER SIXTEEN
Crossing swords

Having watched Maffi depart, Charlie couldn't wait to call Corinne.

"That's it! Gotta be. Hinche is up north. A man in a tie. It's gotta be Pinay. That bastard!" an excited Corinne said after he had filled her in.

"Whoa. There are a lot of places north of Port-au-Prince. There are a lot of men in ties. Don't get ahead of your skis. Even if these clues lead back to Pinay, it doesn't tell us who killed Sanctis. Or if it was a hit, who ordered it? You say it was Pinay, but that's not proven. What about the telescope? That's a straight-up robbery right there."

"But she just told you. Maffi told you. He hired them! Come on! …… I just have a feeling."

"We could just be looking at a robbery-murder that has nothing to do with Pinay."

"No, my feeling is right: Pinay hired Sanctis' killers."

Charlie liked to be a wise ass, to joke around. But he was also hyper-rational when he focused on a problem. Slow to draw conclusions and always wanting more proof. Tangible proof. Part of that was his J-school training. Part was an innate skepticism that had probably nudged him towards journalism in the first place.

"That's great. Feelings are fine. Nothing wrong with them," said Charlie. "They can be good for you. But until you have proof you should keep your mouth shut, especially if Pinay is backed up by Evans and he's as dangerous as you suspect. For now, the tangible evidence points to a robbery. That much we know."

The next time Corinne saw the limping obstetrics chief it was in the bedlam of Notre Dame des Douleurs's crowded maternity ward.

She was holding the hand of a first-time pregnant teenager who, when Pinay showed up, was howling in purple pain from unproductive labor.

"Okay, let's go, move over," he ordered. "Move!" he barked when Corinne refused to let go of the hand. Speaking loudly, she began running down the checklist of the scared teen's vitals.

"Labor started last night about eleven …"

Pinay cut her off.

"I can see she's in labor," he growled. "Prep for a section."

A C-section in Haiti is a crapshoot. Wait too long in unproductive labor and the baby could die of fetal distress. Cut open the mother in this humid, bacteria-filled environment, where clean water is scarce, and she could die of an infection.

Corinne suggested they still had time for more evaluation.

"Prep her," Pinay repeated. "If you won't, get me a nurse who will."

There was no masking the loathing between them. Pinay demanded obedience. Corinne wouldn't bow.

Everyone on the ward could see it.

In the end, the scared teen went under Pinay's scalpel and delivered a healthy baby boy.

That night, back at Saj Fanm, in-country director Annabelle asked if she could see Corinne privately in the second-floor nook that was her office. As Annabelle spoke, she calmly stroked the kitten, Jean Claude. He rolled onto his back and jabbed the air with his front paws like a boxer at a speed bag.

"I heard some of the nurses say that you and Dr. Pinay are crossing swords."

"Crossing swords? That's one way to put it. He's such an arsehole. Treats the women in labor like they are robots. … A Goddamned garage mechanic shows more compassion during an oil change. Gets paid extra for C-sections so he overprescribes them."

Corinne thought of opening up, confessing her suspicions about Pinay's role in Sanctis' murder. She felt she could trust Annabelle, but what if she was wrong? What if Annabelle took her words straight to Pinay?

For a moment Annabelle said nothing, then spoke slowly and deliberately.

"I won't argue with your assessment. He can be a difficult man. But he runs the *salle maternite*. As a director of the hospital, he signs off on all personnel assignments. He could ban you from the hospital. Wouldn't need a reason. Could just say that you've been at it too long. We would still be able to send you out with the mobile clinics. But as far as the hospital goes, Pinay could pull your plug."

Corinne thought about that, and what would happen if she upped the ante by telling Annabelle that Pinay steals from the hospital. Even if Corinne couldn't tie the embezzlement to Sanctis' murder, that allegation by itself would be enough to embroil Pinay in scandal. That was her ace. But should she play it? She felt like blurting out her suspicion but held her tongue.

Charlie had advised her to "zip it until you can prove it." That was not her natural inclination, but she knew he was right.

The thought of possibly losing her hospital privileges hit Corinne hard. She enjoyed going out with the mobile clinic and knew that its work was critically important for the women living far off the grid. But the maternity ward at the hospital is where she shined, Macguyver-like, with competence and flair.

There was the time that an anxious junior nurse-midwife ran up to her holding a totally limp newborn, with its chest faced down on one of her hands and its damp stubby arms and legs draped on either side of her forearm. The baby girl looked like a soggy Raggedy Ann.

Carefully, Corinne took the lifeless lump in one hand. With the other she used a rubber aspirator to suction off fluid from the baby's nose and throat. She did it again and again until a sudden spasm showed her that the baby was starting to breathe on its own. A few more convulsions and the baby cried. The nurses' cheering gave way to relief and laughter.

Another time, on a day that was uncharacteristically chilly, with gusts causing the palm fronds to clatter, Corinne and another nurse were helping a woman in the final pushes of a painful delivery. At almost the exact moment that the baby's head crowned, the mother lost consciousness. Corinne caught the baby and slid her out of the birth canal. Her colleague worked the bellows of a manual respirator to resuscitate the passed-out mom.

Corinne feared that the newborn, a low-birth-weight girl, was getting cold. Normally the baby would have been placed, skin-to-skin, in contact with her mother. But this mom was out cold.

"Hold her for a second," Corinne said, handing the baby to an attendant. Then she slid an arm inside her scrub shirt, reached back, unfastened her bra, slipped off the shoulder straps, and pulled it out through an armhole like a magician pulling a rabbit out of a hat.

"Voila!" she said, theatrically. "Hand her back to me." Corinne reached under her shirt and tucked the baby into her cleavage, the natural warmth of nature's incubator.

When the mother revived, the baby went onto her chest under a dry towel. All in a day's work at the *salle maternité*.

If Corinne remained so visibly at odds with Pinay, the maternity-ward part of her job, the part she was most passionate about, and where she so clearly excelled, was all at stake.

"Okay," she told Annabelle. "I will try not to antagonize the bastard. But he doesn't make it easy."

While Corinne gave little thought to the missing telescope, Charlie was privately disturbed by what its disappearance could mean. Privately, because he wasn't ready to share that part of his thinking with Corinne.

She believed, down to her toes, that Pinay had Sanctis killed, so she chalked up the telescope's theft to happenstance. The way she saw it, whoever came to kill Sanctis grabbed the scope as an afterthought, a side crime of opportunity, perhaps without even knowing the scope's function or worth.

That was possible, sure.

But Charlie also looked at the situation from inside out. He worried that the crime was conceived as a robbery. Not a hit. Not an assassination. A robbery, plain and simple, which went awry and turned fatal.

Everyone in town knew that Sanctis had the fancy stargazer. He loved to talk about all the planets that he had seen up close. Word on the grapevine was that the scope probably wasn't the only valuable thing that the privileged Haitian-American doctor owned. Under those circumstances, it was quite possible that the roughnecks had come to rob him and when Sanctis fought back he was garrotted with his own stethoscope. If so, murder was not the original plan. Charlie's well-trained instincts told him it was entirely possible the killing had nothing to do with Sanctis having caught Pinay pilfering pills.

And what about the missing eyes? Gruesome, surely. But a tactic common to any number of superstitious thugs trying to cover their tracks. Okay, not any number, Charlie conceded. Probably a small number. That might help narrow the field of suspects.

Corinne was emotionally invested in her theory about Pinay. Outwardly, Charlie supported her. But privately he sifted the sparse evidence, generating more questions than answers. Why would someone steal something so expensive and unique that would be almost impossible to fence quietly in Haiti? Why take the scope and nothing else? Maybe the robber or robbers planned to take more, got spooked and fled fast after the killing? Maybe. Maybe. Maybe.

Charlie knew what Corinne would say if he openly doubted her gut feeling. "The answer is right in front of you, Charlie, yet you're going like clappers in the wrong direction."

He wanted to avoid that conversation unless and until it became necessary. Until then he would hold his peace about his doubts.

CHAPTER SEVENTEEN
Pilfered pills

Among some literature that had landed on Pinay's desk two years after the quake was a sheet on "Neglected Tropical Diseases" - NTDs - and the toll in lives and suffering caused by seven scourges: elephantiasis, blinding trachoma, river blindness, snail fever - and the big three of soil-transmitted parasites: hookworms, roundworms, and whipworms.

"Intricately linked to poverty and inequality," they hit hardest on "hard-to-reach populations ... causing chronic illness, blindness and disfigurements."

"What else is new?" thought Pinay.

But one part of the sheet caught his eye. It described the U.S. Agency for International Development's "drug donation partnerships" by which billions of dollars of medicines were donated by pharmaceutical stalwarts, including Merck, GlaxoSmithKline, Johnson & Johnson and Pfizer. The program encompasses 32 countries, including Haiti, where elephantiasis is a problem in 80 percent of the country.

Pinay poured himself some water, added ice and read on. In a hospital almost devoid of amenities, his lair was equipped with a minifridge connected to a battery that maintained power during blackouts, and a hand-cranked emergency radio that could also generate a charge for his cell phone. Thus fortified, he had holed up in this office on many days, with the cabinet of hospital records behind his desk between two heavily draped windows.

Elephantiasis is a mosquito-borne disease that causes a limb or other body part to become grossly swollen. Lymphatic fluid that normally returns to the bloodstream leaks into the tissue, causing it to balloon.

Pinay had seen the effects. "Monstrous" was the word that came to his mind. Worse, the disease has no cure. Binding the limb can squeeze out some of the leaking fluid, but only temporarily. Prevention is the best path. That means "mass drug administration," reaching every person in the population with a combination of pills. In that effort, public health workers had handed out the pills at schools, markets, churches, factories, and public places. The goal: Kill the parasite in its larval form before it matures into a drug-resistant worm a year later.

If an entire population takes the drugs regularly, the volume of larvae circulating in people and mosquitoes falls so low that no new transmissions occur. That's herd immunity.

What a massive undertaking! What a giant opportunity for fraud, thought Pinay. In Haiti, everyone has a side hustle. The busboy who doubles as a hire-car driver. The chambermaid who sells bruised fruit on the roadside in the afternoons. The Ministry of Tourism official who runs an unofficial B&B.

These drug-donation partnerships, if played right, thought Pinay, present an opportunity for someone like him to embezzle and traffic drugs with no one the wiser.

Yet Pinay's world of medicine did not intersect with the supply chain of the NTD medicines. It was out of his reach. But reading about it opened his eyes. What if he aimed lower, say, at the patent medicine market? Those drugs were donated too, and more importantly he had access to them.

He could regularly cadge thousands of pills at the hospital, distribute them via the network of itinerant pill peddlers, and nicely, quietly, invisibly supplement his income.

Pinay rose from his desk and peeked between the drapes. He saw a few agaves growing in the gravel. Sunlight refracted off an oily puddle. A moto driver was tuning his engine. A vendor hawked *sachés dlo*, the ubiquitous packets of sanitized water, slaking thirsts across Haiti a few swallows at a time.

That settled it. And that was the side hustle he had run for nearly a decade in an illicit partnership with Evans, who controlled the Port-au-Prince pill trade. It all had worked so invisibly and so well, all had gone so according to plan, until that nosey Sanctis Beauvoir had come along and stumbled on the scam.

CHAPTER EIGHTEEN
Smug twat!

It had been a week since Charlie and Maffi's lunch at the Desir, where she told him what she had heard about the two gangbangers from Evans' crew. All across Port-au-Prince now dissent was rising. Getting in and out of Cité Soleil was made more treacherous by the frequency and unpredictability of the anti-government demonstrations. The protests against JoMo's corrupt regime were increasingly fierce, and the gangs were taking advantage of the chaos to step up the pace of their crimes, including kidnappings.

His editor Kathy had asked him to stay on for a while to cover the chaos.

Many days, Junior's pickup had to slalom around upturned paving stones, barricades and burning tires.

As a reporter, Charlie's inclination was what he described as "careful risk-taking." But as he plotted each day's reporting efforts, his Twitter feed buzzed with constant reminders of the U.S. State Department's more cautious approach:

Reconsider travel to Haiti due to crime, civil unrest, and kidnapping, was the tweet he woke up to one morning.

Protests, tire burning, and road blockages are frequent and unpredictable it said. Violent crime, such as armed robbery, is common, and incidents of kidnapping have occurred. Local police may lack the resources to respond effectively to serious criminal incidents, and emergency response, including ambulance service, is limited or non-existent. Travelers are sometimes targeted, followed, and violently attacked and robbed shortly after leaving the Port-au-Prince International Airport.

That, Charlie thought, must have been what happened a few days earlier to a French couple that had flown to Haiti as part of an adoption process. The couple had been set upon, robbed, and shot to death almost immediately after arriving.

It was their first trip to Haiti. They were slated to meet the two children they were adopting, a brother and sister, and stay for two weeks for the required get-acquainted socialization.

Upon arrival at Toussaint Louverture International Airport, the couple got into a taxi that had been booked for them by the French Adoption Association. Witnesses say they were set upon and killed the moment they arrived at their hotel in the Delmas district. Adoption officials suspect the assailants tracked the couple from the airport. There'd been no arrests.

The next morning, the French Ministry of Foreign Affairs had weighed in:

"It was with great emotion that we learned of the deaths of two compatriots in Haiti following an assault. We express our condolences to their families and loved ones. ... As soon as it was informed, our Embassy mobilized. It is in contact with the local authorities so that all light is shed on this tragedy. ... [The Ministry] recommends to French citizens to postpone any trip to Haiti until further notice, except in case of absolute necessity, the whole of the Haitian territory is to be avoided."

Avoided? Well, it's a little late for that, thought Charlie.

Clearly, neither the United States nor France wanted their citizens anywhere near Haiti. But here was Charlie, bird-dogging a story like he always did, only this time he had added reasons for digging in: his growing attraction for Corinne and his worry about her mental and physical well-being in a country descending into anarchy.

Drying off after he showered, he heard Aaron Neville coming from the MP-3 player he'd left on the nightstand. Neville's distinctive falsetto warbled *Can't Stop My Heart from Loving You.*

Charlie loved that tender ballad, which expresses a man's devotion to the woman he loves, and her skepticism that what they have will last.

The melody had him daydreaming again about Corinne and wondering what she was doing at that moment. She was devastated and enraged by Sanctis' murder. Charlie worried that when her rage was ascendant, she might do or say something rash. Clearly, Sanctis was the victim of a robbery. That much was clear. Throwing around allegations that he was killed on the orders of Pinay to protect a drug hustle was dangerous speculation.

He hung up his towel and punched Corinne's number with a still-damp finger. She answered on the first ring.

They had barely exchanged hellos when she began venting about Pinay. "Such a jerk. … Awful … arsehole." Her voice skipped and jumped like a needle on a worn vinyl record.

She was filled with a simmering rage. "I can't even look at him! He disgusts me. I want to throw up … or say

99

something. Let him know that I know. Smug twat! Thinks he is getting away with murder. Unless I say something, he will."

Charlie kept his voice soft and soothing, scrubbing it of the panic he was feeling at the thought of Corinne shouting wild accusations down the corridors of the hospital.

"You'll be out on a limb and Pinay will happily saw it off. He'll ban you from the hospital. He'll undermine you with the staff. He'll set you up to fail and make your life a living hell. … Really, you just can't say anything yet. Maybe sometime, if we can find more evidence, but please, understand, it may also never be."

Corinne smoldered. In her head, she bristled at Charlie's words, but eventually bowed to the realization that he was right. She needed more leverage if she was going to bring down Pinay.

"Look, all right," she said. "I know I am consumed by this. But you're the only one I can talk to, love. I wish we could have more time together at the Désir. Talking with you clears my head."

Charlie over-analyzed her words, as he always did, lost in thought about what they meant. Did she mean more time together as an item, as a couple? That sounded good.

Or did she mean she needed more input from the friend-turned-amateur therapist and sleuth that Charlie had become?

Was at the Désir just an afterthought? Or did it define the limits of their togetherness? Love? Was that love, like love? Or just her being British? Corinne's voice pierced his racing thoughts: "Earth to Charlie. Are you there?"

"Sorry. Lost my train of thought. Anyway, Maffi's been great, hugely helpful. The clinic story came together. She found someone who knew the whole history of its transformation. Turns out that a Vodou priestess, a *mambo* from *Bois Neuf*, went to see the gangbanger who had somehow acquired the abandoned house and was using it for hostages. Sounds like he had forced out the previous tenant. Long story short, the mambo visited him in prison. She told him, 'You have done so many bad things in your life, you need to transfer the house to a good cause if you want peace in the afterlife.' Otherwise, she told him, he would wander forever as a zombie. She spoke to him harshly and framed the transfer as a necessity, not a request. 'It is a demand that originates in the spirit world,' she told him. Pretty slick, huh?

"The mambo had extracted the gangbanger's promise to turn over the building. On the strength of that verbal commitment, the nonprofit that supports the clinic took a risk and renovated the building. By the time the man got out of prison, the clinic had been operating for two years. Cool story? No?"

"Very cool," Corinne agreed.

To keep her mind off Pinay, Charlie kept talking about what he had witnessed in the city.

The Haitian police, in white SUVs with snorkel exhausts, were using tear gas and live ammunition on the anti-government protesters, he said, and the country's food and fuel shortages were getting worse. Ordinary law enforcement was non-existent.

"We were driving out of Cité Soleil when we saw a crowd stripping an abandoned satellite police station of everything - its sheet metal roof, furniture, police gear, everything. Maffi said she had never seen anything like it. The day before, cops from that post had fired tear gas grenades and live ammunition at the demonstrators. People were angry, so they took the place apart, dismantled it piece by piece."

"When was that?"

"Yesterday morning. I interviewed a man who scurried off with a piece of corrugated steel. *Pep la* - the people - are taking whatever they can to make their houses better, he said, because "they are tired of getting soaked when it rains.""

"The demonstrations are having an impact on us up here too," said Corinne. "Not the violence per se, but collateral damage. Volunteers that normally come to us from America are staying away. We're running out of the supplies they used to bring with them in their luggage."

Most importantly, she explained, they were almost out of Clean Delivery Kits, the essential supplies they call "CDKs," which they need for their mobile unit.

The kits, distributed for use in remote villages, contain important items for conducting hygienic deliveries under less-than-sanitary conditions.

"We give out about 150 kits a month," said Corinne. "We're down to 50 in storage. It's getting bad."

"Not good," said Charlie, sounding empathetic, but more interested in getting a read on how Corinne was coping. She kept talking about the kits. The razor blade, surgical gloves, absorbent sheets and gauze in a CDK, she explained, reflect the World Health Organization's five principles of cleanliness in childbirth, known as "the five cleans" - clean hands, clean delivery surface, clean cord-cutting tool, clean cord ties and clean care of the umbilical stump.

Charlie wasn't really interested in that level of detail, but happy to hear Corinne talk passionately about something other than how much she detested Pinay. He loved how fiercely she cared for the expectant mothers, even as he wished she'd tone down the fierceness when it came to Pinay.

"With the kit shortages and everything else you are dealing with it sounds like an everyday shit show."

"T'is and more," she said. "But the courage of these women who give birth in remote villages or at our grotty hospital is no joke. They are brilliant."

Charlie had witnessed the gore of war. He had seen wounded men bleeding profusely, and non-combatants shredded by shrapnel.

He had seen mayhem and the final hours of many lives.

But for all his witnessing, he had never witnessed a birth. Sometime, he thought, if he ever got the chance to see a life come into the world, it might change him for the better.

CHAPTER NINETEEN
Love in the time of cholera

A small resurgence of cholera in 2019, a month after Sanctis' murder, had people fearing a reprise of that first October after the 2010 quake when Haiti's Ministry of Public Health and Population had announced the country's first case in over a century. The epidemic that eventually would kill nearly 10,000 people had begun in the rural Artibonite Valley, not far from Corinne's hospital.

Medical investigators later concluded a likely source of the infection was sewage leaking from a U.N. base that housed peacekeepers from Nepal, where the disease is endemic. Their base was above a tributary of the Artibonite River, central Haiti's all-purpose laundry, car wash and source of drinking water.

Responding to concerns about the new outbreak, Annabelle called a staff meeting.

"We all know cholera is bacterial and comes from fecal contaminated food or water. So redouble your efforts on the five cleans," she said. "Keep an eye out for any signs of diarrhea, vomiting or dehydration in our women."

Corinne knew she should be paying closer attention, but the black dog of depression was breathing down her neck. Blood pounded in her ears. Perspiration glistened on her forehead. She ran a hand over her sweaty scalp. Outside the temperature hovered around 85 degrees.

Meanwhile, in Port-au-Prince, Charlie was alone at

breakfast at the Desir, scrolling through news sites on his phone when he saw a mention of the small outbreak of cholera. Just a handful of cases, still manageable, he thought, but cholera in Haiti always bore watching.

The morning sun felt good on his face. He had a growing desire to be with Corinne, to hold her hand, to make her problems his problems, to solve them together. He wasn't a fan of Gabriel Garcia Marquez, whose magical realism wasn't Charlie's thing. Charlie leaned toward earthy realism, and ground truth. But the title of Marquez's novel, *Love in the Time of Cholera*, seemed to sum up his passion for Corinne.

He hoped she felt the attraction too. He could be an insufferable wise ass. He knew that. His rationality in the face of her emotionality could get on her very last nerve. But she was learning that she could count on him, on his focus, strength and loyalty in a crisis. If it came down to open warfare with Pinay, she would want Charlie in the foxhole beside her. At least he hoped she would feel that way.

CHAPTER TWENTY
Secrets of the living dead

Looking out over some sharp bends in the meandering Mississippi, Tulane University's School of Medicine was bathed in sunshine on that fall day in 2018.

Having returned to New Orleans for their 10th Class Reunion, Sanctis and his med-school buddies, Antoine Chery and Joseph Jean, were at the campus food court when they heard the drumming and hustled out to join the parade for *Fet Gede*, the Haitian Day of the Dead, celebrated annually on November 2 as a sign of respect for deceased friends and relatives.

Krewe du Kanaval, the energetic band of drummers, dancers and musicians founded in New Orleans to celebrate the city's cultural ties with Haiti, was on the move in the Nola way … sashaying down city streets behind a vanguard carrying instruments. The women wore flouncy skirts of red and purple; the men, made up to look like the Vodou father of the dead, Baron Samedi, wore black-and-white face paint.

Among the trio of friends, Antoine was the cutup, loud, always teasing, "*Ale! Ale! Reveye mo yo!* Make some noise," he shouted. "*Reveye mo yo!* Wake the Dead!"

At the other end of the personality spectrum, Joseph was the quiet one. An introvert, he carried a cymbal in the marching band but rarely struck it.

Sanctis wore a deep purple jacket, the signature color

of *Fet Gede*. He was happy to be among fellow Haitians reveling in their common culture.

Thousands of Haitians had landed in Louisiana in the early 19th century after Haiti's revolution. By 1809, New Orleans had more than 10,000 of them. By the second decade of the 21st century, however, Nola's Haitian-born population was down to 1,500, among them a diminutive man called Ti-Jean, a *bokor* – or Vodou witch doctor - who presented himself as a soothsayer and intermediary in prayers to the Vodou deities called loas.

Marching alongside Sanctis, Ti-Jean touted the potency of his black magic. "I know the secrets of the living dead," he said. "You doubt? You come. You'll see. *Demen swa*. Tomorrow night."

Sanctis had heard the legends about bokors who created zombies using a paralyzing brew of pufferfish nerve toxin and then brought them back to life to do the *bokor's* bidding as undead slaves. That was a mainstay of Vodou folklore, and it left him doubting.

Now Ti-Jean, this gnome-like man, was offering him a chance to eyewitness a zombification and to put his skepticism to the test.

Sanctis said yes to the invitation. Antoine and Joseph wanted in, too.

The next day at dusk the three of them arrived at the *bokor's* two-room shotgun shack in the city's lower Ninth Ward. Its clapboards were splintered and buckled; its purple paint peeling. Inside-out car-tire planters held lanky Trees of Heaven, which flanked the front door. The inside was furnished with a threadbare Victorian sofa that would have looked at home in a Wild West whore house.

There were votive candles in glass jars, strands of multi-colored beads draped on lamp shades, human and animal skulls, a half-empty bottle of Barbancourt, stick-figure *veves* painted on the walls and a framed oil portrait of Mary, mother of Jesus. Scrawled in script on the back wall of the living room: "*Tous les voudousaints sont des freres et sœurs,*" all believers in Vodou are brothers and sisters.

Seated on the sofa was an unkempt homeless man that Ti-Jean had paid $20 to participate. Sanctis, Antoine and Joseph sat opposite the sofa on creaky straight-back chairs.

"First," said Ti-Jean, raising his palms and lifting his gaze, "I call on Papa Legba to open the gates to the spirit world." Legba is a tall, shadowy *loa* with the power to collect souls and assign them roles in the afterlife. Ti-Jean was dressed for the ceremony in a white suit and cape.

As a sacrificial offering, he flicked a splash of Barbancourt onto the shack's pine floorboards. He mumbled words that seemed neither Creole nor French nor English, and then … "*Ai. Bobo, amen.*"

Blending languages, he called on the snake-like, sky deity Damballa to amplify his power as a *bokor*. "*Ade due Damballa,* tout-puissant. *Donnez-moi le pouvoir, je vous en supplie!*"

Shoulders hunched, chin down, the homeless man fidgeted and waited.

Ti-Jean held a small glass with a few ounces of liquid in front of a lit candle and added some Barbancourt. The appearance of the rum bottle got the homeless man's attention. Ti-Jean instructed him to down the contents of the glass in one swig. Handed a second identical drink, he downed that too.

It looked like he was going to swoon, as Ti-Jean had

said he would. But instead of slipping away gradually, his body jerked with a violent seizure that threw him to the floor, flapping like a fish drowning in air. Ti-Jean's eyes widened. He didn't speak, but the horrified expression on his face said clearly, "This is not how it is supposed to go."

The man's body became rigid. In a final burst, he vomited a river of blood that splattered everywhere, including on the shoes of Sanctis and his friends.

"What the fuck?" blurted Antoine.

Joseph, mute as usual, looked terrified.

To Sanctis, it appeared the man had suffered an aorta-bursting aneurysm and was hemorrhaging profusely, drowning in his own blood. Within two minutes he lay motionless. Sanctis pulled a stethoscope from his jacket and checked for signs of life. Respiration? Nothing. Pulse? Not even one beat.

This was no Vodou parlor trick, no reversible paralysis brought on by a fish's neurotoxin. This anonymous homeless man, who likely wouldn't be missed by anyone, was dead!

"Go now. I will handle this," said a rattled Ti-Jean. "You must never speak of this. You were never here. You understand? None of this happened. If you are indiscreet, I will know because the *loas* will warn me. Then I will call the authorities and implicate the three of you. You will lose your licenses to practice medicine, followed by a worse curse."

It seemed like an empty threat because calling the authorities would necessarily bring the heat on Ti-Jean too. But the trio was not about to test him.

Picking their way out of the Lower Ninth on pitch black

streets, they made their way in silence back to the campus.

Sanctis never learned what became of the homeless man's body. He never saw Ti-Jean again.

But three months after the botched ceremony, while working at a hospital in Miami to be near his widowed mom, Sanctis was stunned by an article he saw online at Nola.com, the website of the *New Orleans Times-Picayune*.

"Death Defies Explanation," read the headline.

The 10-paragraph article described the sudden death of his friend, Antoine, who had collapsed while jogging. Paramedics pronounced him dead of an apparent heart attack. The article described him as a dedicated amateur athlete with no prior cardiac problems, who worked out at a gym, ran marathons, and watched his diet. Friends quoted in the story said he was the fittest person they knew.

Two weeks later, yet another shock: The apparent suicide of Joseph by carbon monoxide poisoning. Authorities had found him slumped at the wheel of his Honda Civic. One end of a garden house was inserted into his car's tailpipe and held in place with duct tape. The other end was passed into the car's passenger compartment through a window that had been opened just a crack. Investigators said the engine idled for hours until it ran out of gas. Again, the newspaper reported the astonishment of friends. They knew Joseph as a quiet, introspective man, who had never shown any propensity for self-harm. Why would he kill himself?

The first death shocked Sanctis. The second scared him.

Was it a tragic coincidence that two of his robust and healthy friends had died so unexpectedly? Or was the *bokor* covering his tracks, systematically killing off witnesses to the failed zombification?

When dwelling obsessively on that question became too much for Sanctis, he reminded himself that he would be going to Haiti soon, and hopefully beyond the reach of Ti-Jean's clean-up operation - if that indeed was what this was.

CHAPTER TWENTY-ONE
Teargas

The air was dry. The sky was clear. A screeching racket of gulls sailed over Route 9 headed for the docile sea behind Cité Soleil.

But six miles east, in the business district of Delmas, demonstrators fed up with the widespread food and fuel shortages, double-digit inflation, weakening currency and a dictatorial government were demanding that President Jovenel Moise resign. Elected in 2017, his government had been dysfunctional for months because opposition parliamentarians refused to confirm his political appointees, and because Moise refused to call for new elections even though his term in office had expired. Politically, he was a dead man walking.

Street musicians with drums and cymbals kicked off the mobilization. It looked at first like a carnival parade except for the faces contorted with fury at high-ranking officials, including Moise, whom they accused of embezzling more than $2 billion in Venezuelan oil subsidies.

Waves of protesters swarmed the streets, flowing like lava past shuttered shops and a Western Union office guarded by three men with pump-action shotguns. Some demonstrators wore surgical masks or bandannas to cover their mouths and noses. Bare-chested men fashioned balaclavas out of their stripped-off tee shirts. Car tires stacked two high were set ablaze, producing curtains of black smoke. The steel-belt remains of burned-up radial tires covered the ground with ashy nests of coiled wire.

"*Viva Ayiti libre,*" they chanted, clapping hands above their heads. A few carried signs that read, *Demisyon Jovenel*, and in English, "Jovenel Moise must leave now!" One carried a sign that read, "*Jenes la bezwen travay*" - the people need jobs.

Some carried short tree branches, bristling with green leaves, which they shook in rhythm with the chanting. Near the front of the crowd was a white pickup truck blaring kompa from a boombox. Men on motorbikes zig-zagged around the edges of the crowd like a cavalry of iron horses.

Up ahead, a cordon of special-forces police stood their ground, shoulder-to-shoulder behind transparent riot shields. They held batons and wore tan camouflage fatigues, helmets, and shin and knee protection. They were intent on dispersing the protesters. They made occasional forays into the crowd, which scattered, regrouped, and started marching again, this time throwing rocks at the cops.

That's when the police fired tear-gas canisters, which sailed toward the protestors trailing plumes of eye-burning white smoke. After that came volleys of live fire from police shotguns. The first victim to fall was a man wearing a tee shirt emblazoned with the logo of Digicel, a popular cell phone company.

The next casualty was a woman in a gauzy, blue hair wrap. She was struck at close range by a canister that hit her squarely in the upper chest. She was dead on the spot from what appeared to be a crushed windpipe. Four people dragged her from the scene, one on each arm and leg.

In all, five people died - one by trampling - and several police officers were injured in one of the largest and most violent street protests in months.

CHAPTER TWENTY-TWO
Fabi?

Having just returned from a sunrise hike to the old sawmill, Corrine stood on the compound's front porch and used a twig to pry clumps of mud from the soles of her Wellies. Haiti's fertile, sticky soil clung like chewing gum.

In one corner of the compound, smoky tendrils spiraled from a small fire where the maintenance crew burned paper trash and fallen palm fronds. A mechanic tinkered with the engine of the clinic's forever balky SUV. A staffer hung freshly washed, detergent-scented scrubs, underwear, bras and socks on a line strung between trees.

Corinne checked her phone and found a fundraising message from Medecins Sans Frontieres that was packaged with an old video from 1999, the year MSF won the Nobel Peace Prize. Like Medicins du Monde, Medecins Sans Frontieres was an important medical relief organization.

"We are not sure that words can save lives, but we know that silence can certainly kill," said MSF's president. "We speak … with a clear intent … to assist … provoke change … reveal injustice."

The remarks were about humanitarian relief on a global scale. But in her state of mind, and in that list of virtues, Corinne heard a call to seek justice for Sanctis.

Downstairs after her shower, she found her colleagues gossiping over the remnants of breakfast. Jocelyn, a Haitian nurse, described her recent visit to the orphanage.

"You know, it was the usual. Heart filling and heart breaking at the same time, especially the dormitory where the babies are."

"I know the feeling. I've held those babies," said Corinne.

"This was different. The nuns were rocking babies on each arm, standing close, talking quietly. It was about the woman killed at the Delmas demonstration. Her only child is at the orphanage. That's what the Mother Superior told them."

"Oh dear God," said Corinne. "A boy or a girl?"

"A girl. Four years old."

"On her neck? Is there a mark on her neck? A birthmark. Like a star," Corinne implored.

Jocelyn shrugged. "Dunno."

"Is it Fabi? Fabilene? Fabi?"

Corinne's trembling voice rose an anxious octave with each repetition.

CHAPTER TWENTY-THREE
Jimmy Griye

In the aftermath of Sanctis' murder, Evans had maintained his distance from the gimpy Pinay.

Pills, after all, were just a part of Evans' criminal activity, and the doctor's sloppiness had put everything at risk.

"*Gate san* – rotten blood! That asshole must take care," said Evans, his lips wet and tingling from a bottle of rum that he passed around with his crew. The group included two moto-riding brothers, plus Evans' brother-in-law and a knife-carrying driver-bodyguard they called Blade.

They were five in all and committed crimes of opportunity - robberies, kidnappings and a protection racket that demanded fees from vendors at outdoor markets. Blade would steer Evans' white Nissan Xterra up to the edge of a market and his enforcers would hop out to collect the tribute. Failure to pay resulted first in a trashing of the vendor's stall, and the next time a thrashing. Evans remained in the car and rarely showed his face.

U.N. peacekeeping troops had withdrawn from Haiti in 2017 after 15 years, saying they had helped to re-establish law and order, a claim that by 2020 was demonstrably false.

With police forces diverted to deal with the protests against Jovenal Moise, Haitian law enforcement had virtually no enforcement power, investigative capacity, forensic ability or functioning judicial system. Gangs loyal to

"JoMo" operated with impunity. Bribe-hungry officials made anything possible. Institutions that should have mattered were hollowed out by the rot of corruption.

The 2010 earthquake had damaged the National Penitentiary and allowed 3,000 inmates to escape. This provided the gangs with an infusion of experienced thugs. That's when the two brothers joined Evans. They rode motos, carried guns, surrounded victims and robbed them in plain sight. Travelers prosperous enough to have arrived on a flight were frequent targets, like the poor French couple had been. Gang members followed new arrivals from the baggage claim and set upon them after their taxi reached a good spot for an ambush.

Sometimes the gangsters shot into vehicles stuck in traffic to panic or kill the driver and rob the passengers. Other times, they barricaded a main route, like National Highway #1 leading north from Port-au-Prince, and extorted anyone trying to pass. Police would arrive to clear the road eventually, but not before individual motorists as well as trucks loaded with merchandise had fallen prey.

Home invasions were part of the repertoire, especially in the relatively affluent suburb of Petionville. Evans' thugs would show a gun, fire it in the air to raise the fear factor, tie up their victims and make off with cash and cars.

The kidnappings fell into three categories: hostage-takings for ransom; proxy kidnappings, and express kidnappings. Some victims were well-to-do Haitian business owners. Foreigners and Haitian-Americans were particularly prized because it was thought they had relatives with money, who would always pay to get them released.

In the proxy kidnappings, which Evans called "tiger

traps," they nabbed victims and forced them to unlock an office safe after hours or break the seal on a commercial truck.

Designed to be quick and profitable, the third category, express kidnappings, were short-term ordeals. Evans' crew snatched victims, often foreigners, and forced them to make withdrawals from ATMs. Sometimes they held the hostages past midnight to extract a second day's daily limit of cash before ending the torment.

Having drained one bottle of rum, and half of another, Evans' crew hit the afternoon streets looking to "get paid."

The moto boys stomped their kick starters and peeled off to stake out the airport parking lot. Evans grabbed his brother-in-law and with Blade at the wheel, headed to Marche Salomon, the crowded downtown market where tribute would be paid.

The fearsome Evans answered to no man save one, Jimmy Janvier, the notorious cop turned capo of Haiti's most powerful confederation of gangs. Brash, ruthless and potbellied, Janvier had been fired from the Haitian National Police for his involvement in a raid that became a bloodbath because he had designed it to achieve that result. Over 14 brutal hours, opponents of the ruling party were systematically dragged from their homes, shot and hacked to death. Corpses were dismembered, set ablaze or left on trash piles. Eleven women were raped; 150 homes looted and razed. The unmistakable message: Conform or die.

A month later, police issued a warrant for Janvier's arrest and quickly found that he was untouchable, a Teflon Don, surrounded by bodyguards 24/7 and immune from prosecution because of the favors he did for officials in

Moise's *Tèt Kale* party. At their behest he unleashed his network of thugs to pound down dissent in opposition neighborhoods or inflate pro-Moise turnout at staged rallies. Officials who played the game provided him with weapons and tactical vehicles.

Known by the alias *Griye*, meaning "grilled," because he burned down neighborhoods, he insisted it was just a childhood nickname, applied long ago to distinguish him from so many other little Jimmies in the slum where his mom sold grilled chicken – *Poul Griye* – on the street.

Evans was in the car and his crew were making the rounds of their protection racket when he was interrupted by a sound that always took precedence, "Dun-dun-dun-dun-dun" - the Jaws-theme ringtone he had set for *Griye*.

"Tomorrow, 4 p.m., Pont-Rouge. *Vini lou*" - come heavy - is all he said and closed the line.

Okay, thought Evans, he's calling for pistols, machetes, hammers, knives, chains and Molotovs. But why?

Given Griye's paramilitary style of command, it was way above Evans' pay grade to inquire. He knew the role his crew was expected to play whenever the boss dialed up a state-sanctioned attack on dissenting civilians. Unquestioning obedience was part of the deal that allowed him to pursue independent endeavors like the kidnappings and pilfered-pill dodge. He tried telling himself that if he ever got into deep trouble with his criminal freelancing, Griye would use his juice to save him, but he knew that was wishful thinking.

Situated near Chancerelles, La Saline and Cité Soleil, three strongholds of anti-government activity, Pont

Rouge is where Haiti's revolutionary leader and first emperor Jean-Jacques Dessalines was murdered in an ambush in 1806. Near the black obelisk that is a monument to Dessalines, someone had spray painted the word *Jistis*. At the appointed time, Griye's confederation had assembled there. Some wore purloined police uniforms supplied by government contacts. Griye handed out assignments.

The impostor cops would order people onto the street where Evans' crew would dispatch them with savage blows to the head. Several were beheaded. At the end of the slaughter, a pile of body parts was hauled away by tractor. Evans and his men heaved two oozing corpses into a muddy pigpen, where a brown sow and two snuffling piglets feasted on their remains.

CHAPTER TWENTY-FOUR
Acc-u-sations!

Later on, Corinne never could explain why she exploded with the fury of a hurricane on that particular day. Even in the heat of the moment she knew it was not a smart move.

It had been a month since Sanctis' murder. A month of seeing Pinay shamble around the hospital with his stunted leg and toxic personality, apparently unafraid of being revealed. She fantasized about the vicious punishment she would exact if it were up to her. Each day that passed, each day that she saw him swan about with impunity, burned like acid on her heart. Maybe it was because of that gnawing ache that she confronted Pinay. Maybe it was because she so desperately wanted to unmask him and couldn't live with herself unless she sought justice for her friend.

Whatever it was, it happened quickly at the deserted end of a covered walkway when no one was around. Pinay was headed to his office. Corinne's shift in the *salle maternite* was going to start in half an hour. She fell in step with him as she spoke.

"I know about Sanctis," she said defiantly.

Pinay stopped, drew himself up, made a face like she was just a nuisance in his path, and started walking again.

"We all know about Sanctis," he said. "His death was a tragedy."

Blood thrummed in Corinne's ears. "A tragedy? Is that what you are telling people?"

"What are you talking about?"

"Sure, play dumb," she said. "You can dummy up all you want. But I know. I know. I know you had Sanctis killed!"

"You are out of your mind, woman. Insane. *Posede*. Possessed. Sanctis was robbed. And sadly he was killed in the act. It happens. What is wrong with you?"

Pinay's denial - and his quick pivot, turning the tables on Corinne to accuse her of instability, infuriated her even further.

She raised her voice and her accent turned more clipped and British. "You don't give a fiddler's fuck, do you? You fucking had him killed! I know you did."

"Acc-u-sations!" said Pinay, sarcastically. "You are insane. You have no judgment. You are unfit."

There it was. The ploy Pinay could use to undermine her. Unfit … and on her way to a sacking?

With that, he walked away abruptly and slid from the sunny outdoors into the dark corridor that led to his office.

Annabelle had warned Corinne about challenging Pinay's authority. Charlie had, too. When Pinay said Corinne was unfit, he was inches away from saying, "You're fired."

For some reason, she didn't understand he wasn't banning her from Notre Dame des Douleurs. At least not yet.

CHAPTER TWENTY-FIVE
Throw a punch?

Having finally unloaded on Pinay, Corinne felt better than she had in weeks, even though she hadn't really laid a glove on him. Her sleep was less fitful. That alone seemed like a win.

The next morning, she was up early enough to hear the roosters crowing, and left for the hospital on the back of a moto-taxi at precisely 6 a.m.

She always used the same driver, Anel, a wiry man of about 30, who made his living hustling passengers around town. Every morning he picked up Corinne for the bumpy one-mile ride to Notre Dame des Douleurs.

She climbed aboard behind him on the bike's spongy, leatherette seat. With one hand she gripped a chrome bar that ran crosswise near her crotch. With the other, she gripped Anel's belt near the small of his back. It was such a practiced ritual, they didn't need to speak.

The single headlight of Anel's moto shot a beam into the predawn darkness. Already the air was thick with humidity. The day would be a scorcher. Anel drove slowly as he slalomed around an obstacle course of potholes, craters, ruts and gullies.

They were on a smooth, paved, uninhabited stretch of the road, picking up speed and passing an intersection about a quarter mile from Saj Fanm when two motorcycles from the shadows suddenly fell in behind them. One positioned itself a few feet behind Anel and Corinne. The other pulled up on their left side. As the bike in the rear forced the pace, Anel had to speed up, and so did the cyclist that flanked them.

In a country where motorcycle helmets are a rare luxury, both menacing riders wore one, enclosing their heads in shiny, black, plastic bubbles. They were dangerous and anonymous.

"What's happening?" Corinne shouted into Anel's ear as the bikes approached at 40 miles an hour with the rider in the rear pushing the pace.

"I don't know. Hold on."

At that point, the driver on the left drifted into Anel's lane forcing him perilously close to a ditch on the right side of the road. Across the ditch was a thicket of thorny shrubs.

"Hey!" Anel shouted. "Hey, HEY!" He looked to his left at the encroaching biker but all he saw was his own re-flection in the shiny visor of the guy's helmet.

Their speed was up to 45 mph when the driver on the left came close enough to push his black-booted right foot against Anel's left thigh. For a moment, Anel's bike swerved, then recovered. *"Manman pute!"* Motherfucker! The trailing bike kept pushing the pace.

The biker on the left came at them again, this time with his right foot cocked and extended like a battering ram. Anel tried to swat it away, but the harasser's boot made solid contact with the teardrop gas tank of Anel's bike. He lost control. His front tire caught the edge of the ditch and the bike pitched forward. Anel and Corinne were thrown clear over the muddy ditch. They landed near each other atop the lattice of thorny thatch. The faceless bubble heads roared off into the thin light of the rising sun.

Corinne disentangled her scrub shirt from the branches. The collision had caused the motorcycle's scalding hot tailpipe to contact her right calf, causing a painful, second-degree burn. She looked over at Anel and could see that his left shoulder was dislocated. He howled in pain and lamented the condition of his bike, a total loss.

"*Moto mwen an! Li fini. Ki kaka sa!*" My bike. It's finished. What kind of shit is this? he cried.

"Did you hit your head? Are you dizzy? Can you stand?" Corinne was worried that Anel might have sustained a concussion. She had worn a helmet. Like most for-hire moto drivers in Haiti, he had not.

He said his head hurt and that his vision was blurry. Freeing his body from the branches, he stood up and braced himself.

Corinne looked down at her arms and saw numerous small cuts where the thorns had slashed her. Thin streaks of blood ran down her forearms and dripped off her elbows. She was badly shaken up, but nothing felt broken. She didn't feel concussed. By some stroke of luck, landing on the thin branches of the interlaced shrubs was like landing on the mat of a trampoline. Her main worry was the burn on her leg. "Gonna leave a scar, for sure," she thought.

The area was devoid of activity. No pedestrians. No drivers. No witnesses. For a few minutes, the only sound was Anel's painful yowling. Then the "clip-clop" of a two-wheel wooden wagon pulled by a farmer's mule. Corinne waved him down. He was skeptical, unsure, if he offered assistance, what he was getting himself into. Corinne gave him 1,000 gourdes - about $10 - to have him take them to Notre Dame des Douleurs, where Anel unleashed a blue streak of curses as doctors applied the necessary pressure to set his shoulder back into place.

"What the hell happened?" asked a nurse in the ER. She unwrapped a large square of gauze to cover Corinne's calf wound and set aside a mostly empty, flattened tube of antiseptic cream. "Looks like we're running low. Last tube in the drawer," she said as she squeezed the remainder onto the gauze before placing it gently on Corinne's burn.

Running low on antiseptic because of the pilfering by that bastard Pinay, Corinne thought. Now she would wear a scar on her leg as a permanent reminder of his loathsomeness.

Dazed, but stable enough to be released, she left the hospital, hailed a moto driver from the pack standing by at the entrance, and had him take her back to Saj Fanm. She called a friend at the *salle maternite* to say there had been an accident and she would not be coming in.

An accident? Even as she said it, it didn't feel right. Surely there was a better word to describe the targeted assault that could have killed her and her driver. But for public consumption, what else could she call it?

She scrolled through her telephone's "recents," got to Charlie's name and stabbed his number. He answered on the first ring. Corinne began speaking at hyperspeed.

"I had hot words with Pinay. I accused him, and the next morning two goons on motos tried to kill me. That's no coincidence. They tried to make it look like an accident, to kill me! And Anel? What did he do to deserve almost losing his life? His moto, the most valuable thing he owns, is destroyed and lying in a ditch. He'll wear a sling for at least a month. His shoulder may never be the same."

"Are you okay? What are you talking about? What happened? … Who's Anel?"

"My moto driver. We were run off the road and nearly killed this morning."

"Holy shit. Are you hurt? Where did it happen?"

"On the road to the hospital. My forearms look like someone went at them with a cheese grater. I'm wrapped in gauze from elbows to wrists. My leg has a second-degree burn."

"Jeezus. … What else?"

"Nothing noticeable."

"Concussion?"

"Don't think so. I was wearing a helmet."

"Okay. Thank God for that. What do you mean you had 'hot words' with Pinay?"

There was an edge in Charlie's voice - sternness masking fear. "We talked about this, Corinne. I told you …"

"You did, yes. You said I need evidence. That I shouldn't risk a premature confrontation. But that fucking bastard and I were alone when I confronted him. Nobody saw us. I wanted to rattle his bony ass, make him worry. Sure, he scares the bloody shit out of me and everyone else. He scares all of us. He is vindictive and dangerous. He is mean. He worries me all the time. So I wanted to turn the tables. Scare him. Confront him. Throw fear into him. It kills me that he is getting away with this. I needed to throw a punch."

It sounded to Charlie like that metaphorical punch had

been momentarily satisfying for Corinne but had only suc-
ceeded in putting a bull's eye on her back. She was a passionate person, always in the moment. She felt the importance of situations in real-time. Emotionally, she was
always way ahead of Charlie. He admired her for that. But
that trait came with risks.

He was wired differently. Real-time feelings often
eluded him, even as he routinely hoovered up all the jour-
nalistic details of any situation. As a war correspondent, he
could witness the most awful gore and inhumanity and still
retain enough emotional distance, enough cosmic aliena-
tion, to report effectively and file on deadline without it
wrecking him psychologically. He wasn't unaffected by
what he saw. He just compartmentalized it.

"Throw a punch?" he said, repeating her words. Neither said anything for 10 seconds although it felt longer.
Then Charlie spoke. "Corinne, what the fuck were you
thinking?"

"I want to start following him. See where he goes, who
he meets with. Every lie has weight, Charlie. He won't be
able to carry that weight forever. I want to be there when
he can't hold it up anymore."

"You do that, and you will get yourself killed," said
Charlie. "Or maybe he won't have you killed. He'll have
you kidnapped and held for ransom. A pretty British nurse
ought to be worth a penny - if there is anything left of you
after you've been gang raped by thugs a thousand times.
Don't count on Boris Johnson negotiating your release. Besides, you have no proof of Pinay's alleged involvement.
Remember?"

Corinne caved. "What was I supposed to do? Pinay

holds every card. I wanted to come at him."

Charlie heard the quavering in her voice and decided not to push the conversation further. He was scaring her, compounding her fear. She put up a tough façade, but he could hear, deep down, that she was terrified. He imagined her warrior's face crumbling.

"First, listen to me. We are going to get through this. You and me. Together. We'll get through this. Let that sink in."

Now it was her turn to parse sentences: "… get through this … you and me." She was comforted by the sound of that. It had the ring of a vow.

"Second," he said, "I have an idea. Someone who might be able to help us."

CHAPTER TWENTY-SIX
C-squared, mon vieux

The email labeled "A blast from the past" hit Jean Belizaire's inbox over a weekend. He opened it on Monday at the FBI's field office in Miramar. The 20-acre facility north of Miami employs 1,000 agents and support personnel. The ultra-modern glass-and-steel building, on a campus lined with palms, is one of the busiest field offices in the bureau system. Drug cases, immigration cases, anti-terrorism investigations, breaches of cybersecurity – FBI-Miami is where so much is set in motion.

Belizaire, a U.S.-born Iraq War veteran, was a rarity in law enforcement circles, a Haitian-American special agent, whose nicknames - John Belly, a.k.a. JB - were coined by colleagues not up to the challenge of correctly pronouncing either part of his name.

That little tradition had begun during his first FBI posting to the Boston field office in 2007. He had an apartment in the Mattapan section of the city, on the top floor of a Seaver Street three-decker, with a view across the street into the playground of the Franklin Park Zoo.

Sculpted to look like zoo animals, the playground equipment featured a giraffe-neck slide and a Panamanian golden frog that rocked back and forth on huge springs.

On his days off, Belizaire had drank coffee and watched the children play.

An administrative transfer in 2015 sent him to Florida,

the state with the nation's largest Haitian-American population. Of approximately half a million Haitian-born immigrants in the United States, half lived in Greater Miami. He and his Haitian-born wife Mirlande were in their element and happy to be in the Sunshine State.

On his neat desk sat a framed photograph of Mirlande, a registered nurse. Next to the photo was a Lucite box containing a Marine commendation, a green ribbon attached to a gold medal from his tour as a bomb disposal technician. There was a birthday card from his mother, who raised her son in Boston and, after her husband died, moved back to Petionville.

Belizaire settled in with the cup of black coffee he had picked up at a Dunkin Donuts drive-through, swept the transcript of an investigative wiretap off his keyboard and clicked open the email.

"Hey, JB,

It's Charlie Carter. Long time no speak, buddy. Hope you and Mirlande are enjoying Florida's sunshine after cold winters in Beantown.

Anyway. … I am in Haiti at the moment reporting on a medical clinic in Cité Soleil and confronted by a troubling situation. It involves the murder of a Haitian-American doctor and a suspicion that he was killed to keep him quiet about a theft he discovered from a program that delivers U.S. medical-relief supplies to Haiti.

There is more. Much more, and probably not a good idea to unspool it in this email. I could use your advice. Any chance I can call soon to fill you in?"

JB put down his coffee. He leaned forward, hands clasped, forearms resting on his thighs, with his face just inches from the screen as he reread the email. If that crazy C-squared was nosing around in Cité Soleil, he was already taking risks. The pacification of Cité Soleil had been one of former President Rene Preval's few achievements after taking office in 2006. But it didn't last. It was only natural that the gangs would come back to the sprawling slum that had always been their stronghold. Under Moise they were back in force. The anti-government demonstrations roiling the country since JoMo took office in 2017 were another safety concern. Getting mixed up in any way with the perpetrators of U.S. foreign-aid fraud was the capper. It seemed that his crazy journalist friend was always stirring up some shit, always pushing the envelope.

They had met in Boston in 2011 when both were chasing down the whereabouts and background of a fugitive gunman who had killed two women and wounded five people in brazen attacks on two abortion clinics in the city.

The shootings happened on a cold morning a few days after Christmas. The attacker struck and fled, managing to elude a massive manhunt by local and state police and FBI agents, which included helicopters and police dogs.

Charlie was on the Globe's metro staff at the time as part of a rapid-response team assigned to fast-moving, breaking news stories. JB had been months into an investigation of a fentanyl ring when he got pulled into the abortion case.

Police described the gunman as white, under six feet tall with a dark complexion, dark curly hair, and black jacket and pants. They said he used a semi-automatic, .22-caliber rifle. The attacks occurred about a mile apart on busy Beacon Street in Brookline.

Witnesses said the gunman stormed into the Planned Parenthood clinic shortly after 10 a.m., somehow gaining access despite the locked door controlled by a buzzer. His first victim was the clinic's 25-year-old receptionist. She was struck in the neck and died at the scene. A female counselor and two male volunteer escorts in the waiting room were wounded in the barrage.

About 10 minutes later, the gunman, carrying a black duffel bag, entered the nearby Preterm Health Services clinic. The receptionist there also died in a hail of gunfire. Wounded were another woman and a male security guard, who managed to return fire before ducking behind a door.

At a news conference on the steps of the Brookline police station, Massachusetts Gov. Bill Weld, a Republican who supported abortion rights, denounced the attacks and said state police would be deployed to safeguard clinics.

"No matter where we stand on the issue of abortion," President Bill Clinton said in a statement, "all Americans must stand together in condemning this tragic and brutal act."

Reporters poured in from across the nation, but Boston and New England were Charlie's stomping grounds and he felt extra pressure to score a scoop.

Witnesses he interviewed said the attacker fled on foot, jumped into a small car that was parked nearby and sped off. That night, a law enforcement source told the Associated Press that the man authorities were seeking was a 24-year-old hairdresser who lived alone and moved frequently. A handgun, ammunition and a store receipt found in a duffel bag that he left at the second clinic helped police learn the identity of the suspected shooter, who was still on the loose.

Following up on the same leads, Charlie had crossed paths with the FBI investigators as they both sought former neighbors to interview at the various apartments the suspect had rented.

"Back off," JB had said, flashing a badge at Charlie after they arrived at the same time at an apartment building in New Hampshire.

"What's your name?" Charlie pushed back gruffly. The agent blew past him and said nothing. Not an auspicious start to a relationship that would end up lasting decades. But Charlie earned JB's respect with an article he published the next day that described the suspect's aberrant behavior at a church service in New Hampshire just a few days before the rampage.

At a Catholic Mass, he had marched down the center aisle spewing obscenities and complaining that the parishioners were "too cowardly" to do what it takes to truly end abortions. It was a telling detail in a compelling article about a gunman on the run.

A source at the church told Charlie that the man had called himself "a soldier" in "the Army of God," the extremist group responsible for clinic bombings, doctor harassment and other anti-abortion violence. The group's spokesman lived in Chesapeake, Virginia, and the suspect was likely headed there, the source said.

At the urging of FBI public affairs, Charlie agreed to delay reporting that detail, holding it back for 24 hours so that agents could stake out the spokesman's house. Sure enough, just hours before the start of the New Year, the suspect turned up in nearby Norfolk, and fired several non-lethal shots into a clinic there before police arrested him.

Charlie's one-day pause in reporting the suspect's escape to Virginia was deeply appreciated inside the FBI's Boston field office.

So much so that when Charlie wrote a widely read, moment-by-moment recap of the case, a so-called "tick-tock" for the Sunday paper, JB was the unnamed FBI source who confirmed that the suspect had the Army of God's spokesman's name and unlisted phone number in his pocket at the time of his arrest.

During recesses in the alleged gunman's six-week trial, Charlie and JB got to talking and the seeds of a friendship took root. Swiftly convicted, the man was sentenced to two consecutive life terms in prison. Two years later, when he was found dead, alone in his cell with a plastic garbage-can liner over his head and knotted around his neck, a presumptive suicide. Neither Charlie nor JB was surprised.

Their bond intensified when they discovered that they had both been in Iraq for the U.S. ground invasion in 2003. Charlie was embedded with the 3rd Battalion, 5th Marine Regiment in southern Iraq, riding in an Assault Amphibious Vehicle, headed for Baghdad past the infernos of sabotaged oil refineries. JB was with a unit that cleared improvised explosive devices and abandoned vehicles off the main highway to the Iraqi capital.

"We signed up to serve. We had to be there," JB told Charlie the first time they met discreetly outside of work for a drink. "When things got really bad or dangerously stupid, we used to say, 'Embrace the suck, Marine! Embrace the suck!' But you came voluntarily and embraced it with us. That took real guts. Or dangerous stupidity," he said, bursting with laughter.

Charlie was flattered but had to admit he was scared to death most of the time and never embraced the suck.

"Me neither. Never embraced it," admitted JB with an even heartier laugh. "Did anybody, ever, really?"

Before returning to his work on the wiretap transcript, JB tapped out a short reply to Charlie's email.

C-Squared, *Mon Vieux*,

Nice to hear from you! But what have you gotten yourself into?

As it turns out you lucky bastard, I will be in Haiti at the end of this week. You might remember that my mother comes to the U.S. once a year for her annual medical check-up, and I return with her to see her safely back to Petionville. Our flight lands at noon on Friday. Let's plan to grab dinner Saturday. Forget about the outdoor restaurant at that hotel that you like so much. We can do better than that. Much better.

Byento!

JB

JB's two-hour flight from Miami landed on time. Instead of wearing his usual dark suit and repp stripe tie, he stepped off the plane in a polo shirt open at the neck, black pants creased to a razor's edge and driving moccasins, no socks. A Haitian friend had offered him the use of his gray Nissan Xterra, with its high-clearance, springy, quick-twitch suspension. Even though JB rarely had occasion to drive in Haiti, he hadn't lost his touch. He bullied his way fearlessly into five-way intersections. He passed vehicles in traffic with mere inches separating his side view mirror from theirs. He slalomed around potholes as big as tank traps. After dropping off his Mom at her apartment in Petionville, he swung by the Desir to pick up Charlie and Corinne. Charlie had asked her to come down from Hinche to join them for dinner. If JB was going to be of any help, Charlie said, she would have to open up to him.

Dressed for a night out, Charlie and Corinne made a handsome couple. They were waiting in the Desir parking lot when JB pulled in, parked, jumped out and bro-hugged Charlie.

Charlie made the introductions.

"*Enchante*," said JB. "I've heard a lot about you."

That was an understatement. Charlie had spoken of Corinne to JB repeatedly, especially after a few bourbons at The Tam, the dive bar they frequented in Boston's theater district. Amp up Charlie's blood alcohol level and invariably he veered into the existential. He'd go on a riff about the need to recalibrate his work-life balance. He'd wonder if he and Corinne could go from the "friend zone" to something deeper.

"You'll have to ask her," JB had said. "*Pas de risque, pas de gloire*. No guts, no glory."

Yes, Charlie had spoken to JB about Corinne and now the three of them were in the Xterra, bounding uphill into Petionville on a winding two-lane road whose most treacherous turns were barely illuminated by the dim glow of wax-candle lanterns.

"I predict you're going to like this place," said JB as he

pulled into the parking lot at *Au Coin des Artistes*, a Petion-ville *boîte* known for its grilled fish and Creole barbeque.

Popular with well-to-do Haitians and expats, the restaurant had the look and feel of an open-air cellar, with wooden latticework walls and a grill that pumped out brochettes of conch, charred goat, and Caribbean side dishes of crab gratin and grilled plantains. On a terraced part of the cellar were tables covered with canary yellow linen cloths and protected from the elements by the overhang of the adjacent building.

"Nice place," said Charlie, savoring the ambiance. "A different Haiti."

"Yeah, it's not all slum-and-rum. Some people here live well. Wait'll ya taste the fish," said JB, who proceeded to order for the three of them. When the waitress was safely out of earshot he asked: "So what's the trouble here? Your email mentioned theft, robbery and murder. That got my attention."

Charlie and Corinne looked at each other. After a pause, Corinne spoke first.

"Charlie told you that I work at a hospital. A doctor-administrator there is stealing donated medicine. My friend, Dr. Sanctis Beauvoir, caught him red-handed. Then my friend was strangled and mutilated."

"And robbed of a valuable telescope," Charlie chimed in. "Sanctis was a U.S. citizen, Haitian-American, who came here to help. The stolen medicines included USAID donations. That's why I reached out to you. I thought the FBI could do something."

"Forget the telescope. It wasn't a robbery. I am 100 percent sure that the administrator, Reynard Pinay, is the one who had Sanctis killed," said Corinne.

"One hundred percent? You're sure? On what evidence?" said JB. Corinne thought she heard sarcasm in his voice. She wondered if it was worth opening up to this American fed. Did he mean to help, or just shoot holes in her story? Her eyes darted toward Charlie.

For a few seconds JB said nothing and sipped his beer. Then: "I checked. Apparently we heard about the murder through our legat in the D.R."

"Legat?" said Corinne.

JB explained that the FBI maintains "legal attache" offices - "legats" - throughout the world. The one in Santo Domingo, Dominican Republic, has jurisdiction in Haiti. "We heard about the murder, but nothing about drug thefts. Nothing about a telescope."

"A U.S. citizen murdered. U.S. foreign aid - donated drugs - ripped off. This should concern the FBI," said Corinne. "Right?"

"Yeah, but a straight-up robbery, even a robbery-murder, would be a local matter. Here's the deal, *zanmi'm yo*," said JB. "The FBI stations agents overseas to build relationships with local law enforcement, intelligence and security services. The goal, ultimately, is the protection of America."

When the waitress arrived with the appetizer, the trio paused to savor the butterflied jumbo shrimp cooked in Triple Sec, lime juice, dark rum and cayenne pepper. Charlie's eyes went wide appreciatively as he sampled the dish.

Swigging beer in between bites, JB continued.

"It's not clear to me yet whether this would fall under

our purview. Here's what we have authority to investigate on foreign soil: Specific violent crimes committed against Americans and American interests overseas and in some instances crimes committed by Americans overseas. Those crimes include non-terrorism related hostage-takings, kidnappings and killings, assaults on U.S. federal officers. We investigate violent crimes on U.S. Government property, and murders of U.S. nationals by other U.S. nationals. We investigate crimes aboard aircraft and crimes on the high seas like piracy and cruise ship crimes involving U.S. vessels or U.S. persons. The FBI also works to track down U.S. wanted fugitives who fled overseas."

"It seems the relevant part of all that is 'violent crimes against Americans and American interests," said Charlie. "That's what happened here."

"You might be right," said JB. "But it's more complicated. In 2008 the FBI created the International Corruption Unit to oversee the increasing number of investigations involving global fraud against the U.S. It oversees several International Contract Corruption Task Forces to combat the misuse and waste of taxpayer money."

"Setting aside all the acronyms and task forces, the theft of USAID donations is a misuse of taxpayer money, isn't it?" said Charlie.

"Correct. There also is language in the regulations that authorizes investigations of 'items and services invoiced without delivery,' and 'diversion of goods.'"

"Plus murder! Sanctis was murdered," said Corinne, "and Pinay had a motive. If Sanctis had revealed him he would have lost his status as a hospital director, his access to all of those poor women that he tees up for C-sections, not to mention his lucrative side gig pilfering drugs. What more do we need?"

"Me? Evidence," said JB. "I need evidence."

"What about the attempt on my life? I'll carry that burn scar on my leg for the rest of my days."

JB paused for a second. "Charlie told me something about a motorcycle accident …"

"It wasn't an accident."

"Any witnesses?"

"I could have died. My driver too."

"I know. Were there witnesses?"

"It was bloody dawn in the Haitian countryside. No one was out on that part of the road. … "

"Look, I'm not trying to give you a hard time," said JB. "But these are the kind of things that you'll need if you want the Bureau to get involved. I'm on your side. I just need something to work with. Do we know if Sanctis was into anything that could have put his life in danger? Anything risky? Who knew he had that telescope?"

"Everybody knew," said Corinne. "He always talked about it. It's why he liked living on the outskirts of town, with less light pollution."

"We'll have to run all of that down. Assuming we arrest your guy, what's his name, Pinay, we're gonna try him in the United States. Extradite him, arraign him, *tout sa*. If we move too quickly, without a proper foundation, he'll lawyer up and we'll just have to kick him free. You don't want that. I don't want that. I will keep in touch. I'll keep thinking about our options. But I have to go back to Miami tomorrow afternoon."

At this point he turned from Corinne and made

lingering eye contact with Charlie.

"Mirlande and I have an appointment … again … at the fertility doctor." He raised his glass as if to toast and forced a smile. "Still trying."

CHAPTER TWENTY-SEVEN
Son of a bitch!

The next evening, Corinne sat alone at the far end of the Saj Fanm veranda soaking the tips of her fingers in warm soapy water, preparing to paint her nails. A breeze rustled the palm fronds. Moths congregated around a bare bulb. The chameleons so evident in the daytime were tucked deep into the cracks of a stone wall.

Invariably, in the *salle maternite*, Corinne was wrist-deep in her patients' secretions. Her nursing school professors had taught her that chipped nail polish was a breeding ground for bacteria, so she rarely wore it on duty. Off-duty was another story. Painting her nails was one of the few luxuries she allowed herself in Haiti. It was her downtime, her me time. The brushstrokes forced her to concentrate, but at the same time her mind was free to wander, to speculate and rewind scenes from her life, the I-told-you-so's and I-shoulda-saids.

Adding to the peacefulness of the moment was the sweet gospel sound of an Eva Cassidy soundtrack that Corinne had stored on her phone.

The song - *Oh, Had I a Golden Thread* - is a Pete Seeger classic, but Cassidy infuses it with feminine soulfulness. Its lines about the innocence of newborns, and the bravery of the women who bring them into the world, made her feel proud of her chosen profession.

Chewing her lips and squinting to concentrate, Corinne

loaded the brush tip with the acqua laquer, touched it to her pinky where the cuticle meets the quick, and gingerly dragged out the first brushstroke. She had admired the soft pastel color on one of the volunteers who had come through and the woman kindly left the bottle behind for Corinne with a note, "For the hands that help people out."

Calmed by the familiar ritual, Corinne's thoughts floated free. Until Charlie's recent return to Haiti she hadn't seen him in a very long time. Their lives were on separate tracks. But here she was, on the eve of their next … what should she call it? … Get-together? … Rendez-vous? … Date? … Whatever. But this much she knew: She wanted to look pretty for whatever she called it, and she didn't need a psychoanalyst to understand that motivation.

Outwardly, Charlie was quite different from Mars Joseph, the Haitian man she began seeing on a lark and dated for a year.

Mars was born in Cap Haitien, Haiti's northern coast port city, a slow, 150-mile drive from the capital, or faster by puddle jumper if you had the airfare. In Cap Haitien, Mars was a welder and hobbyist cook with a flair for tangy marinades and flashy knife skills. Everyone said that his soup joumou was to die for.

What brought him to Port-au-Prince was a career reset with World Central Kitchen, the humanitarian food-relief group founded by Washington, D.C. chef and restaurateur Jose Andres. Devotees proudly displayed WCK's "world-map-in-a-frying-pan" logo on their tee shirts and chef's coats like badges of courage.

WCK had been doing heroic work for years and had become well known as the team that pumped out hundreds of thousands of hot meals for the desperate people of Puerto Rico after Hurricane Maria crippled the island and its food supply in 2017. Filling the vacuum left by the U.S. government, which critics decried as not doing enough, Andres, a naturalized U.S. citizen who'd been born in Spain, responded with people power.

Two years earlier in Haiti, WCK opened *Ecole des Chefs*, a cooking school in Port au Prince. WCK's professional culinary-arts training program offered a five-month curriculum that prepared aspiring chefs for their first jobs in commercial kitchens. Mars jumped at the chance for hands-on training at a school led by Mi-Sol Chevallier, one of Haiti's most respected chefs.

Buoyed by a scholarship, he joined the school's first class of 40 students. Their training included meal production, kitchen hygiene, how to run the "front of the house," budgeting, ordering, butchering, portioning - in short, everything a restaurant chef needs to know. The school, a new structure built in Delmas, featured a state-of-the-art kitchen and full dining room for training and hosting events.

With the skills training came a heavy helping of humanism. Through their periodic deployments to crisis zones, WCK volunteers experienced first-hand the psychic nourishment that came from serving hot comfort food to refugees made vulnerable by wars and natural disasters. Responding to the violent protests and civil unrest that began rocking Port-au-Prince in 2019, WCK provided hot meals to the city's most vulnerable communities, serving more than 4,000 people in one weekend.

In addition to providing quality meals, WCK's "Chef Relief Team" trained the students for disaster activations.

They taught them the best recipes for mass feedings and showed them how to prep, pack and deliver meals en masse wherever they are needed.

Corinne didn't know anything about Mars the first time their paths crossed at a WCK fundraiser. But she knew what she saw standing before her, serving *griot* on the buffet line: A tall, slender, devastatingly handsome man, whose hair - a springy inch of curly thatch – was as shiny and black as a bowling ball. The starched whiteness of his chef's coat made his espresso complexion appear luminous.

"*Li nan griot*," it's griot, Mars said as he ladled a portion onto Corinne's plate along with sides of red beans and rice. Considered a national dish in Haiti, the *griot* was made from pork shoulder using a traditional recipe that called for washing the meat in citrus juices instead of water because clean water is hard to come by. The meat was marinated in *epis*, a mixture of Haitian herbs, vegetables and spices, cubed and braised until tender, then deep fried until golden brown and crispy. The drippings from the preparation were used to make the accompanying sauce, *sos ti-malis*.

"*Bon apeti che*," a smiling Mars said, shooting Corinne a wink. He exuded charm. During a break from serving, he dropped by Corinne's table to flirt.

"In French West Africa, where my ancestors come from, *griot* means poet or storyteller." He leaned in close: "Can I tell you a story?"

"That would be okay," said Corinne, taking a moment to savor the fact that this slightly younger man with incredible confidence and charisma was hitting on her. "Yes, well, okay," she said. She was charmed.

"Then I'll have to see you again," said Mars, securing her number and making a date for the following weekend. "*Byento*," he said, and hopped back to the serving line.

That date began a routine of regular visits, mostly on weekends, and mostly spent in bed, glistening with post-coital perspiration. Corinne didn't worry about where it all was leading. "He's fun," she said to herself, "and the shagging is brilliant."

Mars spoke of his dream to one day open a high-end Haitian restaurant in Miami, but until then, he said, he was happy to serve in "Andres' Army," responding to disasters and crises by bringing food to the world's displaced and hungry.

He had yet to deploy to a disaster zone, but his expanding role as back-field support for WCK's Chef Relief Team limited his free time until his dates with Corinne died a natural death.

"Fun while it lasted," she thought, accepting the reality that the relationship was "really never more than a fling."

Her feelings for Charlie were intense in a different way. She always thought of him as smart and reliable. But he was stepping up his game now. Talking to JB had made her uncomfortable, as if her answers to his questions were somehow deficient. She knew those conversations had to happen and she was grateful that Charlie had stood by her when they did.

For the date that she had prepped for by painting her nails, she led Charlie on the hike that she used to take with Sanctis, past the "camel's hump," out to the "old sawmill" and back.

"I walked these hills with him, Charlie. He was just

as real as you and me. But now he's gone. Brutally erased. Someone has to answer for that."

"Yes," said Charlie, "someone."

Before they parted, Charlie told Corinne he was changing his plans. He had planned, after having filed his clinic story, to use a month of vacation to go bonefishing with a guide around Turks and Caicos. Easily spooked, bonefish are super elusive, which is why Charlie thought that stalking them with a fly rod and reel was more like an even fight. Hunting with a gun or bow wasn't his thing. But he could spend all day covered up against the blistering sun just trying to get a bonefish to bite. He had never caught one.

Charlie took Corinne's hands in his, gently kneaded her fingers and softly harmonica-ed his lips across the gloss of her lacquered nails. He said he would use the month to help her bring down Pinay if the evidence warranted, or at least come to terms with Sanctis' death. "I'll take an apartment for the month in Hinche," he said. "I'll be here for whatever you need."

Before bed that night Corinne called up another song on her phone - *Pearls*, by Sade. The lyrics, which evoke the agonizing struggle of a Somali woman trying to keep heart and feed her family in the face of a famine moved Corinne to tears almost every time.

The next morning, fortified with the memory of Charlie's words – "I'll be there for whatever you need" – she steeled herself to go back to the hospital where she couldn't avoid running into Pinay. She dropped in first at the crowded outpatient clinic to see if anyone there was an obvious maternity patient. Seeing no visible pregnancies, she moved on.

Inside the door of the *salle maternite* she stopped at the open-faced wooden cabinet that the nurses used as a communal locker for personal odds and ends, tampons, chewing gum, hair ties, and in Corinne's case, a bottle of lens cleaning solution for her contacts. She put in her lenses when she got to work and switched to her glasses for the moto ride home. It was such a part of her daily routine that she hardly had to think about it.

While she poured the lens cleaning solution into a hard plastic case, some of it spilled and ran down her fingers. It was then that she noticed the smell of acetone and saw that her nail polish was starting to dissolve. Someone had replaced the cleaning solution with nail polish remover.

"What the fuck? What the fucking FUCK?" Corinne blurted, turning heads. If that corrosive stuff had gotten into her eyes it could have blinded her or scorched her corneas so badly that she would be left with blurry vision for the rest of her life.

"That son of a bitch," she shouted. "THAT SON OF A BITCH!"

CHAPTER TWENTY-EIGHT
"Belizaire, exam room 2"

The waiting room at Caring Conceptions, Miramar's fertility and IVF center, was crowded with half a dozen anxious couples. JB and Mirlande took seats near the magazine rack and waited for their names to be called. He scrolled mindlessly through his phone. She skimmed a Prevention magazine article titled, "12 Things That Could Be Messing With Your Guy's Sperm." Sounds like a Cosmo headline, she thought, not Prevention.

"If your quest to get pregnant isn't going so well, don't automatically assume that you're the culprit," the article began. "Though women usually get most of the blame for fertility problems, a third of cases are caused by issues related to the man."

Was that supposed to make the women here feel better? Mirlande thought as she looked around the waiting room.

Some patients were in their early thirties and impatient to be seen. Others were over 40 and terrified by the tortuous ticking of their biological clocks. Young and old, they were there for a range of services that included egg donation, sperm donation, recurrent miscarriages, semen analysis, in-vitro fertilization, pre-implantation genetic screening and other conditions that required Assisted Reproductive Technologies, what the doctors there liked to call the "ART" of fertility treatments.

Every case was different. What all the couples had in common were their brave game faces trying to mask the physical and emotional stress of repeatedly failing to conceive.

"I want to be a parent, not a patient," an exasperated Mirlande complained to JB each time they scheduled another appointment.

Forty-three-year-old JB, and 37-year-old Mirlande, had been at it for almost three years, with growing sadness, miscarriages and bouts of depression. Time after time JB had administered the intramuscular injections of hormones by plunging a long, hypodermic needle into Mirlande's hips until they were sore and covered with bruises. JB was told to avoid saunas, hot tubs, steam rooms, even heated car seats - anything that might overheat his testicles and affect the size, shape and motility of his sperm cells. Although he loved his morning coffee and evening nightcaps, he tried to limit his consumption of caffeine and alcohol. He was as attuned to Mirlande's ovulation cycles as she was. All to no avail.

The treatments landed Miri on a slew of mailing lists, including the one for Resolve, the National Infertility Association. Their typical letters, like the one she received that morning, told her mostly what she already knew: Infertility affects millions of Americans — one in eight couples, or about 10 percent of the population. Only half of those affected seek medical treatment; those who do tend to be white, older, wealthy, and educated. Depending on where in the country a couple seeks treatment, a single cycle of IVF costs about $11,000.

Sometimes Mirlande and JB bickered over the

punishingly high cost of the treatments, which drained them financially and emotionally. After so many failures it was tempting to just give up and move on. They'd thought of buying discounted leftover fertility meds online, but that seemed too risky. Instead, they kept coming back to Caring Conceptions in the hope that their investments of time, emotion and treasure would bring them the treasure of a child.

"Belizaire, exam room 2," the receptionist announced.

Mirlande stood up and clapped shut her magazine. "Here," she said to JB, "we go again."

Back at his desk at the bureau, JB combed through a file of investigative leads for a case that involved cocaine trafficking, money laundering, a child custody dispute and possibly the contract murder of a Haitian-American woman. The principal locations of his sleuthing on this case would be Palm Beach County — and perhaps Port-au-Prince if the investigation took him there.

"This one's the gift that keeps on giving," he told his supervisor. "There are enough leads in here for four investigations."

According to the file, the target of the investigation was 33-year-old Etienne Marvel, alias "Prantout," who smuggled hundreds of kilos of cocaine annually into the United States using Haiti as a transshipment point for Colombian cartel product. Prantout, a naturalized U.S. citizen, was married to a Haitian-American woman and had split his time between Haiti and South Florida until he became the focus of an FBI drug warrant. He narrowly escaped arrest by slipping onto a Haiti-bound flight from New York disguised as a woman.

Leaving his wife and children in Florida, he made Haiti his base of operations. When the kids, a 6-year-old boy and a 4-year-old girl, came for a visit, he enrolled them in school and refused to send them back to the U.S. That drew the ire of the wife and her mother, who vowed to take him down. The grandmother sent her son, a Desert Storm combat veteran, back to Haiti on a mission to snatch back the kids. Within a day of his arrival, however, he got the devastating news that his mother, the children's grandmother, had been shot to death in a Miami parking lot. The grieving son returned to Florida, suspecting that a hit had been ordered by Prantout, whose alias, roughly translated, means "Take it all."

JB was formulating a plan to advance the investigation when his phone rang. It was Charlie, sounding more nervous than he had at their dinner a week earlier.

"I know you are busy. I'm sorry to call," Charlie began. "But you've got to hear this. Someone sabotaged Corinne's contact lens solution with acetone - nail polish remover. It was vicious and could have been disastrous if she hadn't noticed it in time. She is panicking. Needless to add, she is sure Pinay is behind it. Like you, I am all about gathering evidence, establishing proof, but frankly at this point I don't see who else it could be."

"So it's escalating," said JB.

"Yeah, and I'm afraid o f where it will lead. I'm gonna move up to Hinche to be near Corinne. You know how I feel about her. All I need is a room with a bed.

One of the Saj Fanm security guards has a room I can rent near the compound."

"Okay, clearly someone is screwing with her. Trying to hurt her, but also messing with her head," said JB. "We don't know what it's related to. Maybe it's not Pinay. Maybe it is. Maybe the goal is to scare her so badly that she'll quit. That's one way for him to solve his problem. Get her off his back. If it's him. But it could be someone else entirely. Just tell her not to confront him anymore, and to keep her head on a swivel. You too."

"She's not gonna quit. She cares too much about her job and about Sanctis. She wants justice. Wants Pinay to pay for the murder."

"I get that. But she's a nurse, not a cop. We don't go on hunches. We go on evidence. And how do we know it's Pinay? Remind her."

"I will."

"And FYI. I've been assigned to another case that could bring me back to Haiti sooner than I expected. We'll keep talking. There might be a role for the Bureau in your problem. Like we used to say in Iraq, 'I got your six,' but you need to be extra careful."

Federal guidelines governing FBI investigations state an agent has 30 days to "assess" an allegation without first having to get a supervisor's approval. No "probable cause" or "reasonable suspicion" is required as long as the assessment has an "authorized purpose" and "defined objective." After 30 days the agent must get permission to keep probing. JB, a cautious investigator, thought it best, even if not required, to put Sanctis' murder on his boss's radar right away, along with some of what he was hearing.

"Don't know yet if there's anything to it," he summed up.

"Thanks for the heads up," said the chief. "Be sure to keep me in the loop."

CHAPTER TWENTY-NINE
Why am I here?

Charlie's second-floor room was in a building of white-washed stucco near Hinche's outdoor market and its famous cathedral. The room had a wobbly table with a cracked wicker base, two mismatched chairs, a two-burner electric hot plate for cooking between rolling blackouts, cold running water that you wouldn't want to drink, a chipped toilet with a broken seat and a saggy mattress on a Harvard frame above a herd of dust bunnies. The mosquito netting that hung from the ceiling had been mended countless times.

The cream-colored cathedral - Our Lady of the Immaculate Conception - was often cited as "the first church constructed in the Americas." In truth, that honor, if accurate, belonged to the *ancienne* cathedral built on the site five centuries ago. The current cathedral, built in 1997 and wrapped with a gorgeous array of small and large clear-glass windows, seats 2,000. On the first Sunday after Charlie moved in, he was the lone *blan* in a sea of noir parishioners that filled its pews. A lapsed Catholic, Charlie went to the church to scope it out, more for reconnaissance than for worship. Was it possible that Pinay was there? Charlie watched the pews empty out, looking for a man with a pronounced limp. After counting ten of them, he stopped counting.

In Hinche he was glad to be near Corinne, who had

taken JB's "head-on-a-swivel" advice to heart and was being hyper-vigilant. That's what the situation called for, certainly. But Charlie also knew that her hyper-vigilance was a symptom of the post-traumatic stress she was suffering, probably because Sanctis' death had been so sudden and violent and she hadn't taken any time to mourn. Her anxiety led her to call Charlie multiple times a day, checking in with her whereabouts and to hear his voice. She wasn't just being careful; she was positively jumpy, a state so unlike the focused calm she brought to hospital emergencies.

Having filed his clinic story and started his vacation clock, Charlie's time was his own, and Corinne's welfare was his chief concern. She was still every bit the tough veteran nurse. But her confidence was shaken. If Pinay could order a hit on Sanctis and get away with it, what else could he do? Who else could he hurt? And what if her hunch was entirely wrong?

Another mystery fueled her anxiety. He could have fired her but he hadn't.

"Why am I still here?" she asked Charlie.

"It is surprising. Maybe he figures he's better off keeping you close, in sight and busy with work rather than outside with plenty of time to do mischief. But I don't really know. I'm just glad you're still here and have your patients to keep you from going crazy."

He just wanted to make Corinne feel safe and supported. He wanted her to feel the security of knowing that he was all-in on Team Corinne, even if he harbored doubts about her theories on Sanctis' demise. He just wanted her to be able to get some sleep.

She was coming over frequently after work. Some nights they'd go to the *Coin des VIP* bar on Rue Ste. Catharine, with its peach-colored walls, thatched roof, barred windows and concrete floor inlaid with oddly shaped slate tiles. Red cloths covered the white plastic patio tables which were surrounded by white plastic chairs. Overhead there was a ceiling fan and written in fancy chartreuse script on the pass-through to the kitchen, was one word: *Bienvenue.*

Other nights they stayed at home and Charlie slapped together a stir fry on the hot plate.

On the nights that Corinne came directly from the *salle maternite* she'd leave her clogs outside the door, wash her feet in Charlie's bathroom sink, sponge bathe the rest of her, and slip on a white guayabera that Charlie had picked up on an assignment in Cuba. The men's large tropical shirt fit her like a mini dress.

After eating they'd usually tap into a bottle of Barbancourt, relaxing as the double-distilled, fermented sugar cane juice of Haiti's premier rum warmed their throats with every swallow.

In a sea of religious stations, Charlie kept the dial tuned to their favorite, Kompa Mix Radio.

"In the *salle*," Corinne said, swaying to the beat, "when a woman's labor is not progressing, we stand her up and gently shuffle-dance with her. The music calms the mother. Gravity helps the baby drop."

She closed her eyes and shifted rhythmically from one bare foot to the other. Charlie, bare-chested and barefoot in cargo shorts, held her and they danced.

He took her hand, held it against his face and inhaled.

Then he draped it over the back of his neck. He reached under the guayabera and stroked her back. Slowly, he traced every vertebra. The back of his hands brushed the sides of her breasts. She leaned in and nuzzled his shoulder.

It was happening. Charlie felt himself crossing the threshold, out of the "friend zone" into something more.

Intoxicated by the rum, music and closeness, they parted the gauzy mosquito netting and lay down on the bed, hungry for affection as they crawled on and into one another.

Later, Charlie awoke first and savored the sight of her sleeping soundly.

CHAPTER THIRTY
Haitian men with braids

JB's pursuit of the coke trafficker Prantout began in *Ti Ayiti*, Miami's "little Haiti," where Prantout operated an Afro-Caribbean art shop and was a benefactor of its Cultural Complex, an act of largesse that also was one of the ways that he laundered his drug proceeds. His criminal case file showed that before his return to Haiti, he had lived lavishly in a four-bedroom, $2.5 million home on Battersea Road in Coconut Grove. The house had a large swimming pool, rooms that opened onto marble-tiled porches, Jacuzzis, an expanse of manicured lawn and towering palms surrounded by box-cut hedges. JB drove out there to interview the estranged wife. She came to the door in sandals, a shiny mauve pedicure and a Boho print maxi dress. JB showed her his credentials. She led him to the living room, which was furnished all in white and worthy of a spread in Architectural Digest.

"My husband didn't involve me in his business affairs," she said, attempting to set the parameters of the interview. She offered JB not so much as a glass of water.

"Are you divorced? Or just separated?"

"Call it what you like. He's not welcome here."

Hmm, thought JB. That's no answer.

"For someone who didn't know anything about the business, it looks like you did pretty well for yourself."

Generally, JB was a polite interviewer, but he didn't like

it when subjects attempted to blow smoke up his ass. Chloe Marvel was giving him no reason to trust a word she said. "Look," she replied, "I put up with his shit for years. Now he's trying to steal my kids. Whatever it is you think you see around here, believe me, I earned it."

Okay, so she wanted her kids back. She might need JB's help to do that. He could use that to his advantage.

"Did he ever bring his associates here to the house?"

"He did. They'd park their tinted-window black Escalades in the driveway, then go around back by the pool. He never let them come inside."

"What did they talk about?"

"I couldn't say."

"You couldn't say, or you don't know?"

"Agent, I'm not playing with you. I told you he left me out of his business affairs."

"And that's the way you liked it?" JB wasn't letting up.

"That's the way it was."

"What did these men look like?"

"Men. Haitian men."

"Big? Small? Bearded? Bald? …"

"Big. Some had braids. I never paid them much mind. Like I said, they never came into the house."

JB knew from the case file that the muscle and mules employed by Prantout were former members of Port-au-Prince gangs. In the U.S. they presented themselves as importers of Haitian art and artifacts, supplying shops like Prantout's. On their social media profiles, they left out the part about smuggling drugs.

"Any idea where his associates are now? Where they live?"

"Nope. … Miami?"

The surly, two-word answer told JB the interview had reached the point of diminishing returns. He pulled out his business card. No sense pressing any harder at that moment. He might have to circle back to her down the line.

"Thanks for your time, ma'am," he said. The look on her face conveyed her annoyance at the ma'am. "If you think of anything, here's my number."

He wouldn't wait by the phone.

CHAPTER THIRTY-ONE
Try the conch

Sheets of rain lashed the thatched roof of Monty's Raw Bar in Coconut Grove, a Tiki-chic watering hole. The bayside *boite* is where Miami police detective Mateo Adolfo had agreed to meet JB for a law enforcement tete-a-tete. The white noise of the downpour provided a curtain of privacy for their conversation. Also helpful were the random peals of thunder that reverberated across the channel from Key Biscayne. It was 4 p.m., a classic late afternoon South Florida soaker.

"So the lovely Mrs. Prantout - I'll remember her name. Joey? Zoe? Chloe, that's it, Chloe Marvel - told you to be on the lookout for 'large Haitian men with braids,'" said Adolfo. "Well, *mierda, Tio,* around here that's 30,000 people."

Born in Puerto Rico, Adolfo had joined the Miami police force a decade ago and rose quickly from patrol to the criminal investigative division, the detective unit he called "the House of Dicks." He was short and powerfully built, with a goatee trimmed perfectly, as if traced with a template, and an off- kilter set to his jaw that made it seem like he was always speaking snidely or conspiratorially out of the side of his mouth, even when he wasn't, which was rare.

He said his department had long suspected that Prantout had "much more going on" than just the *Ti Ayiti* art shop.

The hinky Haitian had landed hard on the Miami department's radar - and on the FBI's as well - after a Port Miami longshoreman, who was surreptitiously clearing Prantout's shipments of contraband, got caught on a surveillance camera tossing a few pilfered packets of coke into the trunk of his car.

Stealing from the head of a cocaine cartel is "seriously dumb shit," said Adolfo. "Had Prantout caught him, his fingers would have been systematically broken, one by one, then snipped off, joint by joint with a bolt cutter. They'd pound three-inch nails into his ear canals. That would be for starters."

The hapless longshoreman decided it was preferable to cut a deal with the cops. Arrested, he was forced to name names, which put Prantout in law enforcement's crosshairs.

"That's when Prantout fled back to Haiti on a bogus passport dressed as a woman," said Adolfo. "Most of these guys couldn't pour water out of a boot if the instructions were on the heel. Prantout's different. He's smarter. Even before the federal indictment, we were profiling him and his entourage. We think he is protected in Haiti by a kidnap-extortion gang, and that he still runs the coke distribution scheme here through his merry band of braided-hair assholes."

Given all of that, JB thought, why in the world had his wife - estranged wife, ex-wife, whatever she is - ever sent the children to Haiti on a visit to see him in the first place? She didn't seem stupid. Clearly she knew more than she was letting on. But if in fact Prantout had her mother gunned down, or knew who did, then all bets were off.

"From what we've been able to piece together, the gang that protects him in Haiti specializes in kidnap for ransom, especially U.S. nationals and well-to-do Haitian Americans for whom they ask high prices," said Adolfo.

Since neither lawman was going back to his office, they ordered another round, a Presidente, the D.R.'s premium beer, for JB; Johnnie Walker-rocks for Adolfo.

"I just finished a Haiti case … the gang was called Delmas," said Adolfo. "A combination of Haitians and Haitian-Americans. Real lowlifes. Kidnapped two girls on their way to school. When their usual driver came to pick them up, he was ordered out of the car at gunpoint. Gunmen snatched up the first student, gagged her and stuffed her in their car. When the second girl came out of her house, she realized something was wrong and tried to run back inside but was grabbed and told they would kill her classmate if she didn't come with them. She got in the car.

"The Delmas crew held the girls in some crappy-ass safe house while they negotiated with one of the girls' grandfathers, who lives in Coral Gables. The initial demand was $200,000 - package price for both girls - with a threat to kill them if the money wasn't paid. After three days the grandfather, through a Port-au-Prince intermediary, paid a much lower price and the girls were released unharmed but scared to fucking death."

"Real nice fellas," said JB.

"Yeah, and it felt real nice taking them down. Joint operation. Cast of dozens. A full-court press. We're lucky it came off without a leak."

The HNP, as the Haitian National Police are known,

were widely seen as corrupt, inefficient, under-resourced and no match for the groups known as the *baz* – the heavily armed gangs affiliated with and protected by mainstream political factions. The criminality is brazen. One notorious scheme involved a Colombian drug lord who paid off the HNP to protect his precious loads. The drugs came in on small planes that landed at night on dirt roads graciously illuminated by the headlights of HNP cruisers.

"I don't have to tell you," said Adolfo. It's a never-ending story. Bribe-hungry police. Tip-offs. Warnings ahead of raids. Impunity for the gangsters. The average citizen, living on two bucks a day, is SOL. But for you, my brother, I've got something."

Adolfo, who had gone to Haiti a time or two to follow leads, had a trustworthy Haitian police source he was willing to share with JB on a confidential basis. Lacking arrest powers on Haitian soil, JB would have to team up with a Haitian cop for searches and arrests. Even with no one eavesdropping, Adolfo didn't want to risk saying the name out loud in the bar. He wrote it on the back of his business card and skimmed it over to JB the way a blackjack dealer hits a player. "This guy is on the level. He is honest. He'll help you. But you gotta protect him."

They had agreed that Adolfo would leave the restaurant first so they wouldn't be seen in the parking lot together. JB picked up the check, which seemed only right since he was the one who had sought the meeting. The rain had stopped. Wisps of steam rose off the parking lot's black asphalt. JB decided he would stay, have another beer, order take-out, and bring it home for dinner with Mirlande.

Adolfo swirled the melted ice in his glass for a final

swig and pushed back from the table.

"Try the conch," he said, "it's their specialty."

CHAPTER THIRTY-TWO
"Don't honey me!"

"The fresh air will do us good," said Charlie as the weekend approached. He had convinced Corinne to join him in a five-mile dirt track trek that would take them from the outskirts of Hinche to the petroglyph-covered grottoes, sparkling waterfalls and aquamarine pools at Bassin Zim, a natural attraction in Haiti's central plateau.

Instead of crashing down into the basin below in a freefall, as most waterfalls do, these frothy falls cling and crawl over the face of the mountain, giving the impression of a wide, undulating lace curtain.

"Looks like an avalanche," said Corinne. "Like no waterfall I've ever seen," said Charlie.

They had barely arrived on that Saturday when they were set upon by a pack of teenagers, each wanting to be their guide, to show them the caves and the safest ledges from which to plunge into the pools below.

"*Gid, mesye, gid?*" they called, touting their guide services, shouting over one another. Charlie picked out the hungriest-looking kid, pulled him aside and handed him a 500-gourde note, about $7, a relative fortune. The kid beamed and drove it deep into a front pocket.

"*Oke, montre nou,*" Corinne said, and the boy led them to the first cave. As they crossed from the 90-degree heat into the cave's cool entrance, a cauldron of bats left their perches, circled 50 feet overhead and rose higher into the cave's black recesses.

"The guidebook says these wall carvings were done by indigenous Taino Amerindians before colonization and immigration," said Charlie. Corinne nodded.

Inside the cave they followed their guide, sloshing through the ankle-deep water on the cave's floor, which was studded with rocks and stalagmites. Green moss covered the walls. They steered clear of an archway under which hung a massive nest of wasps.

"It's getting a little creepy," said Corinne. "Let's go out to the pools. I'm ready for a swim."

They had worn T-shirts and shorts over their bathing suits. They stripped those off, kicked off their sandals and tiptoed in. The water was refreshing, cool but not numbing. They stayed in long enough to rinse, then lay atop two towels and dried quickly in the sun. As they got up for another dip, Charlie touched a wet hand to the back of Corinne's neck and made a sizzling sound – *tzzsssss*. The cool hand startled her. She kick-splashed him.

An afternoon of nonsense was part of Charlie's plan to distract Corinne from any thoughts about Sanctis, Pinay or the hospital.

They dug into their backpacks for tomato sandwiches, packets of water, granola bars, mangoes and the spiky fruit called corossol. With its bitter skin and sweet flesh, corossol is more than a snack. "Guidebook says it's a home remedy for everything. Head lice, bedbugs, leprosy, cancer. That should protect us against anything we'll encounter today," Charlie teased. "Me? I'm doubly protected. I'm here with my own nurse!"

Their teen guide hung around long enough to be

rewarded with a half sandwich. Charlie and Corinne lay silently on their towels, soaking up the sun, lizarding.

"You won't believe what happened yesterday. We admitted a girl with an obstetric fistula. Fourteen years old. Had a hole between her rectum and vagina caused by a long, obstructed labor."

Charlie wasn't sure where this story was going but it was off to a grim start. "Jeez," he said.

"She was from a remote village, in labor for two days with her insides getting torn apart by uterine contractions. The baby died. The community took up a collection of a few gourdes to transport her to the hospital. They bore her down the mountainside on a litter made of a door that had been taken off its hinges. She came to us in agony on the back of a moto. We cleaned her up. But with feces leaking into her vagina, she smelled awful."

A grim start and not getting any prettier, thought Charlie.

"She desperately needed surgery, but Pinay refused because of the stench. 'Not in my O.R.,' he said. 'Send her to general surgery.' That meant she would have to wait a few days, reeking, in shame, distraught at having lost her baby, parked alone on a gurney in an outdoor alcove to spare the other patients the stink. "Pinay is such a bastard," said Corinne. "We have got to get him."

When Charlie finally spoke, he reached for a note of empathy, but it came out sounding critical. "Corinne. … Honey. … It's not healthy, Corinne. This obsession with Pinay. He is awful, sure. But your mental health …"

"Don't honey me!" she spat, sitting up suddenly. "Obsessed? You think I'm obsessed? He had Sanctis killed,

God dammit! What's wrong with you? As far as I am concerned, you're not obsessed enough!"

CHAPTER THIRTY-THREE
"I'm not doing bugger all!"

"JB, it's Charlie. Have you got a minute?"

JB pushed away the Excel spreadsheet he was building to track Prantout. He hunched over his phone and leaned in to hear better. All around him at the FBI's Miami field office colleagues were on their phones, staring at computer terminals or huddled in knots of conversation.

"Hey C-squared. *Tout bagay anfòm*? You okay?"

"I'm alright. We're alright. I guess. But Corinne is really stressed. Now that you've had time to think about Sanctis' murder, do you have any good ideas? Is there anything that we can do? That you can do? Corinne won't let it go. It's causing friction between us."

"Okay, you know that Haiti is different, right? Of course, you know. If I were working on this case stateside there are a thousand threads that I would want to pull. That might not be possible in Haiti."

To begin with, he said, there is the condition of the crime scene.

"Any footwear impressions? Tire tracks? Anything left at the scene?"

"I don't know. ... Neither do the police, probably. From what I can tell, they're not investigating."

"In a weird way, that might be a good thing. The biggest contaminants of crime scenes are investigators, coroners, witnesses, anybody who accidentally or carelessly tramples everything. In your case, the half-assed investigation could be a blessing because the crime scene wasn't badly disturbed. There might be clues there even now, two months after the killing. What about the way that Sanctis was strangled? Any reason to think that someone was trying to scare him, and that the death was accidental? Was the twist on that stethoscope's rubber tubing tied left hand over right? Or right over left? That could tell you something about the handedness - the hand dominance - of the assailant.

"That's how a serious investigation would proceed. Where's the telescope? Was this – *Bondye*, I hate this term – a robbery gone wrong? Was it an assassination? What's the motive? Who had it in for Sanctis? Were any patients or their families angry at him for some reason? Do you know? Make a list of potential suspects that doesn't include Pinay. I would want to know the condition of his hyoid, the u-shaped bone where the spine meets the neck. The hyoid gets fractured in 50 percent of strangulations. Its condition might indicate if Sanctis was strangled with the tubing or if the stethoscope was added afterwards like a bow on a sick present."

That last bit of inquiry left Charlie speechless.

"Strangulation is asphyxia by closing the blood vessels of the neck or the airway. It happens three ways: by hanging, by ligature or by manual pressure. A constricting band, like the stethoscope's tubing, might not be strong enough to crush the hyoid. But if that bone is broken, then Sanctis might have been choked out first by a forearm across the neck, or another way."

JB was not trying to be grisly, it was just the nature of

a homicide investigation.

"His eyes were removed," said JB. "That's what you told me. What kind of tool was used? Clean cuts from a switchblade? Rough gouges from something like a spoon? Either way, that could be a clue. I think you see what I'm getting at. For the Bureau to commit our resources to an international investigation, we need something to go on, something more than a nurse's hunch."

Charlie thanked his friend. Later, when he told Corinne about the call, he dialed down the gore. He explained that JB would not proceed without at least something tangible to support her allegation. If it went forward on such slim beginning evidence it would fall flat without bagging Pinay.

"Then we'll just have to go out to Sanctis' place and look around," she said immediately.

"You think that's such a good idea? The people who killed him could be watching the place. …"

"Watching? Why? For what reason? That makes no sense. And what if they are? So what? Are we supposed to do nothing? Let them murder a doctor who stuck it out through all the hardships here to alleviate local suffering - and we do what? Nothing? Bugger all? We do bugger all? I am not doing bugger all, Charlie. You can come with me to his house, or not, but I'm not doing bugger all."

Corinne's blood was up and there was no way Charlie would let her go alone. They rented a moto for a few hours from a driver at a taxi stand and drove themselves to Sanctis' place on a sunny day. They set the moto on its kickstand and walked to the back of the house. Several hard rains since the killing had dappled the ground where Corinne had discovered Sanctis' body. They used sticks to push aside the weeds as they searched for clues.

"See anything?" said Charlie.

"Not yet."

They came across the pop top from a soda can, shards of brown glass still attached to a torn Prestige label, an empty, soggy pack of Comme Il Faut cigarettes. "That's Pinay's brand," said Corinne.

"And the brand of about a million other Haitians," said Charlie.

"None of this - or all of it - could be relevant," said Corinne. "Sanctis didn't smoke. So what's that cigarette butt doing here?"

Then she saw it.

It looked like a gray pebble nestled among other pebbles. She poked at it with the stick. On closer inspection, it was a shiny amulet, an inch and a half square, shaped like a bell with an eyelet at the top and an inscription. "This could be something," she said.

She lifted it with the tip of the stick and saw that it was made of silver or pewter. She wiped off the mud and revealed the depiction of a skeleton riding a motorcycle in raised relief on one side of the bell, and on the obverse, two words: "*Ekip*" and "Evans" – Evans' crew. Corinne read it aloud.

"What?" Charlie said in disbelief.

"Evans. Crew. It says Evans Crew. I don't believe it."

Corinne tucked the bell inside a surgical glove for safekeeping. She always carried a pair, the way Charlie carried a pen and paper. Tools of the trade.

Before returning the moto to its owner, the couple rode a few kilometers out of town on the Rue Paul Eugene

Magloire, Hinche's main thoroughfare, to the Comfort Plus Hotel where they sat on the elevated patio above a kidney-shaped swimming pool. They ordered vanilla-infused Haitian lemonade and took advantage of the free Wifi. They opened the Internet on their cell phones and used Google Images to try to figure out the significance of the tiny bell.

They were scrolling intently when Corinne said, "Got it! Motorcycle bell." She passed her phone to Charlie so he could read the link.

"The use of bells as a channel for positive energy dates back to antiquity," the entry read. "Across cultures, continents, and religions, bells have been rung to banish evil spirits at ceremonies, funerals, and even in everyday life. Many serious bikers attach bells to the bottom of their rides - a decades-old custom believed to ward off mishaps and mechanical failures."

"Those sons of bitches," said Corinne, "I'll bet there is another bell just like this one on another motorcycle, the one that ran me and Anel off the road."

"Maybe," said Charlie. "Maybe it's the same guys. Maybe not. Either way, it still doesn't prove a Pinay connection."

"We'll get there," said Corinne. "Oh, ye of little faith. We'll get there. You have to tell JB about this. Is he helping us? Shouldn't he be here? When is he going to get involved?"

CHAPTER THIRTY-FOUR
Dyab blan!

A few days later, carrying a tin of home-cooked beans, fried plantains and dirty rice, Charlie met Corinne for lunch at the hospital. On days when she could take a break they ate on a bench under the white blossoms of an almond tree.

"We have three women in labor in the *salle* right now," she said. "All just a few centimeters dilated. Not ready to push. They'll be a while. What have we here? … Oh, nice, beans and rice … mmm, and still warm. Brilliant."

They were into second helpings when they noticed a commotion at the hospital gate. A stream of badly-burned people was arriving in ambulances and private cars. Some were motionless under gurney sheets. They were wheeled directly to the hospital's morgue.

From a driver rushing back out to retrieve more victims, Corinne and Charlie learned that a truck delivering gasoline to the Total service station on National Highway 1 had exploded, killing seven people and injuring at least 30. Witnesses said the tanker truck, which had evaded a carjacking earlier that day, had hit a wall, spewing gasoline that came in contact with a vendor's outdoor grill. The truck exploded, igniting the victims, incinerating four nearby houses and destroying two dozen cars and motorcycles. Hinche, like many Haitian towns outside of the capital, has no fire department. Staffers of a nearby U.N. post helped contain the flames.

"It's going to get crazy around here," said Corinne. "The Department d'Urgence will be pulling us from all over to staff the emergency room. I'd better run back to the *salle*."

As she turned to leave, Charlie tagged the back of her neck with a quick peck. "Good luck."

Free to wander because of the buzz of activity, Charlie looked around the hospital grounds - a handful of white, one and two-story buildings with concrete floors, red tile roofs and a swath of green painted on the lower six feet of the walls. Some of the walkways were paved; others were hard-packed dirt. The central courtyard, which had once been planted with grass and shrubs, was a naked field of rocks and random agaves.

He followed a walkway past the *salle maternite* to an intersecting walkway that led to the administration building. It was his chance to get a glimpse of Pinay's lair. If he ran into anyone who demanded to know what he was doing he would say that he was a reporter covering the explosion and had gotten lost looking for the morgue.

Charlie shoved a reporter's notebook into his back pocket, slipped his pencil behind one ear and walked slowly down the dimly lit corridor. He moved unnoticed past the open door of what looked like a secretary's office. The next door was closed. He moved closer to make out the nameplate and was startled by an angry voice behind him. He hadn't heard anyone approaching.

"No one belongs back here. Who are you?"

Charlie turned. It was Pinay.

He offered up his lost-reporter-looking-for-the-morgue ruse, but Pinay wasn't having it.

"Preposterous! What are you doing here?"

"Nothing. I ..."

"You are lying."

"Really. I came to see my friend ... "

"Your friend is that British nurse. I know who your friend is. I saw you outside."

"We were having lunch when the ambulances ... ."

"Which doesn't explain what you are doing back here."

"I was looking for the morgue and an administrator to interview."

"*Dyab blan*! White devil. You are lying! Show me your identification."

Charlie reached into his wallet and pulled out his Boston Globe business card. Pinay looked at it and threw it back at him. When Charlie bent down to pick it up, he feared that Pinay was about to strike him.

"Leave now, or I will have you thrown in jail. If I ever see you again, I will have you arrested."

To maintain contact with her colleagues, Corinne split her nights between Saj Fanm and Charlie's apartment. That evening, he called her at the compound and told her about his run-in with Pinay.

"What were you doing back there?" she said. "I thought you left when I ran back to the *salle*."

"It's not the kind of spot news I normally cover. But I wanted to know more about the explosion, especially since so many fuel trucks are getting hijacked. It was a chance to snoop around, gain some intel. You said I wasn't obsessed enough. So I went looking for Pinay's office. The door was closed. He came from behind and nailed me. Said he would have me arrested."

"That's the tamest thing he would do," said Corinne.

The next morning, as Charlie left his house, he saw a sand-painting on the ground in front of his door. Its neat lines were made of a yellowish powder, probably cornmeal, although Charlie wasn't about to taste it to find out.

He knew from his readings on Vodou that he was looking at a *veve*, a ritual drawing done to invite the presence of divine spirits. And this one, on the threshold of his home, was the *veve* of Baron Samedi, who Charlie knew was the gatekeeper between the living and the dead. The Baron's *veve* depicted a cross-hatched crucifix on a two-tiered tombstone, flanked by two small coffins floating in air.

"Well *bonjou* to you too, Baron Pinay," Charlie said to himself. Or was somebody else trying to scare him? He dragged the side of his sneaker through the design and stamped hard to shake off the corn meal.

CHAPTER THIRTY-FIVE
"The sickness that keeps them sick."

That night at Saj Fanm, Corinne lay in bed, restless. She had hoped to fall asleep quickly but each time she closed her eyes she pictured the gruesome death mask of Sanctis - red-rimmed black holes where his eyes should have been. Entangled in her bed sheet, she rolled, snorted and wrestled free. She curled into a fetal ball, then stretched out, long and languid, like a dog arching its back. She ran her hands over her hair. Nothing settled her down.

Intrusive memories and insomnia were among the symptoms of post-traumatic stress. After Sanctis' murder, she also experienced self-destructive thoughts, sour moods and emotional outbursts. Charlie had seen similar symptoms in some of the soldiers he was embedded with. Through a private Facebook group, he had kept in touch with them long after his stories about their unit were published. He sent them birthday cards and new-baby presents, holiday greets and condolence cards after one of them died, an apparent suicide. Having entrusted his life to them when they were in Iraq, he felt he owed them more than a "thanks for your service" when they came back home.

On occasions when fear and doubt overwhelmed Corinne, she turned existential, asking herself, "Why am I still in Haiti? What am I doing here?"

She was committed to the life-saving mission of Saj

Fanm, a truly beneficial organization. That would never change. Her quest to nail Sanctis' killer was fresh motivation to carry on. But before that? On more days than not, she had to admit, she felt overdue for a change.

She thought about the winding road that had led her back to Haiti. After volunteering with Care4Calais, she returned to her hospital in Truro, then moved up to London to work as a nurse supervisor for the local office of Medecins du Monde. When she heard about the opening at Saj Fanm, a place she knew well from her stint as a volunteer in 2010, she applied, was interviewed by Skype, and offered a one-year contract subject to renewal. Haiti's heat, even its humidity, would be a welcome change from the dreariness of London, where more often than not overcast skies were the color of wet cement. She told herself that accepting a responsible full-time position in a country rife with daily hardships was the logical next step in the development of her career as a nurse-humanitarian.

In London, she had ridden a bike to the clinic, which was a warren of rooms in a community center in Bethnal Green, an increasingly gentrified part of the city's East End with a large Bangladeshi immigrant population.

Through contact with the Bangladeshi community, Corinne learned that the caste system so closely identified with India was part of Bangladeshi culture, too. Relegated to society's dirtiest jobs – street sweepers, washers, trash collectors, sawyers, and the like - these outcasts experienced descent-based discrimination in housing, education, employment, and the social and cultural spheres.

Outsiders called them "untouchables." They called themselves Dalits – "broken people" – to emphasize that they were deliberately exploited, oppressed and destroyed through generations. When Bangladeshi women in London had marched to draw attention to the plight of Dalits in the U.K., Corinne marched with them. Many wore scarves and threadbare sweaters. One stood out in a delicate saffron sari and shawl. Corinne - with no time to change - had marched alongside her wearing her work clogs and scrubs.

On her bike she had conducted a survey of people "sleeping rough" – living outdoors, with no protection - in the vicinity of the clinic. The survey was in preparation for the launch of a Medecins du Monde mobile clinic to address that vulnerable population's general health needs and offer screenings for HIV, chlamydia, and gonorrhea. Her favorite part of the job was the look on the rough sleepers' faces when she handed them clean socks and gloves.

Whether marching with the Bangladeshis, or surveying the rough sleepers, Corinne felt her career came with the obligation to call out injustice and try to rectify it.

In the U.K., where single-payer health insurance means everyone, even undocumented immigrants, is entitled to a doctor, MdM's London clinic should not have needed to exist at all. But the reality on the ground was different. Many hospitals demanded paperwork, passports, and Home Office documentation, which many people - especially the rough sleepers and the undocumented – didn't have. They feared trouble with the authorities, so they stayed away from clinics.

"It's a vicious cycle," Corinne wrote in her report on the project. "Fear is the sickness that keeps them sick."

Charlie's reappearance in Haiti caught Corinne at a

time when she was maximally stressed. She always liked him, beginning with the time she caught him stealing a look at her at the Désir. She had noticed the shape of his hands, the ridgeline of his knuckles. Muscular forearms added to his appeal. He was her type, and now, the maturity of the passing years had made him even more attractive.

While she wanted more of Charlie's mind, body and soul, she worried that she wouldn't be able to keep up with the intensity of his growing attachment because of her emotional fragility.

On her laptop in a file of old photographs there was one taken a week after the 2010 quake. It showed her, some colleagues from the triage unit, Charlie and a couple of other "hacks" lined up along the Désir's bar. It was a noisy, heady scene and two people standing opposite the group had their cell phone cameras out to capture it.

Corinne hadn't seen that photo in a long time. Now, in her room at Saj Fanm, with Charlie on her mind, she called it to the screen and enlarged it with a double-click. Everyone, of course, looked so much younger. And, as often happens when two photographers face a group, no one being photographed knew exactly where to aim their gaze.

Seeing that picture now, Corinne noticed something for the first time. She was looking in the direction of one photographer. Charlie had his eyes fixed on her.

Clicking through more old photos, Corinne found one that made her smile. It was of her, playfully posed in front of a large round target painted on a chewed-up wall, with a hatchet stuck squarely in its red bull's eye. The picture was snapped at Celtic Tossers, the axe-throwing club favored by hipsters in her hometown of Truro, population 20,000, Cornwall's only city, and five hours from London by car. On a lark with one of her girlfriends, Corinne had tried the trendy sport and liked it, which is how her portrait, with victorious thumbs up, had come to take its place in the club's online "Gallery of Tossers." Amazingly she had hit the bull's eye on her first throw. When she explained to Charlie the lewd meaning of tosser, he couldn't stop laughing. "A jerk-off, huh?" he said. "Congratulations."

As the only child of a postman and a Year 10 teacher of literature, Corinne read voraciously and had excelled at school. Her first love, however, was the sharp-eyed, velvety Border Collie she got when she was 16 and named Puccini. She had raised him to be a therapy dog and volunteered weekly at the Royal Cornwall Hospital where he provided cuddly comfort and was a favorite in the pediatric cancer ward. Decked out in his royal blue "Therapy Dog" jacket, Puccini sidled up to patients' beds, extended his sable snout to their outstretched hands and luxuriated in their delighted stroking.

Corinne had trained as a nurse at Royal Cornwall and volunteered with Puccini in her off hours. One of the patients they visited, nine-year-old Amanda, had advanced bone cancer. Corinne and Puccini had met Amanda shortly after her right leg had to be amputated below the knee. The child was scared and deeply depressed but perked up whenever Puccini, whom she called "Poochie Softie," came around.

When Corinne moved up to London before landing the Haiti job, she had asked Amanda's family if they would look after 10-year-old Puccini. The Haiti offer brought the issue of Puccini's long-term future to a head.

"Poochie Softie needs a good home. I think you can provide that. Would you take care of him?" Corinne had asked the little girl.

"But my leg …"

"Oh, Puccini doesn't care about that. He knows you'll walk again. But he will want to sleep with you in your bed. Would that be okay?"

"Yes," said Amanda, smiling. "He's such a good boy."

"He is a good boy. After you get out of the hospital and finish your rehab, you'll have to bring him back here to help the other kids. Can you do that?"

Amanda nodded, mouth agape, eyes wide, absorbing the importance of the assignment, but unsure what to say.

Earlier, in private, Corinne had cleared the arrangement with Amanda's mother.

"I'm going to tell her that your family is taking over the therapy-dog gig," she told the mom. "But between us, there is no obligation. That's just my cover story with Amanda. I want her to have Puccini and build a lasting bond with him. I have seen the comfort he brings her. You've seen it too. It will help with her recovery. I'll be leaving soon for Haiti. I will miss Poochie Softie dearly. But he'll be living the life he trained for. Me too … I hope."

CHAPTER THIRTY-SIX
"Alo, ti cheri."

It was Corinne's first time back at the Sisters of Charity orphanage since learning that Fabilene's mother had been killed at the opposition march. Charlie accompanied her.

"We haven't told the little one," said the Mother Superior, Sister Alouette. "Please don't say anything." Corinne and Charlie nodded solemnly.

Corinne had been telling Charlie about the remarkable orphanage. Now he would see it for himself.

Dressed identically, the 50 boys and girls sat stockstill, side by side on long, child-sized wooden benches. To Charlie they looked like "little old souls."

"Some are older than they look," said Corinne. "Starvation stunts their growth."

The boys' hair was clipped close to the scalp. Some of the girls wore it that way, too, facilitating hygiene. A few, like Fabilene, had box braids or nappy twists secured with brightly colored barrettes. Almost all had the reddish-gold tinge to their hair associated with childhood malnutrition.

"Hypochromotrichia," said Corinne, "lack of melanin to the hair shaft. Doctors aren't sure why it happens."

Charlie grimaced. "That's a helluva word."

When Fabilene saw Corinne, she ran straight to her.

"*Alo, ti cheri. Alo Fabi,*" Corinne said, scooping the child into her arms. Fabilene seemed not to remember the sadness at the end of Corinne's last visit.

Corinne introduced Charlie. Fabi looked skeptical. Who was he? Who was he to Corinne? More importantly, was he going to be an ally, or a rival for Corinne's attention?

Seeing the intimacy that the little girl shared with Corinne, Charlie was awed. He'd seen Corinne with newborn babies. She always exuded a protective aura. But this was different. This revealed a maternal instinct he hadn't seen in her before. He was charmed just watching Corinne gently trace the beauty mark on the back of Fabi's neck. The child reached back and ran the fingers of one hand through the hair on the nape of Corinne's neck. He could have watched them cooing and snuggling all afternoon. But he stepped away to give them privacy, and immediately was set upon by two little boys who wanted to run repeatedly between his legs.

That night at Charlie's apartment he and Corinne talked about the orphanage and the feelings it stirred in them. Corinne said it made her recognize that she probably would like to be a mother someday.

"I'm a woman," she said. "I have the capacity to bring life into the world. At least as far as I know I do. Sometimes I think it would be a shame not to try."

Charlie said he had never thought seriously about being a dad. If it ever came about, he said, he'd want to be an all-around good one, not just a good provider. A father who was supportive both emotionally and materially. Was he fooling himself to think he had the makings of a good parent? He thrived on headlines and deadlines, new stories, new countries, new experiences. Could he have all of that and parenthood, too? Would something have to give? And if so, would he make the right choice?

"Did you and Molly ever talk about having children?"

Charlie was startled by Corinne's sudden use of his ex-wife's name.

"We didn't. We thought there would always be time to have children. Given how things turned out, I'm glad we never did."

They talked about Fabi, who was brought to the Sisters of Charity by an overwhelmed single mother who loved her but couldn't feed her, and how fate, in the form of an errant tear gas canister, had intervened to make Fabi a true orphan now.

"It breaks my heart," said Corinne. "Most of those children might someday return to their homes or at least come to know their mothers."

She was silent for a long time. Then she looked directly at Charlie and said, "In a case like Fabi's, she really could be adopted."

In the quiet that followed Charlie asked himself: Was there a deeper meaning in Corinne's words? Could the two of them, two white people not from Haiti, successfully raise a Haitian child? Would they have to be married? Could they prove they were committed to the child without marriage? Without it, could they prove they were committed to each other? Was any of that even possible? Besides, in a case like Fabilene's, weren't foster care and local adoption the better options? What was he thinking? Forget about raising a child. He and Corinne had never even discussed making their lives together. Now who was the one getting out ahead of his skis?

Charlie had written about Haitian foreign adoptions in

the years since the earthquake, particularly in France, where his parents lived, and he could frame the story around government statistics. His article ran prominently on the front page of "Revop," the Globe's Sunday Review and Opinion section.

In 2009, 653 Haitian children were adopted by French parents, Charlie wrote. In 2010, the year of the quake, 1,000 were. But in the post-quake chaos, many of those adoptions turned out to be under-the-radar arrangements, part of a lucrative kids-for-cash scheme that bypassed Haitian government authorities. When the scandal was revealed, Haiti halted all foreign adoptions.

Two years later, foreign adoptions resumed with tougher regulations. "What happened after the earthquake pricked our conscience. We owed it to these children to do better," an official in charge of international adoptions told Charlie.

In 2011, Haiti signed the Hague Convention of 1993 "On the Protection of Infants." Then its parliament updated its law, re-emphasizing the requirement that the birth parents knowingly consent to giving up their parental rights.

What a mess, thought Charlie. All of these children in need, and a wonderful couple like JB and Mirlande, who desperately want a child but are childless.

As night fell, he lit a candle for mood lighting and poured an inch of Barbancourt into two jelly jars.

Sharing the experience of the orphanage with Corinne deepened their intimacy. They'd been more honest and unguarded with each other than they had ever been. Together at the orphanage they had brought an hour of comfort to little children hungry for food and affection. They felt nourished by the experience, too.

He kissed her passionately as they moved toward the bed and lay naked, nestled like spoons in a drawer, savoring the taste of each other - and the sting of Barbancourt - as they drifted off.

While Corinne was dreaming and talking in her sleep, Charlie thought he heard her mumble "Fabi." A few moments later he thought he heard her say "Pinay."

CHAPTER THIRTY-SEVEN
Take a pill

On the broken sidewalks of Croix des Bouquets where she hustled clients, she called herself Jolifleur, pretty flower, but to the neighborhood regulars who saw her every day she was *Dam grenn lan*, the Pill Lady.

Stocky and dark-skinned, with brittle twists of hair tucked behind her ears, she had a wide smile, a sweaty top lip and buck teeth as big as Chiclets. A pink rag that had been a T-shirt was rolled into a ring and placed atop her head to cushion the weight of the yellow plastic tub that held her wares. Anchored in the tub was a two-foot-high cardboard column wrapped with multi-colored lozenges, capsules, and pills, all in blister packs.

Weaving among the market ladies selling their tired tomatoes stacked precariously in pyramids, Jolifleur sang out: *Pran yon grenn, pran yon grenn, pran yon grenn* - "Take a pill, take a pill, take a pill."

Many Haitians preferred to self-medicate rather than seek formal treatment because the public hospitals were frequently on strike, the government health services inconsistent, and the private clinics too expensive.

For Jolifleur that meant a cash-and-carry opportunity to earn $2 to $24 a day.

For example, Fluconazole, a prescription antifungal medication, sold for $7.15 in a local pharmacy but could be bought on the street for $3.20. A single pill could be purchased for as little as 30 cents.

Jolifleur's regular rounds took her past the *charbonnier*, a tiny woman dwarfed by stacks of blackened wood that had been burnt into charcoal for cooking fuel. Coated head to toe in coal dust, she wasn't her natural shade of dark brown. She was tar-paper black, with rheumy eyes that shone yellow within deep sockets.

Near a gaggle of teenage boys admiring an older man's shiny moto, a customer approached the Pill Lady. She was a woman in her twenties, leading a five-year-old boy by the hand. She explained that the child had an inner-ear infection that caused him excruciating pain. She lacked a doctor's prescription for the antibiotic amoxicillin. Even if she had a 'scrip, she said, she lacked the money to buy a full box of capsules at a pharmacy.

As the child pressed a hand against his aching right ear, the mother said she wanted to buy three amoxicillin capsules, but with so few gourdes in her tattered pocketbook, she had to settle for two. It was a loving gesture, but not nearly enough medicine for proper treatment. Given the child's age and weight, the Pill Lady told her, the proper amount is two doses a day for at least five days.

Na wè – si Dye vle. "I'll see you again, God willing," said the forlorn mother. She grabbed her son's hand and dashed to catch a tap-tap.

CHAPTER THIRTY-EIGHT
When it's murder

Having nabbed the PortMiami customs manager, turned him into an informant and set him free to avoid suspicion, JB was making progress connecting the dots of Prantout's cocaine smuggling network.

He knew his target used legitimate international trade in artwork and handicrafts to disguise his illegal shipments. Prantout arranged just two or three shipments a year from Colombia via Haiti to minimize his risk of getting caught. Rather than land the coke in the U.S. at a remote location, Prantout brought it in through the port of Miami using an unwitting, reputable shipper whose loads were less likely to be vigorously inspected.

A critical part of the operation was avoiding the all-seeing container-truck inspections performed by the low-dose X-ray scanners mounted overhead in the tall arch of a drive-through portal. That's where the customs manager, who was bribed $2,000 a month, earned his keep. If he saw that one of Prantout's containers was destined for an inspection, he "randomly" assigned it to himself and diverted it from the machine.

One technique that Prantout used to disguise the contraband involved decorative ceramic tiles, framed with a border made of wood, which his shop sold as trivets and wall hangings. Some of them bore the red-and-blue insignia of Haiti's flag. Others bore cheeky sayings, like "If you mess with me, you mess with my Haitian boyfriend, and you don't want to mess with him," or "Made in America, with Haitian parts." The half-inch thick tiles were six inches square. A stack of 12 measured six inches high.

Smuggling in the coke was a game of camouflage. First, a sizable center square was cut out and removed from 10 of the tiles, which were then stacked. Two uncut tiles from the dozen were set aside and reserved to cap the top and bottom of the hollowed-out stack. The resulting cavity, which measured 3 inches square by 6 inches deep, was large enough to hold a half-kilo of bagged cocaine. The stack, capped at both ends with the uncut tiles, was carefully glued together, wrapped in bubble wrap, and put in the middle of a crate surrounded by indistinguishable stacks of undoctored tiles. As a precaution, the "hot" crates were checked to make sure that they weighed the same as the "clean" ones.

"What do you know about the economics of the operation?" JB asked the informant during an interrogation.

"Zip. I know what he pays me. That's all," said the man.

"And that is …?"

"Two large a month. Like clockwork. I never have to worry about getting my money. Beyond that I don't know anything. Don't know who he sells to, or what happens to the drugs after they leave the port."

"If you do know something, now is the time to tell it. If you hold back, it'll kill your plea deal."

"I'm telling you I know nothing. That's everything I know."

"How much do you figure Prantout grosses in a year?"

"You don't believe me, do you? I told you. I don't

know what any of it is worth."

In the car on the way back to his office, JB thought about how little the customs guy claimed to know, and of that stanza from Bob Dylan's *All Along the Watchtower*.

At his desk, JB did some rough calculating. Let's say Prantout brings in 200 dozen of those trivets every six months, and just 10 percent of the load is doctored. That's 20 disguised stacks hiding a total of 10 kilos of cocaine. And let's assume Prantout paid the wholesale price of $18,000 per kilo. Depending on the drug's purity and how much he steps on it with adulterants, he can push it out to the street at $40,000 to $100,000 per kilo. He invests $180,000 and walks away with $400,000 to $1 million - every six months.

Not only that. He seems to have kidnapped his own children, and maybe had his mother-in-law shot to death after she and he were seen arguing. JB had a sense that Chloe Marvel was in on the action. Had her now-deceased mother been in the game too?

JB was ready to start making the case on paper. He typed out an affidavit for a criminal complaint. When he got to the part about probable cause, he summarized what the customs guy had told him.

"Based on my knowledge, training and experience, and the facts set forth in this affidavit," JB wrote, "I have probable cause to believe, and I do believe, that Etienne Marvel, alias 'Prantout,' conspired, in violation of Title 21, United States Code, the Controlled Substances Act, to commit crimes against the United States, specifically the importation, possession and distribution for sale of cocaine, a schedule II dangerous drug."

The case for extradition would be more complex. Although the U.S. and Haiti have had a bilateral extradition treaty in effect since 1905, the treaty doesn't name drug offenses as grounds for extradition. In fact, when the U.S. Pure Food and Drug Act, which required accurate labeling of contents and dosages, was passed in 1906, cocaine, heroin, cannabis, and other such drugs continued to be legally available without prescription so long as they were accurately labeled.

But the extradition treaty offered other grounds for snagging Prantout. It grants extradition for: bribery, such as the payoffs to the customs official; forged documents, such as the falsified container-inspection records; and the kidnapping of minors, such as the refusal to return his children to his wife in the United States.

"There's enough here for the U.S. Attorney to make a case," JB reported to his boss. "And a murder charge, if it turns out that he had his mother-in-law killed. When it's murder, extradition is always granted."

CHAPTER THIRTY-NINE
Peyilok

While JB was closing in on Prantout, the anti-government protests in Haiti were escalating, consuming the capital in flames and fury.

Many streets in Port au Prince were blockaded with debris. Police fired tear gas on demonstrators throwing rocks. Universities suspended classes. In February, the government announced it would cancel all remaining Carnival celebrations "to avoid a bloodbath."

Demanding the resignation of President Jovenel Moise, demonstrators scattered bricks, oil, burning tires, an upended light pole and overturned ice cream carts on the roads leading to his house. For the first time, Charlie saw signs emblazoned: *Lanmo Jomo* – Death to Jovenal Moise.

Citing a resurgence in murders and kidnappings, and the impotence of law enforcement, the protesters decried the country's mounting insecurity. The U.S. State Department raised the travel warning for U.S. citizens to Level 4 - Do Not Travel to Haiti.

Charlie and Corinne were drinking coffee in his apartment as the morning sun burst through a beat-up shade.

"It's a shitshow down in P-a-P right now," Charlie told Corinne after he got off the phone with Maffi. "Maffi says even the streets of Petionville are flooded with protesters."

They tuned their radio to VOA Kreyol, the Voice of America's Creole service. Corinne interpreted as they continued getting dressed.

In a sign of the worsening chaos, police officers, who demanded improved working conditions and the right to bargain collectively, attacked an army headquarters in the city. Moise called it "a coup attempt." Police said the army fired on them first.

The widespread demonstrations, known as *peyilok*, "closed country," sent a stream of more than 250 patients to the 25-bed, Doctors Without Borders hospital in the Tabarre section of P-a-P.

"We knew we were meeting a need ... but the situation is even worse than we imagined," the MSF project coordinator told VOA. He said that gunshot wounds accounted for more than half of the hospital's admissions.

MSF, which has worked in Haiti since 1991, estimated that the 2010 earthquake, which collapsed two of its three medical facilities, had wiped out 60 percent of Haiti's health care system. An estimated 10 percent of Haiti's medical staff left the country or lost their lives, including 12 MSF staff.

A decade later, amid the escalating political and economic crisis, Haiti's medical system was again on the brink of collapse, with facilities struggling to provide basic services due to a lack of staff and shortages of drugs, oxygen, blood and fuel.

The renewed strain heightened the relevance of Charlie's clinic story. Because of its gangbanger connection, it also neatly incorporated the current climate of violence. Newswise, it was a lucky coincidence.

In a climate of mayhem, there was a fresh massacre in La Saline, a hotbed of anti-Moise activity, where gangs killed 26 people over two days, while police failed to intervene. Some eyewitnesses said it appeared the gangs and the government were complicit in the attacks. The government denied the allegation.

The VOA broke in with a live report from the outskirts of Pelerin, Moise's well-to-do neighborhood, where a cordon of police with riot shields, tear gas and water cannons were holding back the demonstrators. The voice of an angry man being interviewed could be heard over the crowd.

"What's he saying?" Charlie asked Corinne.

"He said the demonstrators are at the edge of an abyss, and that this is an uprising, not a protest."

With the turmoil of *peyilok* roiling Haiti's streets, Charlie's Globe editors had asked if he wouldn't mind pausing his vacation to produce a "quick hit" first-person story about how it feels to be in the heart of a Haitian political demonstration.

He typed out a budget line for that story and read it to Corinne before filing it. He thought it was an evocative telling of one day in Port-au-Prince when his driver Junior made a wrong turn, they got boxed in by thousands of demonstrators, and had to get out of the truck.

"Marchers, protesters, swarms of them, lathered with sweat, filled the avenues shoulder-to-shoulder, curb-to-curb. They leaned forward, lurching en masse into a speed walk." Charlie kept reading the budget line aloud, searching Corinne's face for any reaction. "Before we knew it, the crowd was trotting in spooky unison, pressing forward as one. All it would have taken to unleash panic would be for an instigator to fire a shot and holler, Everybody Run! People are routinely trampled in these stampedes. The in-between times - between the trot and the shot - are very scary."

"Whoaaa, wait a minute," said Corinne. "Swarms? Instigator? Don't you mean the people's popular movement, led not by instigators, but by leaders who respect Haitians' hard-won right to live free from dictatorship and oppression? Describing the action without the reasons for the uprising tells only half the story."

Charlie nodded. It was just like her to cut right to the political heart of the story. "You need that element," said Corinne. "And spooky? Spooky? Seriously?"

Charlie knew she was right. A budget line is supposed to hype a story, grab an editor's attention, set the article up for good display. But pure hype, without a sober explanation of what motivates the action, is shoddy journalism.

"I'll fix that," said Charlie. "And spooky? What? Does that sound racist?"

CHAPTER FORTY
Light of my life

Feeling confident that the case against Prantout was solid, JB called Mateo Adolfo, the Miami detective, to say he was ready to reach out to Adolfo's trusted contact in the Haitian National Police.

"If you are truly close to an arrest," Adolfo said, "it's best to go there and speak to him in person."

That made sense, thought JB, and while there he could visit with his mother and check in on Charlie and Corinne.

Before going, he wanted to interview Sanctis' mother, Jesula Beauvoir, a widow who lived alone in Coral Gables, not far from the University of Miami, where she worked as a housekeeper. Sanctis' body and personal effects had been shipped back to her. The interment, next to her husband in a family plot, had been private.

JB arranged to meet the grieving mother at her one-bedroom garden apartment in the modest neighborhood called Little Gables.

It was 6 p.m. when JB arrived and showed his credentials. She had the tired face of someone who collected trash, restocked bathrooms, and pushed a vacuum over acres of student-center carpeting. She was polite. She offered JB a glass of water as she led him to the sofa. But she was wary, hesitant to re-experience the pain of losing Sanctis, to go through it all again unless the FBI really meant to solve his murder. She pulled over a chair from the dining table, which had a white lace tablecloth covered with clear plastic.

On a side table was a statuette of *Le Marron Inconnu*, the unknown slave, with a conch to his lips, trumpeting the call to rebellion. Next to it was a framed, three-panel photo collage of Sanctis: In a coat and tie at his high school graduation; a cap and gown when he finished college; a spotless lab jacket at his "white-coat ceremony" after medical school.

Above the sofa was a large reproduction, hand painted in primary colors, of a classic Haitian market scene: women in hair wraps, others with baskets on their heads and live chickens at their feet; men shouldering heavy green stalks bristling with bunches of unripe bananas.

"Mrs. Beauvoir, I am sorry about what happened to your son. Thank you for making time to see me."

He asked to be forgiven for having to ask uncomfortable questions. Did she notice anything amiss? What could she tell him about her son?

Jesula Beauvoir sat with her hands folded in her lap. She gave a pursed-lip, closed-eyes nod of resignation. In a voice so low JB had to lean in to catch it, she said, "Why are you here?"

"To try to understand why your son was murdered … and catch his killer."

"This happened in Haiti."

"Yes."

"And you are with the FBI. So …"

"You're right. Ordinarily my office wouldn't be involved. But we have reason to believe that this case … your son's murder … has unusual circumstances. That's what we are hearing."

"Hearing how? Unusual how? Who told you that?"

"At this stage that's not something I'm at liberty to say."

"Agent Belizaire, I am his mother. Sanctis was my only child. You have got to tell me something."

Hoping to reassure her, JB thought it might help if he started by telling her about himself.

"Like your son, I am a Haitian-American. I know the culture. I know the country. I have enormous respect for the people of the diaspora, especially the ones like your son who have gone back to help in whatever ways they can."

"That's what Sanctis said before he went to Haiti. He wanted to help," said Mrs. Beauvoir. "Like when he was 16 and carried Narcan just in case he needed to help someone who overdosed. … Going to a country with Haiti's health problems, he wanted to help. But he said it in a funny way. He said, 'I want to be infectious.' That's what he said. 'I want to be infectious.' He wanted to infect the Haitians with his passion for public health and human rights."

"I get that," said JB. "Getting to the bottom of what happened to Sanctis would be my contribution to a healthier Haiti, one where violence does not escape punishment. Where thugs don't enjoy impunity. Telling me more about Sanctis can help me pursue justice in his name."

He had found his pitch to keep her talking. But it was more than a convenient pitch. He meant it.

Jesula Beauvoir sighed. She reached for the manila folder that held the paperwork of Sanctis' violent death: the autopsy performed at the Hopital de l'Universite d'Haiti; the death certificate; the transit label for his body and personal effects issued by the U.S. Embassy in Port-au-Prince; the Haitian Customs export permit; receipts from the Ange Bleu Funeral Home for the casket, embalming and preparation of Sanctis' remains for shipment.

Jesula Beauvoir held the file in her lap, still trying to comprehend how the life of the only child she bore and took such pride in had been reduced to a sheaf of bureaucratic forms.

"He was the light of my life," she said softly. "Especially after his father died."

"When was that?"

"Four years ago. Cancer. Roudy was a smoker."

"Did that motivate Sanctis to go into medicine?"

"He was already in med school when Roudy was diagnosed. … But we had a neighbor when Sanctis was growing up. He was an orthopedic trauma surgeon, with extraordinary skills and insight into human nature. Ghastly accidents brought him his patients. He used to say, 'I fix broken people.' Sanctis liked the sound of that."

"Did Sanctis want to be a surgeon?"

"For a time, yes. But general medicine was a faster route to earning a living, which became more important after his father died."

"How did he end up doing the work he did in Haiti? It surely wasn't to get rich."

"When he saw that I was going to be alright after Roudy died, that my job at the university was secure, he said he wanted to use his skills in the place where Roudy and I were born. He had the luxury and privilege of starting his life here in America. That's what he said. Working there was his tribute to us."

"Were you in regular contact?"

"He'd call a couple of times a month, mostly on Sundays using What's App."

"Can you think of anyone who wanted to hurt him? Do him harm? Did he mention anything? Anyone he was spending a lot of time with?"

"No. I always allowed him the privacy of his personal life. Sanctis came out to us when he was in college. It was hard for Roudy to accept. We didn't pry. I knew he was gay. I wanted him to be happy. I didn't pry."

"Was he involved with anyone in particular in Haiti?"

"He never said. I didn't pry."

"What else should I know about Sanctis?"

"He was compassionate, even as a child. Always included all the kids on the playground while some of the other kids formed cliques. He was always mature beyond his years. Even his elementary teachers said so."

"That must have made you proud."

"He always made me proud. In college, at Tulane, through the Big Brother program, he mentored a 9-year-old boy whose parents divorced bitterly. The mom, who was sad and lonely, joined Parents Without Partners and was desperate for a positive male influence for her son. Sanctis stepped up. He saw that boy weekly. Took him to ball games and bowling. Paid for it all, too. That boy grew up to be a bus driver in New Orleans. Years later, out of the blue, the mom reached out to Sanctis to let him know what an important influence he had been on her son during a critical time in her family's life."

"That had to make him feel good."

"It did. Sanctis had no siblings. It was a new experience for him to have a little brother. He enjoyed it."

Jesula Beauvoir continued with the string of poignant memories that emerged from her soul. In high school, Sanctis began carrying Narcan after a friend OD'd and nearly died. In med school he found time to volunteer at an HIV/AIDS clinic in New Orleans.

"We didn't talk much about that, but he wrote about it in the journal he started when he went off to college. I was surprised not to find it in his personal effects."

"Wait, what? He had a journal?"

"Sort of a diary, I guess, with a red leather cover and a small, heart-shaped padlock. He didn't share it with me. But he wrote in it. All the time. ... That's what he told me. I thought I'd get to read it now."

"Just one more question, Mrs. Beauvoir. Is there anything out of the ordinary that you think I should know?"

"Maybe this," she said. "A month before Sanctis was killed a small man who said he was a friend of Sanctis and needed to reach him came to see me. Sanctis had never mentioned him. He said he owed Sanctis something. Something he had to give him urgently. When I asked if it was money, he said it was private and couldn't tell me. I thought maybe he was someone Sanctis knew from the New Orleans' gay community. He was nervous. I didn't want to make him more uncomfortable. He was insistent so I told him how he could find Sanctis in Haiti. I hoped I wouldn't come to regret it. Did I do wrong?"

"No, no, Mrs. Beauvoir. What was his name?"

"He said people call him 'Ti-Jean.' He was a *petit homme*. No bigger than me."

Networking with a contact at the New Orleans Police Department, JB learned that Ti-Jean was known to the local cops by his given name, Littlejohn Emmanuel, a swindler, practitioner of Vodou, and "person of interest" in the deaths of Antoine Chery and Joseph Jean because traces of pufferfish neurotoxin were found in the tox screens after their autopsies. "He hasn't been seen around here in a while," JB was told. "You find him, hold him. We have questions for him too."

Consulting the manifests of U.S. airlines with direct flights to Haiti, JB discovered that passenger L. Emmanuel had flown from New Orleans to Port-au-Prince five days before Sanctis was murdered.

CHAPTER FORTY-ONE
Strike a pose

Back in the office, JB was on the telephone and riled. At the other end of the line a perplexed Charlie absorbed the flak.

"When were you going to tell me that he was gay?" said JB.

"What …?"

"Your boy Sanctis. Was gay. Murdered. Gay. Murdered. And … gay. Did you think that might have been worth telling me? Might have been relevant?"

"I never thought about whether he was gay," Charlie shrugged. "He was Corinne's friend. She never said anything. I never asked her. Is it relevant? Besides, how do you know?"

"Yes, it's relevant. Or it could be. His mother told me he was gay. And if you understood LGBTQ life in Haiti, you'd know why it very well could be germane."

While consensual sex between adults of the same gender is not illegal in Haiti, JB explained, public opinion generally frowns on it. LGBTQ people are not specifically protected from discrimination. They are not included in the country's hate crime laws. Households headed by same-sex couples do not have any of the legal rights of married heterosexual couples.

"Gay people - the slur is *masisi* – are frequent targets of harassment and attacks," said JB. "Some have been killed.

The flavor in Haiti may be French, but it's not cosmopolitan Paris. It's not London. Not Miami. Not New York. Being gay in Haiti, in and of itself, might have been enough to put Sanctis at risk."

Charlie checked in with Corinne and told her what JB was saying. She said she and Sanctis talked about many things, but not their sexuality. She knew he sometimes spent weekends in Port-au-Prince. He said he had a friend that he stayed with. She didn't press him. Their jobs at the hospital were hard enough. Wanting to get away for a weekend from time to time was only natural.

Although they gossiped freely during their frequent jaunts in the Haitian hills, they never spoke about boyfriends or girlfriends. He was private in that way; so what?

Had they been two women regularly tramping through these grassy glades, she thought, they surely would have gotten around to the subject of partners – past and present. That was an essential difference she noticed between her female and male friends. The men were surfers, the women, divers. The men skimmed the surface of emotions; the women plumbed the depths. Sanctis defied the stereotype. He could be remarkably perceptive about his colleagues' personalities and their motivations. He was easy to talk to in so many ways. Easier than most of the men Corinne knew.

But she also sensed in him a strong reluctance to share anything about his romantic life.

"A handsome guy like you must have broken hearts back home when you committed to long-term work in Haiti," she probed one day.

He parried with humor. "Oh yeah," he said. "When

word got out that I was leaving for Haiti, the local cardiac care unit was overrun with broken hearts."

"Seriously? Are you going to doctor-joke your way out of this conversation?"

Sanctis smiled. Apparently, he was. He raised a thumb and forefinger to his mouth and pantomimed that his lips were sealed and locked. She let it drop.

Strike-a-pose was a game they made up and played as they walked along. On the command – "strike a pose!" - they took turns dropping into classic yoga positions. Downward dog, Sun salutation, warrior, and all the rest. The person not posing gave the poser a score for style and precision. They played round after round, teasing and guffawing like teens. The only rule: You couldn't strike the same pose twice in a row.

"Strike a pose!" Corinne would suddenly command, and immediately Sanctis would swivel his hips into Warrior.

"Uhhhhhhhhhh … 9.5," said Corinne. "Your front thigh was not perfectly parallel to the ground."

"You're tough," he said. "Just wait till I rate your thighs."

Sanctis was smart and verbally quick. There were times when the double-entendres he tossed her way made her feel like he was flirting. She liked that.

"Keep up, or I'll have to lick you into shape," he said one hot day as they trudged along. The silly smirks they exchanged seemed freighted with more than friendship.

There were an equal number of days when Corinne thought of Sanctis more like an older brother, "possibly gay, possibly straight, always ambiguous." She could speculate about his sexual orientation, about what he did on his weekends in Port-au-Prince. This much she knew without speculating, while being gay was not a choice, coming out was. If Sanctis was intent on maintaining his privacy, she would protect it too – in life and in death - no matter what.

Wanting to know more about gay life in Haiti and its significance, if any, in Sanctis' demise, Charlie and Corinne used the Saj Fanm WIFI to scan the internet. What they found only reinforced Corinne's belief that if Sanctis was gay, he would have chosen not to live openly in Haiti.

One of the first news stories Charlie and Corinne found was about the suspicious death of a gay rights activist named Charlot Jeudy.

Responding to the social and legal challenges for gays in Haiti, Jeudy founded the advocacy group *Kouraj* - Courage - to raise consciousness and promote acceptance of homosexuality.

"For 40 years we've been talking about democracy in this society," Jeudy said in a 2016 interview. "Since our existence as a people, as a nation, we've been talking about freedom; we've been talking about equality; we've been talking about fraternity. These words, what sense do they make? These words, what value do they have when society can treat us with inequality?"

Jeudy, 34, the nation's leading gay rights activist, was later found dead in his Port-au-Prince home by a nephew who was unable to wake him.

Earlier that Sunday, Jeudy had spent time with his brother, who said that after they parted Jeudy had gone to meet someone near the Champs de Mars, a cruising area. The brother didn't know who he was meeting.

"I always told him to be careful because Haiti is not like other countries," he'd said.

Sources close to Jeudy said he had received threatening and anonymous phone calls because of his activism. While there were no overt signs of foul play, some wondered whether he had been poisoned. The exact cause of his death was never made public.

Outright International, the New York-based support network for LGBTQ groups worldwide, issued a statement and called on the police to conduct a transparent investigation.

"We fear [Jeudy's death] is part of a larger pattern of anti-LGBTQ violence underway in Haiti," the statement read.

"So yeah, maybe now you understand why it could be relevant," JB said the next time they spoke. "Maybe his sexual orientation had something to do with his death. Maybe it had nothing to do with it. I think we'd want to know, so at the very least we could rule it out."

CHAPTER FORTY-TWO
Cave of the vampires

"He never mentioned a journal. Not to me," Corinne said, fussing with the hot plate in Charlie's apartment.

"Yeah. ... Okay ... But his mother told JB he kept one ... since college," said Charlie.

"News to me," said Corinne. "If there is a journal, we've got to find it. It could be the evidence we need to show what Sanctis knew. Pinay must have it hidden in his office or his house. He's got it, for sure - unless he destroyed it. If we find it and it's incriminating, we could blackmail him, and when he pays up, we could turn every-thing over to JB."

"Corinne, that is crazy talk. Besides, Pinay's office is a black hole. Cave of the vampires. Off-limits. If he catches me around there again God knows what he'll do."

"Right. So I'll search his office. You search his house."

"Are you out of your mind? As a reporter I snoop around all the time. We joke. We call it sleuthing. But not by breaking and entering."

"So don't break in. Figure out another way."

"Like what?"

"I don't know. It's your assignment. I've got my hands full with, uh, 'the cave of the vampires.'"

Pinay's house, a corner property in a mixed residential and commercial part of Hinche, was walking distance from the hospital. The one-story, flat-roofed, stucco building was painted yellow with brown trim, heavy carved-wooden doors, and a steel French door for access to the enclosed courtyard. The windows were covered with bars for security. Swirls of concertina wire traced the roof line. It had two bedrooms, two bathrooms, a living room, dining room and indoor-outdoor kitchen. The garden, surrounded by a cement wall topped with barbed wire, contained raised flower beds with red-purple bougainvillea, oleander, a coconut palm and a blossoming almond tree.

"Such a nice house for such a not-so-nice guy," thought Charlie. After first checking with Corinne to make sure that Pinay was still at the hospital, he cased the place. The house wasn't impregnable, not a fortress, but it looked pretty secure. Charlie didn't see an easy way in.

Corinne was similarly stymied at the hospital. Pinay hid in his office for large parts of every day. Whenever he was out, his administrative secretary was in the office next door with her door open, keeping watch. Corinne contemplated a late-night foray. If caught, she'd be fired, turned over to police for prosecution or more likely subjected to some kind of vigilante punishment. No way would Pinay let her off with a simple sacking. What if she found the journal, but there was no entry about the pill thefts? Then what? Ransacking the office was a big risk for an uncertain payoff. There had to be another way.

CHAPTER FORTY-THREE
Guns

The meeting between Evans and Prantout was arranged via What's App, a favorite of drug dealers because of its end-to-end encryption. Even so, they texted in code. "Sunny pitch, rise +6," Evans wrote, instructing Prantout to meet him on the sunny sideline of a vacant soccer pitch in Cité Soleil, six hours after sunrise, which on that day happened to be high noon.

Taking pains to camouflage his appearance and movements, Evans dressed in a red-striped rugby shirt and a white bucket hat. He had Blade drive him to the crowded *Marche Salomon*. For a few minutes Evans shuffled anonymously in the virtual conga line of slow-moving shoppers. Then, at the edge of the covered market, he ducked into the curtained stall of a merchant he knew and quickly changed his clothes. The merchant had fallen behind in his protection payments and owed Evans as many favors as the gang leader cared to demand. Evans dumped the bucket hat. He stripped off the red-striped shirt and replaced it with a black tank top. He exchanged his jeans for cargo shorts, his sneakers for rubber slides. Passing under the draped tarp at the back of the stall, he walked quickly to a motorcycle, whose driver, waiting there by pre-arrangement, whisked him to the soccer field where Prantout waited. Meeting on the far sideline, they were the only people around for 100 yards in any direction.

"We're okay here," said Evans. "You can't see them, nobody can, but I have men stationed around. If anyone approaches, they know what to do."

"If they're snipers, I hope their aim is good," a nervous Prantout said, trying to lighten the mood. Evans didn't laugh; didn't even smile.

The two had known each other since childhood. They had begun doing illicit business together after Prantout moved to Florida and Evans consolidated power in Cité Soleil. Working with Colombian suppliers, he provided the cocaine that Prantout disguised in his shipments of ornamental trivets. Until Prantout fled back to Haiti to avoid arrest, he had paid Evans via couriers who carried stacks of U.S. dollars, which they flattened and smuggled inside vacuum-sealed bags.

"For the next shipment," said Evans, getting right to the point, "I want payment in 9-millimeter pistols and AR-15 rifles. You do that. Then we'll talk about ammunition."

Prantout was taken aback. He knew that acquiring the guns in the United States would not be difficult. "I can get them, no problem. But getting them here might be a problem," he said.

"Yeah," said Evans. "Your problem."

Changing the terms of their business arrangement exhumed old tensions in their relationship. Both grew up with barely two gourdes to rub together. Both had prospered on illicit activity and ill-gotten gains. But Prantout, until he became a fugitive, had lived what Evans thought of as a soft, cushy life in Florida and had lost touch with his tough-neighborhood roots. As tough as Prantout thought he was, Evans always showed him he was tougher.

"What's wrong with the way we've been doing business?" Prantout carped. "What's wrong with money? You have guns. Why do you need more guns?"

"Just hold up your end," said Evans. "I'll worry about why I need guns."

As Prantout left the field he scanned the horizon for snipers. Were they there? Or was that just something Evans made up to fuck with his head and impress him?

JB reached for the business card that Adolfo had given him at Monty's Raw Bar in Coconut Grove that day, the card with the name of his trusted Haitian police contact written on the back. He flipped it over and squinted to make out Adolfo's scrawl above the words, *La Brigade de Lutte contre le Trafic de Stupefiants* (BLTS), the Haitian anti-drug police. It was time to seek the guy's help. JB called Adolfo to let him know that he was going to reach out. They met again at Monty's.

Adolfo parked his black Mustang with its vanity plate - XLNTAY - not visible from the street. He entered the restaurant and found JB sitting at a dockside table with a lineup of gleaming-white sport fishing yachts at his back. Muscular machines with tall flying bridges and whippy outriggers. Behind the boats, seagulls wheeled and cawed. Halyards clanged against sailboat masts.

"*Tio, como esta?*" Adolfo said in that cross-jawed way of his.

"*Mwen byen,*" JB replied.

After the waitress dropped off a pitcher of beer and two sweating chilled glasses – Adolfo thought it too early for his usual Johnnie Walker - they had gotten down to business. JB said the Prantout investigation was ripe for arrest, that soon they would nail him and return the children back to his ex-wife, even if there was something not quite right about her. On a parallel track was the Sanctis murder case, where the apparent disappearance of Sanctis' journal gave JB a reason to interview Pinay - not as a suspect, but for the purpose of gathering information. Subject to what might happen on the ground, JB would need an honest local cop that he could count on.

JB reached across the table and frisbeed the business card in front of Adolfo.

"Am I reading your handwriting correctly? Does that say Kenley Cloud?

"Claud," said Adolfo, "Kenley Claud, and there are a few things you should know about why you can trust him. First of all, he was born in Cité Soleil and still lives there. While he recognizes all of its problems, he hates the public's stereotyped perceptions and tired clichés about the place. The stuff that stains anyone who grows up there from birth. He lives to counter that shit."

Adolfo explained that Claud was new to the force a decade ago when Haiti's national police commander was arrested as the ringleader of corrupt Haitian law enforcement officials who'd helped traffickers move tons of Colombian and Venezuelan cocaine through Port-au-Prince.

The case was part of a three-year probe that netted 14 Haitians, several formerly of Cité Soleil, who held top government and private jobs during the administration of deposed President Jean-Bertrand Aristide. The targets included a former presidential palace security chief and American Airlines' former director of security at the Port-au-Prince airport.

Also snared was the chief of Haiti's anti-drug unit, the division that Claud had his sights on joining if he could rise through the ranks. The case began after an informant told the U.S. Drug Enforcement Administration that the Haitian chief and another ranking police official had seized $450,000 in drug profits from a Colombian trafficker, returned $300,000, split the rest with other corrupt officers and agreed to split the take on future drug shipments passing through the airport.

A disillusioned Claud vowed that he would be an example of honesty in the ranks.

"An honest cop, well, hallelujah," JB said sarcastically.

"Not just honest. With a chip on his shoulder about mass-media stereotypes of Haitian cops - this is what drives him - and it'll work to your advantage. Are there corrupt cops in the Haitian National Police? You better believe it. But Kenley Claud is not - and never will be - one of them."

"I thought you were usually more skeptical than that."

"Listen, it happens here too. In my department. Your shop, probably. Two kids grow up, same tough neighborhood, same deprivations. One is destined for jail, the other, destined to put him there. Kenley Claud is the latter."

JB nodded.

"What's more," said Adolfo, "he is active with *Konbit Soley Leve.*"

JB knew of KSL, the post-quake empowerment movement that built new alliances within Cité Soleil, transformed the world's image of Soleyans and redefined Soleyan identity.

Its philosophy is that the problems of one neighborhood are the problems of every neighborhood, and it's not enough to participate in your own community's development unless it's in solidarity with others.

The goal is "an economy of mutual assistance," which doesn't depend on money, religion or politics. It uses reciprocity as currency. You help me dig out of the mud this week when my streets are flooded, I'll pitch in next week when your shanties need whitewashing.

"Progressive," said JB.

"Yeah, and Claud never misses its Saturday meetings, where no one is banned or kicked out. Even the gangbangers show up so long as they leave their guns outside and do something real to improve the community. KSL's philosophy dovetails with Claud's desire to present a different image of Cité Soleil to the outside world. He wants the world to know there's more than just misery and violence there. There are artists, athletes, electric power companies, soda bottling plants and honest cops like him. It's not all poor, ignorant people who need to be saved or imprisoned. Understand that and you'll understand what makes Claud tick."

CHAPTER FORTY-FIVE
Just so tired

JB turned up the volume on his car's CD player just as Saskya Sky, singing in Creole, leaned into the chorus of Hello by Adele. Born in Thomassique, not far from Hinche, Sky was eight when she began singing at a local church. She immigrated with her family to Pompano, Florida in 2003 and learned English by studying the lyrics of popular songs. Among Haitians, particularly in South Florida, she was a pop sensation.

"*Allo ... soti nan lot aaah,*" she belted, passionately covering Adele's familiar anthem. In the privacy of his black Jeep Liberty, with the windows up and the air conditioning blasting, JB sang along. He noticed that Mirlande's blue VW Golf, with its "Nurse Strong" and "Scrub Life" bumper stickers, was already in its numbered spot in their townhouse community's parking lot.

He found her in the apartment, sitting in the dark with a half-drunk bottle of white wine on the coffee table. He called her name, but she didn't turn around.

"Whoa, Miri, I thought we decided we weren't going to drink during ..."

She wheeled to face him, and he could see she had been crying. He had planned to tell her that his investigation of the Prantout case had advanced to the point that he would need to go to Haiti for at least a few days. Clearly, this was not a good time.

"Miri, what's wrong?"

The two had been in upbeat moods since their reproductive endocrinologist had performed a procedure he called "IVF with ICSI" - invitro fertilization with intracytoplasmic sperm injection - using a thin glass pipette to carefully place just one of JB's sperm cells into one of Mirlande's eggs. It seemed like the longest of long shots, but after five days growing in the laboratory, it paid off. The resulting embryo was transferred to Mirlande's uterus. She was pregnant.

JB tried again. "What's wrong, cherie? *Poukisa ou kriye* - Why are you crying?"

"I lost it," she said, heaving and rocking. "I am sure. It's lost. I know it. I started spotting at work this morning. By the time I got home I was bleeding heavily. It's over, Jean."

JB put a hand on her shoulder, but she recoiled.

Before he could speak, she said, "I'm so tired. I'm just so tired of all of this."

"Did you call the doctor?"

"I'm sick of the doctor. I don't ever want to see the doctor again."

JB didn't know what to say. She seemed certain the pregnancy was lost and was probably right. But she was taking it like a personal failing, like she had somehow let them both down. "I'm sorry," she said through a spasm of tears. "I'm so sorry."

"Don't. ... Honey. ... Cherie. ... Don't. You have nothing to be sorry for. This happened. We are both sorry. What's important is that you are okay, that you are healthy. Are you still bleeding? Are you okay? You should see the doctor."

"I'm okay," she said, sounding more disgusted than concerned about her health. "But this … This is not okay. None of this is okay. We can't keep doing this. I am done, Jean. No more. I won't do this again."

CHAPTER FORTY-SIX
"Your cost of doing business"

It wasn't just a crowded tap-tap. That would have been luxurious transportation.

Instead, it was a 300-horsepower, eight-wheel, 10-gear dump truck, a pugnacious behemoth, blunt-nosed, still with its classic bulldog hood ornament but missing the chrome "C" from the Mack nameplate on its grille. Barely moving uphill at 10 miles per hour, the beat-up truck strained to climb National Highway One, the steep mountain road leading north from Port-au-Prince. With each jerky gear change it billowed black smoke from its exhaust. Riding along in its dirty, dented dump box and clinging to the sides for dear life were 30 itinerant street vendors, headed to an outdoor market, packed in with all their wares.

Close behind and exasperated by the snail's pace but unable to pass was a beat-up red Tacoma pickup with a live sheep tethered in its truck bed. Its driver surged forward several times, attempted to pass, then dropped back.

In the opposite lane, traveling south and downhill was a motorcyclist, a clandestine courier, having just come from Hinche where Pinay had watched him load 100 pounds of pilfered pills and capsules into his saddle bags and hand over an envelope stuffed with dollars.

The biker was rolling fast downhill with no traffic in front of him. He spotted the Mack chugging uphill, thought nothing of it, but then suddenly lost control as the Tacoma veered left into the oncoming lane, forcing the cyclist to bank sharply to the right. The big bike slid out from under him, producing a shower of sparks and the screech of scraping metal as its chassis gouged the pavement. The rider, bouncing like a skipped stone, fell hundreds of feet into a ravine and died instantly. The tumbling bike burst into flame, incinerating it and its cargo.

That night Evans broke with his usual cautiousness and made a personal call to Pinay using a burner phone. No salutation, not even an identification of who was calling. Straight to the point. He said he wanted his money back - *Mwen vle lajan mwen an.*

Pinay chose his words carefully. "It was an accident … That's what the witnesses said. Unavoidable … no one's fault … the cost of doing business, no?"

"Your cost of doing business," said Evans.

Pinay started to speak but Evans had already ended the call. He cocked his arm, wound up like a major leaguer, and pitched the burner into a distant ditch.

CHAPTER FORTY-SEVEN
Where nobody knows you, nobody owes you

The FBI's "legat" in Santo Domingo arranged for a car and driver to meet JB on his arrival at the P-a-P airport. He entered the terminal with Mirlande on his arm. Given her emotional fragility after the miscarriage, she and JB decided she should take personal leave from her job and come along. While JB was in the hunt for Prantout, she would visit with Gladness, the cousin who'd been like a sister to her growing up. Their reunion, JB hoped, could be a balm for Miri's wounded soul.

"Karibe Hotel, Petionville," JB said to the driver.

"*Te dako*" - okay - said the driver, who warned that the usual half-hour drive to the outskirts would take longer because of anti-government demonstrations coming from two directions – *Manifestasyon yo!* - had forced the closure of many roads.

Tucked in a lush, densely wooded garden on the southeastern outskirts of the city, the four-star Karibe, where a night's stay costs more than the typical Haitian earns in two months, can feel like a cosmos of outlandish luxury. It featured a spa, fitness center, boutique, two restaurants, rooftop lounge with panoramic views from the mountains to the bay, an enormous pool with a swim-up bar and cabanas bigger than most Cité Soleil shanties.

"Knowing how the rest of the country lives, this is embarrassing," said Mirlande.

"It is," said JB. "But its buildings are certified anti-seismic. It's got secure parking and the business that I have to do is nearby."

From their room Mirlande called her cousin and arranged to meet for lunch the next day at *Au Coin des Artistes*. They had a lot to catch up on. JB dialed Kenley Claud, having earlier alerted him of his arrival with an encrypted What's App text. They agreed to meet, two days hence, to coordinate the take-down of Prantout.

That night, by pre-arrangement, JB and Mirlande had dinner with Charlie and Corinne at Asu, the hotel's throbbing, over-the-top, rooftop lounge, where affluent Haitians and monied expats mingled in a swank atmosphere. Mirlande knew Charlie from their Boston days. "Happy to see you again," she said. "Me too," said Charlie, adding "I'm sorry. JB told me." Mirlande looked like she was going to cry. Then came another introduction. It was her first meeting with Corinne. JB had given her a preview of what to expect. She appreciated that Corinne kept silent and didn't try to console her about the lost pregnancy.

Behind them, the setting sun painted the sky pink and gold. Splotchy clouds bunched up on the horizon.

The couples shared a round of rum sours and the house specialty, risotto topped with lobster and herbs. Extravagant, surely, but had they been in Miami, London or Los Angeles they would have thought little of it. Here, in this privileged aerie above the city's strife and shabbiness, such luxury felt unseemly but didn't stop them.

"Tomorrow, then, it'll be *fritai*, all day," said JB, speaking of the cheap Haitian street food made from balls of fried dough mixed with spices.

Over a round of after-dinner drinks, he laid his cards face up.

"I know what you want me to work on," he said to Corinne and Charlie.

"Yes, and there've been developments," said Corinne, looking at Charlie. "You told him about the motorcycle bell, right?"

"Yes, he did. But please listen," said JB. "You have to understand, I am here to close a case against a major cocaine dealer. That's my job. That's my assignment. That's why I'm here. If I can help with the Sanctis case, I will …"

"You already said you will," Corinne interjected. Her impatience wasn't pretty. JB shot Charlie a look of consternation, then turned back to address the whole table.

"I will help," said JB. "But it won't be my priority. It can't be."

"Sanctis was a U.S. citizen callously murdered … "

"Possibly because of his sexual preference? Possibly defending his expensive telescope? I don't know what happened. Do you?"

"What? No! Don't be ridiculous. It has nothing to do with his sexual orientation. Telescope? Come on! It's because he witnessed the embezzlement. Because of what he knew about Pinay." Corinne's fire was stoked by her second rum sour.

"You've ruled out that his homosexuality had anything to do with it?"

"For fuck's sake, this is daft," said Corinne, shaking her head.

Mirlande was upset to hear someone speaking so disrespectfully to her husband. She started to speak, "Hey," but JB stuck out his arm to shut her down.

"Look. I get it. You lost someone important. That's not fair. Life's not fair. Death's not fair," he said, aiming his words at Corinne. "But just so we're clear. The cocaine case that I am here to wrap up is miles easier to solve than your friend's murder. We had human surveillance, video surveillance, a cooperating witness and government resources devoted to closing down a major avenue of narcotics into Florida. That's our cocaine case."

Corinne sat mum. Charlie hoped she was thinking of how to apologize.

"Over here, in Haiti," JB resumed, "I've got three possibilities: an assassination to cover up an alleged embezzlement; a robbery gone wrong, and someone I haven't yet told you about, a Vodou *bokor*, suspected in two murders in New Orleans, who might have been stalking Sanctis before he was killed."

Stunned by this last bit of information, Corinne leaned back, pulling in her horns, but JB was on a tear.

"A murdered doctor, no eyewitnesses, little physical evidence, a theory put forward by his friend – you! - no local sources, no snitches, *anyen menm* - nothing at all. And where was he murdered? In a remote province! To solve a homicide, you need sources on the killing ground. Sometimes you have to trade favors with them. Where nobody knows you, nobody owes you. It's going to take time."

Corinne thought about blaming her aggressiveness on the rum sours but that would come off as insincere, a half-assed substitute for the actual apology that was required, so she said, "I'm sorry for the harsh things I said, JB. You don't deserve that."

He nodded and repeated, "Gonna take time."

CHAPTER FORTY-EIGHT
Regret to inform

That night, back at Charlie's place, Corinne sat bolt upright in bed. Charlie rolled over to face her.

It seemed her apology had a short shelf life.

"Do you think your friend is really going to help us?" she said. The clarity and volume of her voice clashed with the hushed lateness of the hour.

"He wasn't encouraging. Not at all. He's always so tetchy, so cheesed off. Treats me like a dolt. Gonna take time."

Charlie blinked and tried to focus. "What time is it? … It's late."

"Four o'clock. I can't sleep."

"Come here and let me rub your arm."

Corinne didn't move.

"It feels like JB doesn't want to make the effort for Sanctis. … All of that stuff about his private life. Pfaff! Do you think we need to know more about his weekends in Port-au-Prince? I don't. We know why he was killed. He caught Pinay red-handed. And that stuff about a stalker? Where'd that come from? It's bollocks."

"Hey, watchit, JB is my friend and it's not bollocks. It's proof he has been working on the case. Can't you see that? He's smart. He has his own way of working. His word matters. He said he will help. Believe him."

"He's always so skeptical."

"He's a cop; it's part of the job description. For

reporters too, for that matter. Plus, remember, he's under pressure. Taking down an international coke dealer who is holed up with the two little kids that he refuses to send back to his wife - that's JB's job-one. He said so. His priority. And as far as I know, he is trying to do it in a very low-profile way, which could blow up in his face, wounding his career if it goes wrong. It's complicated. Let's be patient. Now come here … scoot over here … please."

He reached out and massaged the spot on the top of her forearm near the bend in the elbow where the muscles and tendons cross. She always seemed to carry her stress right there. He had learned he could knead it out by digging a thumb into that spot and applying hard pressure down the length of the radial muscle to her wrist.

After a minute of kneading, he could hear that she was breathing more deeply. After another minute, she sighed and slid back under the covers. More gentle pressure and … "Thanks," she whispered sleepily.

Charlie scooched closer and wrapped her in an all-around embrace. He pressed his lips into the nape of her neck, inhaled deeply, and was intoxicated by the scent of her hair. They spooned. By taking deep breaths in unison with hers, he tried to get her to slow down her breathing.

In the morning he brought up what he knew would be a sore subject.

"You're probably right that Sanctis' sexuality is irrelevant," said Charlie. "Let's prove that to JB. He's working the cocaine case. You're busy in the *salle maternite*. I can nose around Port-au-Prince. I'll be discreet. It'll show JB that we're not locked on a predetermined outcome, that we'll go wherever the investigation leads."

"But I am set on an outcome. It leads to that murderous bastard. What you are talking about is a waste of time."

"Okay. But let me try. Let me sniff around Port-au-Prince and see what turns up."

Thinking, but not saying it, Charlie thought there also could be crime-solving potential in trying to figure out what had become of the missing telescope. In addition to learning what he could about the local gay community, he would see what he could turn up about the telescope's disappearance. He began by trawling the Internet for information about astronomers in Haiti. Farfetched though the theory might be, why not rule out the possibility that some night-skies enthusiast had committed the robbery and murder?

He clicked on a weblink for *La Societe Haitienne d'Astronomie*. If any group was likely to have a rough count of all the fancy scopes and their owners in Haiti, it would be the *Societe*. How many such scopes could there be?

Charlie dialed. The group's president, Guy Anthony, nicknamed "Guy L'Etoile," picked up. From the household noise in the background, Charlie deduced that the organization's phone number and L'Etoile's personal cell were one and the same.

"Monsieur Anthony. My name is Charlie Carter. I am a reporter for the Boston Globe with a research interest in astronomy in Haiti."

So far, so good. Charlie hadn't misrepresented himself. He was a reporter – a foreign correspondent, in fact – for the Boston Globe. He did have a "research interest" in astronomy in Haiti. He hadn't said he was writing an article. Anthony may have inferred that. But Charlie made no promises.

Anthony was a retired gynecologist who had co-founded the Societe and by coincidence had trained at the same medical school, during the same years, as Pinay. After retirement, he joined the astronomy faculty at *l'Ecole Nationale de Geologie Appliquee, Universite d'Etat Haiti.*

"There are not so many, as you say, 'fancy scopes,'" he told Charlie. "In fact, the *Societe* is trying to raise money to add another to the one we already have."

"Are the ones that other people have in private hands?"

"We've never done a census, but I would guess there are fewer than 100."

"Are they located throughout the country or concentrated in a particular region?"

"All over. We have members in all parts of Haiti."

"In the Artibonite Valley?"

"Yes. Why?"

"Specifically in Hinche?"

"Yes, we have a young man there. Why are you asking? What is your article about?"

There it was: his article. What article? If he let Anthony's article comment slide, he would be abetting a misunderstanding.

"My article will depend on what my research turns up. Research is everything. Sometimes, it all falls flat."

Charlie felt it was time to tell Anthony about Sanctis.

"If your member in Hinche is Sanctis Beauvoir, Dr. Sanctis Beauvoir, I regret to inform you that Dr. Beauvoir is dead, strangled during an apparent robbery in which his telescope was taken."

"*O, Bondye!* That is a terrible thing. *Chokan*," – shocking.

"It certainly is. So I must ask you, please be on the lookout for anyone trying to sell an expensive used scope. The name was on the carrying case that was left behind. It's a Celestron NexStar."

"What size?"

"I don't know."

"They come in different apertures. What's the number after the word NexStar?"

"Eight"

"That's their big one."

"How big?

"Eight-inch diameter; 17 inches high. About the size and shape of a cylindrical vase."

"Not so easy to hide."

"That's right."

Charlie laid out his night-skies-enthusiast-gone-bad hypothesis.

"Possible … but not likely," said Anthony. "More likely it was someone not from the astronomy community, someone who didn't know the exquisite quality of these extraordinary instruments. Someone like that who just ends up scrapping it for cash at a metal recycler."

With Corinne back at work and Charlie at his apartment, he punched in Maffi's number. She and Junior swung by to pick him up. They would help him find his way around Port-au-Prince's gay subculture.

"*Masisi* life is very closeted," said Maffi as they set off on the long drive to the city. "No openly gay bars or nightclubs. The party scene happens in people's houses. There are some 'gay-for-pay' hookups, prostitution near the Champs de Mars. But the rest is largely invisible."

There was a time, she continued, when sophisticated, low-key cruising happened on Thursday evenings on the upper terrace of the Montana Hotel, but the earthquake wiped out the hotel and forced that scene underground.

Proposed legislation had also hampered the open expression of gay community life.

One bill presented at Haiti's Parliament included "proven homosexuals" among the people to be deprived of a "certificate of good moral standing," a government-issued document required for acceptance into some universities and an expected part of most job applications. A second bill called for banning "demonstrations of support for homosexuality," punishable by three years in prison and an $8,000 fine.

With Junior at the wheel, Charlie in the passenger seat, and Maffi sandwiched in between, they swung by Ly-sha Beach, a once popular gay meeting place on the bay, but empty when they showed up.

Frustrated, Charlie asked to be taken to the office of *Kouraj.*

"That place has moved three times," said Maffi. "It's always under attack." She called a contact to confirm its current location.

There was no sign on the door at *Kouraj.* A plain-clothes security guard stood out front. Inside, the sparse reception area was decorated only with a rainbow flag. After determining that the receptionist, a transgender woman, spoke passable English, Maffi and Junior left

Charlie and waited outside.

As a journalist, Charlie was practiced in the art of cold-call introductions. Still, this was awkward.

"My friend, well, actually he's my friend's friend, was murdered," he began. "At the time we didn't know he was gay. This happened in Hinche. He used to spend weekends, some weekends, down here in Port-au-Prince. And, well …"

Even as he was speaking, Charlie worried that he sounded a little crazy.

The receptionist's smile was replaced with a wary look. "You know our director was murdered not far from there."

"I recently learned that. Yes. I am sorry for your loss. So … I was wondering … if maybe the man I'm inquiring about, his name was Sanctis, had any contact with *Kouraj*? He was a doctor. Medical doctor. Haitian-American, actually."

Charlie saw a flicker of recognition in the receptionist's face.

"What did he look like?"

"My height, black, medium build, thin moustache."

"Closeted?"

"At least with his co-workers he was. They were unaware."

"There was someone like that a few months ago. He came in asking about gay rights in Haiti and whether he was protected from discrimination and harassment on the job."

"Came in here? Out of the blue?"

"He had a reason. Said a photograph of a naked, underage boy suddenly appeared in his locker at work. It looked to him like it was torn from a magazine. It happened again a few days later. He said he was afraid someone was trying to out or blackmail him.

"We told him that Haitian law does not specifically protect him from workplace discrimination on the basis of his sexual orientation. That is one of the reforms we are pushing for."

"And?"

"There is no and. That was it. We never saw him again."

"And you never will," Charlie said, explaining why.

"*Mortifyan*," mortifying, said the receptionist.

"Yes, it is," said Charlie. He thanked her for her candor.

He stepped outside. Maffi and Junior were parked at the curb. He waved for them to pick him up and looked at his watch. In one hour Corinne would be off work and he could call her.

CHAPTER FORTY-NINE
What's the risk?

Drug investigator Kenley Claud told JB to meet him outside the squat, powder-blue-and-white Haitian National Police control post in Titanyen. The arid, empty expanse of rocky soil northeast of the capital is where more than 150,000 Haitians killed in the earthquake were unceremoniously dumped into mass-burial pits. Hour after hour amid the aftershocks and trauma, trucks dropped the unidentified corpses into backhoe-carved trenches that were 50 yards long, five yards wide and 10 feet deep.

Charlie had spent a forlorn day there after the quake watching the interments in a barren landscape of sand, gravel and scrub grass, where trash and plastic bags blew through like tumbleweeds.

"I am afraid of these corpses, but I have to do this," a worker, sweating inside the cab of her yellow bulldozer, had told him.

The desolation of Titanyen also was where the Tontons Macoutes brought their political rivals, executed them and left them rotting in unmarked graves. Area residents say that hundreds, possibly thousands, were killed that way from the 1960s through the 1980s.

In the privacy of this forsaken place where Haiti's horrors past and present intersected JB and Claud planned their take-down of Prantout.

"Certainly, we know of him," said Claud. "We received

a bulletin from your Justice Department when he fled back to Haiti dressed as a woman. That got our attention. He's been on our radar, but not a priority."

"He's a priority for me," said JB.

"*Dako*," I understand, said Claud. "We know he lives in Petionville at the closed end of a one-lane drive. I have seen his house."

"What's it like? Is it going to be a problem to arrest him there?"

Claud pulled out a color photograph of the house that he had taken on a stakeout. He shot it after JB had sent him the What's App message saying he was coming to Haiti.

"Two stories, white stucco stained with dirt and mold behind a cement wall with a sliding steel door painted green with splotches of rust. Tall palms. No garden. A parking space over a cistern. Near the back end of the property is an outdoor, brick-encased tub for handwashing clothes. Upstairs, three bedrooms. One for Prantout. One that the children share. One for a 15-year-old *restavek* employed as the nanny."

Derived from the French "*rester avec*," to stay with, *restaveks* are Haitian adolescents sent by their parents to other people's homes as domestic servants. The equation is harsh: food and shelter in exchange for housework, and many *restaveks* end up exploited and abused.

"We don't know the exact nature of Prantout's relationship with the 15-year-old," said Claud. "She lives there. Other staff come and go. A washerwoman arrives each morning about 8. A driver shows up at about the same time and sits around smoking cigarettes until he is summoned.

An armed gatekeeper, stationed inside the gate, sits on a stool under an umbrella listening to the radio."

"That's a lot going on. It's a dead-end street?"

"*Wi*, a dead end, unpaved. Road washes out after heavy rains. Erodes the ground right out from under the poured-concrete utility poles, which tilt every which way. A few cars parked haphazardly. At the no-outlet end of the street is a low wall of grapefruit-sized stones, held together with splashes of mortar. Behind that wall, where the hill slopes down gently is an encampment of squatters who came after the *tremblement* and never left."

"Other than the bedrooms, what do we know about the interior?" JB asked.

"We haven't been able to see much. Ground floor is polished stone. Walls are white plaster. Black metal chandeliers, which won't matter since we have to operate in daylight anyhow."

"In the States we usually hit a target's house just before sunrise."

"Not here. Under our penal code, we can't make arrests between 6 p.m. and 6 a.m. unless the target is caught - *flagrant delit* - in the act. The same hours apply to search warrants, our *mandats de perquisition*."

"What's the risk that someone tips him off?"

"High. There's always that risk. That's why we're meeting out here, away from questions and prying eyes at headquarters. When it's time to seek a warrant, I'll contact a justice of the peace I know personally who is discreet."

JB had wondered why Claud had called the "meet" for this out-of-the-way place, where a police car was parked in the shade of a lone mango tree. The words *Servir et Proteger*

– serve and protect – were painted on its side, although it rested on a box where the right rear tire was missing.

"If Prantout resists, what do we do for back-up?"

"It's better if we can go low-key," said Claud. "A SWAT standoff in precious Petionville is bad for us and bad for you."

"We've got to get those kids out of there, the nanny too, before we make a move, otherwise he could take them hostage. Restricting our operation to daylight means we have to deal with the washerwoman, the driver and the gatekeeper too."

"If we greenlight it for 6:01 a.m.," said Claud, "we can be in ahead of the driver and the laundress. The gatekeeper? We'll have to deal with him separately."

JB felt the plan taking shape but was still concerned.

"On that one-way street our approach would be spotted easily," he said. "We need to launch the operation from the squatter's side of that low stone wall. How do we get there?"

Prantout's house overlooked the Petionville Club, a nine-hole golf and tennis center for Haiti's elite. It became famous after the earthquake as a forward operating base for the helicopters of the 82nd Airborne's relief mission that supplied food, water and desperately needed medical supplies. The 56-acre resort opened in 1934, the last year of the 19-year U.S. military occupation of the country.

Two months after the quake, more than 45,000 internally displaced people lived there in a shabby tent city amid the patchy grass and occasional tamarind trees on the club's steep slopes. The homeless used bed sheets, tarps, tires, wood and sheet metal to construct their shelters. In addition to the Airborne's food drops, Catholic Relief Services provided rations of bulgur, peas, a corn-soy blend and vegetable oil.

The actor-activist Sean Penn, through the non-profit he co-founded, Jenkins-Penn Haiti Relief Organization, brought a semblance of order to the sprawl. Church services were held under a blue-and-white-striped tent on fairway 4. An elementary school formed on fairway 5. A temporary hospital on fairway 2.

After almost four years, the refugees were relocated, mostly within the capital, with the help of the International Organization for Migration, the Haitian government and Penn's group. For the next three years, a dedicated crew of caddies and landscapers trucked away tons of debris. They rebuilt the greens and tee boxes. The course reopened in 2016, but 100 families still squatted on a sloping parcel outside the club and adjacent to Prantout's house.

From time to time the squatters come across the low stone wall at the end of Prantout's street to beg for handouts and pick through his trash.

"That can be our play," Claud told JB. "Our people can create a beggar's disturbance to lure out the gatekeeper."

"Our people?"

"Two men and a woman from narcotics special-ops. People I know and trust completely. They'll work with us."

Trust was everything in the operation. Trust in their tradecraft and integrity not to tip off the target in exchange for a bribe. Trust that they wouldn't use the operation to enrich themselves.

The 2015 case of the motor vessel Manzanares made the risk of that last point abundantly clear. The 371-foot Panamanian-flagged freighter coming from Colombia had docked at the privately owned Terminal Varreux in Cité Soleil with hundreds of kilos of cocaine and heroin hidden beneath its cargo of imported sugar.

"The stash was discovered by longshoremen unloading the ship," said Claud. "Someone made a call. Then cars with tinted windows showed up. People, including some identified as Haitian police, grabbed bags of the drugs and sped off. By the time my drug unit arrived two hours later, most of the drugs were gone."

CHAPTER FIFTY-ONE
I'll show her trouble

Pinay arrived late for rounds, passed quickly through the *salle maternite*, and shuffled back to the dark solitude of his office. Evans had demanded another shipment of pills to replace the one that was lost in the motorcycle accident. Pinay would have to check the hospital's inventory to see how much further he could cook the books.

Evans was the threat that Pinay was most worried about. The annoying British nurse thought she was a threat, thought she was onto something, but she was nothing, a gnat, a mosquito. Annoying but swattable. She was in way over her head, thought Pinay, by daring to accuse him in the death of Dr. Beauvoir. Delusional. Pure insanity. If she goes public with that absurd accusation, he'd have no choice but to send her packing, and who could fault him?

Evans was a different story - dangerous. Not someone to trifle with. Backed up by Griye's confederation of gangs, Evans could bring the pain. The pilfered pills were not the biggest part of his criminal enterprise, far from it, but Pinay did not want to find out the hard way exactly how much the pill trade meant to him.

Pinay placed the paperwork for the hospital's inventory alongside his doctored log. If he pilfered more amoxicillin and ibuprofen, he thought, there still would be enough for the hospital and no one would be the wiser. Ciprofloxacin, used to treat more serious infections and diarrhea, was heavily in demand on the street. He would have to figure out a way to filch that, too, while disguising its disappearance from the hospital's stocks.

He stood up and went to his mini fridge for some water. In this place where electricity is sporadic and ice worth its weight in gold, having his own refrigerator was a sign of his status. He was obsessed with making sure that it was always running, that its small ice box was always freezing, and its storage battery always charged. He poured a glass, took a swig, and tried to calm himself with its soothing chill. That annoying nurse wants trouble? I'll show her trouble.

CHAPTER FIFTY-TWO
A baby made by God

Mirlande's lunch with her cousin Gladness blended sweet feelings of nostalgia with bitter tears. They laughed about the comic results years back when they did each other's hair as "schoolgirl cool girls," and used crushed seeds to make hair oil. They cried about the mutual friends they had lost to the earthquake and to cholera. They shared the sadness of Mirlande's lost pregnancy in a clan where big families were the norm.

When Mirlande and Gladness met again a few days later for breakfast at the Karibe, Corinne was seated at another table with Charlie and JB. She had gotten off to a bad start with Mirlande by being so confrontational that night with JB. She went over to apologize.

"*Pa gen pwoblem*," we're all under stress, Mirlande said generously. The cousins invited Corinne to sit and join them for coffee.

They were an incongruous trio: Gladness, who had a six-year-old daughter and a four-year-old son; Mirlande, who was the daughter's godmother, but had no child of her own, and Corinne, who had never even been pregnant in a profession that was all about conceiving and delivering babies.

"She got the family's fertility gene - two kids already," Mirlande said, nodding toward Gladness.

"Actually, family history is not the biggest factor in

fertility," said Corinne, who tried not to come off as a know-it-all but was close to crossing that line. This was emotional ground and she needed to tread lightly.

"Go on," said Mirlande.

"In 20 percent of women, experts don't really know what causes infertility. Family history probably only plays a small role in a woman's ability to conceive."

"For the short time that I was pregnant, I was happy," said Mirlande. "I was ready. I was so ready. It was right there. And then …" – she motioned as if to grab the invisible prize that had slipped through her fingers.

Gladness put a hand on Mirlande's shoulder.

"Then, after I lost it, it seemed that everyone could get pregnant except me. In Miami I'd see Orthodox Jewish mothers with four children under six. The supermarket reserved parking spaces for 'mothers to be,' with a drawing of a damned stork on the sign. Haitian nannies – Haitian nannies! – pushed white babies in strollers all over town. There were mountains of Huggies at the Costco. Everywhere I looked, I was being mocked."

"Cherie … no one is mocking," said Gladness.

"I know, but that's how it feels."

Corinne went to the buffet table and put more coffee in a carafe. She poured some into Mirlande's cup and then served Gladness.

"It's still hot," she said, as a clatter of busboys in white jackets began clearing away the breakfast chafing stands and setting up for lunch.

For a few minutes, the trio sat and sipped in silence.

"What about adoption?" said Corinne. "Would you consider that?"

Mirlande looked over the top of her cup at Corinne, and Corinne wondered if she had overstepped. She had only just met Mirlande. Where did she get off asking such an intimate question?

"Jean is a man. He wishes for a baby made by us."

"And you?" asked Gladness.

"*Mwen*? I want any baby, any baby *fe pa bondye*," any baby made by God.

CHAPTER FIFTY-THREE
You are not here to help me!

JB arose at 5 a.m. and dressed silently in the shaft of light that spilled from the half-closed bathroom door. He tucked his Glock into a waistband-holster, dropped his FBI neck-chain credential inside the collar of his blue-striped polo shirt and left Miri sleeping in their room at the Karibe. The role he'd assigned her in Prantout's takedown would come later.

A rooster in the distance crowed as JB crossed the polished white marble lobby and left the hotel. He sniffed the air. It was the coolest it would be all day and already hot. In a taxi headed to his rendezvous with Claud, he ticked through his mental checklist. Would Prantout go without a fight? Would he pull a weapon, or worse, barricade himself with the children and the nanny?

They had surveilled the house enough to feel confident that Prantout did not have a nest of thugs in there with him, just the armed security guard who manned the gate. They studied the layout - a two-story building of stucco and green-painted cement in a compound on the crest of a hill, surrounded by a high stone wall. Two palm trees towered over an array of flowerpots that spilled over with purple bougainvillea. Near a back corner of the property, opposite the kitchen door, was the outdoor, waist-high stone tub for washing clothes. Two similarly walled compounds flanked Prantout's place on the unpaved road riven with weedy gullies. For the most part, thought JB, the physical challenges would be manageable.

Still, he was apprehensive about proceeding with so little backup, which was contrary to his training and instincts. He was trained in such situations to go in with overwhelming force. An FBI takedown of a significant drug dealer ordinarily would involve six to a dozen heavily armed agents in helmets and flak vests. An exclusionary perimeter would be established with yellow crime-scene tape. Local police would be deployed to guard it. An ambulance would be standing by, as would a SWAT armored wagon.

But in Haiti, preparations for a major, SWAT-style operation would attract too much attention and involve too many loose lips, raising the probability that Prantout would be tipped off. JB and Claud would have to balance the risks of going in, low-profile, against the alternative risk that a more imposing operation could be blown entirely. It reminded JB of his tenure in Boston, whenever he and his FBI colleagues had conducted human-trafficking raids in nearby Chelsea, they never gave the municipal police a head's up courtesy call because local-police corruption was so endemic there. For one last time, JB pondered how the entire operation against Prantout would be so much safer if it could begin in predawn darkness. But the arrest was bound by the hours prescribed in Haitian law.

At 6:01, with sunlight creeping over the horizon, it was "go" time. Two special-ops agents disguised as shabbily dressed squatters vaulted over the low stone wall 20 yards from the front gate of Prantout's compound. From their hiding place behind the huge yellow-green fronds of a giant ostrich fern, Claud and JB watched as the squatter-agents staged a tussle, tugging fiercely at each other's shirts and hurl savage insults.

"*Sispann ou bata!*" – stop, you bastard! one of them howled.

"*Lage kouto a! Lage kouto a!*" – drop the knife! the other shouted. "*Lage li. LAGE LI!*" – Drop it. DROP IT!

Locked on to one another like mating dragonflies, they wheeled and corkscrewed into the steel gate with a resounding crash.

They kept at it, aiming for a disturbance loud enough to draw out the gatekeeper.

"Son of a whore, release me!"

"I'll cut off your balls, you scumbag!"

"*Ede mwen*" – help me! one man shouted as he pound on the gate. "*Jezu, sove mwen*" – Jesus, save me!

With that, the gatekeeper left his post to investigate. He had a rifle slung over his shoulder. When he bent down to have a look at the man who was getting the worst of it, the other man jumped up, threw a cloth hood over the gatekeeper's head, cinched its drawstring, dragged him to the ground, and kicked away the rifle in the direction of JB and Claud, who grabbed it.

The squatter's partner in the ruse jumped to his feet, wrangled the gatekeeper's hands behind his back and cinched them in a pair of black PlastiCuffs. Then they lashed him, standing up, to a tree using a tight cord around his neck that forced the back of his head against the tree's trunk. They pushed the fabric of the sack into his mouth as a gag and added a piece of coconut husk they found on the ground for good measure.

As all of this was taking place, the female special-ops

officer had climbed the utility pole behind the house. She tossed a blanket onto the outward-leaning strand of barbed wire on the perimeter wall and launched herself onto it. Moving like a spider, she eased herself onto the ground inside the compound. She hid behind the outdoor wash tub to await the *restavek* and the children, who routinely came down for breakfast at 7 a.m., an hour before Prantout. The plan called for her to round up the nanny and the kids, trying not to scare them too badly, and herd them into a waiting taxi and escort them to the Karibe, where Mirlande and Corinne would babysit them until the operation was over. Buy them lunch. Take them swimming in the hotel pool. Whatever. Just tell them that the operation was all about protecting their dad, who would join them soon to explain.

With the gatekeeper neutralized, JB and Claud were able to sweep into the compound and take positions on either side of the door to the kitchen, pistols drawn.

Almost immediately their plan began to unravel. The noise of the mock fight had alerted Prantout, who came charging downstairs. Instead of being safely outside the compound with her young charges in tow, the female agent was pinned down with the *restavek* and the terrified kids, crouching behind the stone tub and very much in harm's way.

The moment Prantout's shoes hit the steps, JB hollered, "FBI. Etienne Marvel. You are under arrest. Come down with your hands behind your head and your fingers laced."

Prantout recoiled and charged back upstairs.

"Shit," JB snorted. He and Claud backed up and took cover behind stone abutments.

A moment later Prantout threw open an upstairs window.

To prevent the lawmen from trying to enter the house, he pitched a five-gallon jug of bottled water out the upstairs window. It exploded with a "whoosh" on the stone threshold, leaving a puddle into which he dumped a vat of rancid cooking oil. The slippery slop made the threshold impassable.

"Back the fuck up," Prantout yelled, brandishing a pistol. "I have children in here."

JB took control of the negotiation.

"Actually, you don't. We have them and the *restavek*. Let us get them safely out of here. No one has been hurt. You've got to protect your kids. Give yourself up and you'll get to be with them."

"You fucking took my kids? S*alop, ki kaka sa!* Bastard, what kind of shit is that? Bring them back now or we've got nothing to talk about."

"That's not going to happen. You are going back to the United States. Surrender peacefully and no one, including you, gets hurt. What do you need? What can I get for you?"

JB hoped to keep him talking and distracted long enough for the female agent to sneak out with the kids.

She had gathered them into a huddle and was preparing to dash for the gate when Prantout fired a shot.

The slug shattered a flowerpot twenty feet to the right of where JB stood, an unaimed but potentially lethal shot discharged in anger.

With each passing minute JB worried that Prantout was on his cell phone calling out for muscle. Claud knew from his BLTS intel that Prantout was protected by Evans. Cité Soleil was just a half hour away, maybe quicker by motorcycle. The last thing they needed was Evans and his thugs showing up. JB and Claud had chosen not to surround the house with overwhelming force. For the moment, Prantout didn't know that. If JB and Claud moved quickly, he'd never be the wiser.

To minimize the possibility of outside interference, JB wanted to take Prantout with a minimum of force. A wounding, or serious injury to anyone, would upend the plan.

"Drop your weapon and put both hands out the window. Do that for me, please. Then tell me what I can do to make this situation better for you. Just give me a sign. I can't help you if … "

"You are not here to help me," Prantout shouted and fired again, this time striking the ground just a few feet in front of JB, who returned fire with three quick rounds. Surreptitiously, Claud tried to edge closer to the children until Prantout sent a round sizzling his way and he had to take cover again.

"You are making this situation infinitely worse," JB shouted. "A sentence for drug trafficking can be reduced if you cooperate. Shoot a federal agent, or one of your kids, *Bondye Padon* - God forbid - and you are going away for life. There will be nothing I can do to help."

"*Fout ou!*" – fuck you, Prantout hollered. "You're not here to help."

That exchange was followed by a lull. JB worried that Prantout was using his phone.

The agents disguised as squatters were still in character. They went behind Prantout's house and began scavenging in his trash, maintaining the ruse.

Standing in front of the house JB hollered: "Throw out your weapon and come down slowly with your hands on the top of your head."

No response.

"Prantout?"

Claud worked his way cautiously toward the kitchen door but couldn't get close because of the slop on the threshold. He couldn't enter. But if Prantout charged out he'd be in position to grab him. Meanwhile, if he hurled down another one of those five-gallon jugs, Claud thought, he could be knocked out cold by 40 pounds of flying water.

The female agent looked toward Claud, desperate for a signal that it was okay to dash for the gate. Without speaking, he barred his arms in a cross in front of his chest and shook his head emphatically, No!

"Prantout?" JB hollered again.

What he couldn't see was that Prantout had snuck down the back staircase, opened a ground-floor window and jumped out into the alley where the mock-squatters were picking his trash.

They pretended to pay him no mind. As Prantout began running to make his escape, one of the squatters stumbled as if by accident and tripped him. Then both squatters pounced, prying the pistol from Prantout's grasp and forcing him into handcuffs.

"*Li fè*" – it's done, we've got him," the first squatter said, speaking into a walkie-talkie to signal Claud.

Not the type to waste time collecting high-fives, JB celebrated the successful mission with a simple "*mesi*" to his colleagues. He had more pressing concerns. He photographed the slug-shattered flowerpot, the slop-trap Prantout had created on the threshold, and the open window he had climbed through before his arrest. He called Mirlande at the Karibe to confirm that the kids and the *restavek* had arrived there safely.

"Safe, *wi,* but rattled," said Mirlande. "I feel bad for them."

JB's next call was to the U.S. Drug Enforcement Agency's small field office in Port-au-Prince. He'd have to involve them now.

Contrary to the popular notion that all FBI agents work only on task forces, for the most part they work alone. They can team up with colleagues to corroborate evidence or allay safety concerns, but under FBI guidelines they assume an almost entrepreneurial ownership of their cases. They determine the necessary manpower and resources. JB's low-profile, lone-wolf approach to the Prantout case was within the scope of his authority. Now, having made an arrest, he'd have to raise the operation from below the radar.

As the car that Claud had arranged was carrying the three of them back to the hotel, JB dialed his boss at FBI-Miami.

"We got him, Etienne Marvel, the one they call Prantout …'

"I know."

"What do you mean you know? We only just arrested him."

"And not an hour ago a courier sent by his lawyer, that fancy firm up on Brickell, handles all these creeps, sent over a waiver of extradition. It seems your Prantout wants to come back voluntarily. Lawyer's letter said something about death threats against him in Haiti. If you and your prisoner get moving, you can make Miami by tonight."

JB knew there were typical reasons why some defendants choose to duck a fight over being brought back to the United States for prosecution. For one thing, if eventually they are convicted, they get no sentencing credit for their time served during the months and sometimes years of an extradition battle. For another, they often want to save their money to fight the central charges. It happens. Sure. But the fact that his boss had learned of the arrest before JB could reveal it infuriated him.

He had confiscated Prantout's phone when Claud placed him under arrest.

"Stop the car." JB was angry. He threw open the door, hip-checked Prantout to force him out, and stood beside him. He grabbed his cuffed hands and forced his right thumb against the phone's fingerprint security sensor. With the phone unlocked, JB went straight to its "recents" and there it was: Prantout's last call was to his wife - JB recognized her number - placed at 6:45 that morning, just moments before he was arrested. He must have called her during the lull.

JB held the phone in front of Prantout and pointed at the number.

"So what?" said Prantout. "You thought I should hang around here in prison waiting for Evans to have me killed?"

CHAPTER FIFTY-FOUR
Not taking advice from you

That night's flight to Miami was scheduled to take off on time and a DEA field agent met JB and Prantout at the gate.

Having fired shots during his arrest, Prantout was deemed "a high-risk prisoner," which meant that two armed officers were required to transport him on a commercial flight. JB, Prantout, and the accompanying officer boarded ahead of the other passengers. Prantout made his way down the stiflingly hot jetway with his hands cuffed and shackled to a jingling belly chain. His leg irons had to be removed for the flight. The prisoner and the escorts sat in the rearmost row, adjacent to the bathrooms, with Prantout in the middle seat, the DEA agent at the window, and JB on the aisle.

If there was irony in the image of Prantout being dragged back to America in the same way that his ancestors were enslaved and hauled to Haiti – in chains! – it was lost on him. Halfway through the two-hour flight he began to fidget.

"I gotta pee," he said.

JB looked at him skeptically.

"Come on man, I gotta go. You gotta let me."

"I don't gotta do anything," said JB, studying the lines of Prantout's face, trying to read his intentions.

"Come on, man, I'm not faking."

JB nodded, satisfied that Prantout really had to go.

He reached into his pocket and pulled out the key to the handcuffs. He opened one cuff. Instead of opening the other, he attached the open cuff to the bracket arm of Prantout's tray table.

"You're fucking with me now," Prantout moaned.

JB got up, opened the lavatory door, looked in and satisfied himself that there was nothing in there that Prantout could use as a weapon. He returned to the seats and released the cuff that had been attached to the tray table.

"Go ahead," he ordered Prantout, following him in the aisle. "I'll be outside the door. Don't pee on the loose cuff."

A minute later, Prantout opened the door. He looked relieved. "You didn't have to do me like that."

"You didn't have to shoot at me," said JB. "But you did."

After delivering Prantout to the U.S. Marshal Service in Miami, he called Prantout's wife and told her to be ready for their flight back to Haiti the next day to retrieve her kids. She'd have some explaining to do.

Their morning flight had barely leveled off when JB spoke to Chloe Marvel. "We know you've been speaking to him."

She shot him a perplexed look and held it. He started again.

"We know that you've been speaking to Prantout. We suspected your involvement. Then we developed a reasonable suspicion of your involvement. We got a court order to put a pen register on your cell phone line."

"You tapped my phone? I should sue your bitch asses!! You're out of control, like what the fuck, Belizaire?"

"We didn't listen in on any of your calls. Just record all the numbers that you dialed out. You dialed your husband in Haiti almost every day. One call was for an hour. You spoke to him yesterday. To quote you now, Mrs. Marvel, what the fuck?"

"Is this part of your clever plan to arrest me when we hit the ground? You think I am going to confess something to you on this airplane? After you told me that we are going to see my children? After you made me vulnerable and desperate to do or say anything to see my kids? That's entrapment, *estipid!* Entrapment!"

JB made a coin slot of his lips. "Well, *cherie*, the scenario you just outlined doesn't constitute entrapment. Not technically, anyway. But you seem to know a lot about entrapment, or think you do, for an innocent bystander? Do you know what an accessory to a crime is? Have you heard of aiding and abetting?"

Chloe Marvel sat stock still. She studied JB's face, with a look of disgust on hers.

The only sound was the whine of the plane's jet engines.

"I am just saying that you haven't been straight with me," said JB.

"Oh, *ti mouton*, little lamb, are your feelings hurt? Did I hurt your feelings? Do I owe you an apology?" she said, sarcasm dripping from every syllable.

"No. You don't. But don't worry, *cherie*. You are going to see your kids. As for arresting you … not today. Maybe another time. And you might want to think about cooperating with us. After we make the drug case against your husband stick, you could be charged with conspiracy and that beautiful house of yours could be subject to asset forfeiture. I'd hate to see you dispossessed."

The reunion of mother and children took place in the grand garden of the Karibe, where Mirlande and Corinne had watched them. "*Manman!*" they hollered as they leapt crying into their mother's arms. After realizing that their father was not coming to join them, they hadn't slept all night. Now they wailed and wailed.

"They are tired and still scared," said Mirlande. "There was shooting. They saw things."

"You people are disgusting," said Chloe Marvel.

"There is a gun-trauma clinic at the hospital where I work. The staff say just witnessing an incident involving a weapon, even if no one is shot, can be as emotionally wrenching as being a victim. No one pointed a gun at the children, but they knew they were in danger. A child psychologist can help them express that trauma."

"Who the hell do you think you are? Your husband just arrested mine, *cherie*. I'm not taking advice from you."

CHAPTER FIFTY-FIVE
Our day will come

The next day, after seeing Marvel and her kids off to Miami, JB gave himself permission to lounge with Miri around the Karibe's pool.

When the midday sun proved too intense, they ordered rum punch cocktails at the swim-up bar and took seats on the submerged stools. They clinked glasses.

"Day drinking in a swimming pool. It's all smooth sailing now, baby girl," said JB. "*Sante.*"

"*Sante,*" she chimed.

The anguish of the miscarriage was still fresh for them. Now that they had privacy, JB tried cautiously to get a sense of how Mirlande was feeling.

"How was it seeing Gladness? The other morning at breakfast you looked to be enjoying yourselves."

"She knows my heart. My past. The psalms we sang in the church that we all went to. The first boy I had a crush on. It's been comforting."

"That's great. Did she talk about her kids?"

"Of course." Mirlande was starting to bristle at what felt like an interrogation.

"Was that difficult? Were you sad hearing about her as a mother? It's only natural if you feel a little envy."

"Stop talking to me like a therapist," she snapped. "Gladness is my cousin. She's my friend. I love her. I am happy for her. She deserves all good things."

"So do you, baby. So do I. … Our day will come."

"I don't think so, Jean. We have tried. *Bondye!* … Good God! I don't … I don't want to talk about it anymore."

They dried off in the sun on separate chaises longues, as though retreating to neutral corners. They spent the next two hours wordlessly paging through books and magazines.

At dinner they barely spoke. Finally, JB said he had one more investigation to conduct in Haiti.

"It's the murder of that doctor, the one called Sanctis," he said. "You heard about him that first night at dinner with Charlie and Corinne."

"Oh, I remember," said Mirlande. "I remember."

CHAPTER FIFTY-SIX
Unrecognizable

"Monsieur Carter? It's *Guy L'Etoile, de la Societe.* I have information that will interest you. It could be a piece of hardware from the telescope that you have been looking for."

He explained that the piece was found among the bric-a-brac and used tools for sale by a vendor in a dark corner of Hinche's covered market.

"I'm told it was laid out on the ground alongside rusty machetes, broken calculators, paint-encrusted door hinges, *tout sa.* To the uninitiated, it looks like a telephone handset - white buttons on a black plastic rectangle. One of our members who was passing through Hinche recognized it right away as the computerized hand control of a sophisticated telescope. He bought it from the vendor for a song, and brought it to us, thinking we might need it for spare parts someday. I am holding it now. It's from a Celestron."

Charlie recognized the brand name of Sanctis' scope. "What about the body of the scope, the tube? Where is that?"

"Probably sold for scrap. Fourteen pounds of quality aluminum. Worth about $12 at P-a-P recyclers – melted down and no doubt unrecognizable by now."

Having kept this part of his research private from Corinne, Charlie felt it was time to tell her he had been looking into what had become of the telescope. He called and told her about L'Etoile's discovery.

"It's sad and hard to accept that Sanctis may have lost his life for $12," Charlie said. "We might never know."

"Seriously? Hard to accept? We'll never know? Sanctis wasn't murdered for 10 quid, Charlie. It was because of what he knew and could reveal about Pinay. But great work there, Sherlock. Blinding! Simply brilliant! Twelve bucks? That's more like the worth of all your sleuthing."

CHAPTER FIFTY-SEVEN
Face up ... or down?

To be closer to Charlie and Corinne, and nearer the crime scene, JB and Mirlande decamped to the Hotel L'Ermitage de Pandiassou, a two-story white elephant of French Colonial architecture wrapped with balconies, a red terra cotta roof and Doric columns oddly painted lavender. Surrounded by woods and a scattering of tall palms, it is a mile west of Hinche on the rue Magloire. Not a bad place to stay if you can snag one of the rooms with working internet.

Charlie was happy to hear that they finally had JB's undivided attention. Corinne was encouraged but still snarky.

"I never know with him if he's shining us on," she said.

"He's methodical," said Charlie.

"Methodically slow. But his wife," said Corinne, "she's a doll. Got down on the ground with Prantout's kids. Showed them *Lalin ak Soley*, the hand-clapping game about the sun and the moon."

"Mirlande is a good woman," said Charlie.

"She is that."

The New Orleans Police Department had sent JB a mug shot of the *bokor* Ti-Jean. That night, JB pulled it from his investigation file and studied it.

The test of JB and Corinne's ability to tolerate each other came the next day. He wanted to see the place where they had found Sanctis' body and later on had discovered the motorcycle bell. She took him there. The house was vacant. The weeds around it had grown taller since her last visit.

"Take me through what you saw," said JB.

"We came around back and found him here … on the ground."

"Face up or face down?"

"Face up. I told you, we saw his mutilated face." Corinne shuddered at the recollection.

"Which way was his head facing?"

She pointed to the spot, which sloped away from the house.

"Whoever did this probably came from behind, snagged him with the stethoscope, pulled him to the ground, and crushed his windpipe. Whose stethoscope was it? Was it his?"

"I assumed so, but I don't know."

"Are stethoscopes ever included in the shipments of donated medical supplies?"

"Occasionally. Used ones. Sometimes packaged with used blood-pressure cuffs."

"Was there a moon out that night? I could look it up on a chart. But what do you remember?"

"I don't remember. It was dark. We used our cell phone flashlights."

"Was the house door open or closed?"

"I don't know. His face was all I saw. Horrible black holes in place of his eyes." She shuddered again. "What difference does the door make? Open? Closed? So what? When are you going to interview Pinay?"

"I'll get to Pinay. According to you he's going to lie to

271

me anyway."

"He will. But my mother always said a lie has a shelf life, goes rancid and starts to stink. That's how she scared me into telling the truth."

JB smiled at the folk wisdom.

"We know you found the body a little after 8 p.m. We don't know precisely when he was killed, or why he was outside when you'd think he would have been busy cooking soup joumou. I'd like to know if the door was open or closed. Might tell us whether he knew his killer. Whether he came outside to let in someone he was familiar with. Whether he was attacked at the door, or ambushed."

"He did know his killer … well, not in that way. I'm sure Pinay had him killed. Didn't do it himself. Had it done."

"You're sure?"

"Oh bollocks, JB! Here we go again." Corinne stomped away, wheeled, and came back.

"Do you think Sanctis didn't matter? That it's not important to name his killer? Pinay had Sanctis killed. Had me run off the road on a moto and nearly killed. Poisoned my contact lens cleaner. For fuck's sake, have you been listening?"

"Sounds like you've got it all figured out. Why do you need me?"

"To arrest him, dammit. We need you to arrest him. Bloody hell! When are you going to do that? The sodding Sphinx moves faster than you."

So much for her earlier apologies.

Had JB told her to "go piss up a rope," no jury would have convicted him. Thinking of his friendship with

Charlie, however, and of Corinne's extreme distress, he kept his irritation in check.

Before they left the crime scene, JB took out the mug shot of Ti-Jean and showed it to Corinne. "Have you ever seen this man? Do you recognize him?"

"No. Should I?"

CHAPTER FIFTY-EIGHT
She's a charmer

The next morning JB went alone to the hospital to interview Pinay.

"Special Agent Jean Belizaire," he said, laying down his business card and FBI credential. "Here to see Dr. Reynard Pinay."

The receptionist's eyes darted toward Pinay's office, which was next door.

"He's …. not … in. Can I help you?"

"No, actually. I'm here to see Dr. Pinay. … I'll wait."

"It could be a while."

"I don't mind."

"It could be a long while."

"*Pa fe okenn diferans*" – it makes no difference, said JB.

"Is he expecting you?" said the receptionist, clearly stalling?"

JB turned and smiled. "I guess he will be now, won't he?"

There was no place to sit so he stood like a sentry near the door.

An hour later, Pinay came directly out of his office. He had been in there the whole time.

"Dr. Pinay, I'm Special Agent Jean Belizaire, investigating the murder of Dr. Sanctis Beauvoir for the FBI."

"Sorry to keep you waiting. I didn't know you were out here."

Okay, thought JB. He is more polite than advertised,

but on-brand as a liar.

Pinay wanted to walk and talk. JB said the questions he had to ask were too delicate to be posed in public. He asked to return to Pinay's office. The doctor reluctantly agreed.

JB took a seat in a brown upholstered armchair. Pinay sat on a swivel chair behind his desk. On a table behind him was a framed black-and-white photo of Pinay's father with "Papa Doc" at some kind of ribbon cutting. At the base of Pinay's wastebasket and partially hidden by the hem of the heavy drapes, were two stray items that appeared to have missed landing in the basket - a crumpled sheet of paper; a small heart-shaped padlock with its shackle severed.

Alarm bells went off in JB's head but he kept a poker face.

"So what happened?" he asked.

"Surely you know. Dr. Beauvoir was strangled."

"I know that. By whom? Why?"

"That's what we all want to know. We were all so shocked and saddened."

"Do you have suspicions? Any known enemies? Anyone who wanted to do him harm?"

Pinay said "no" and swiveled his chair several times in a wide arc.

"Was he in a recent fight with anyone? Any patients, former patients or patients' family members who were angry with him for any reason?"

"None of that. Not to my knowledge. No," said Pinay. "He had an argument with a porter, once, but everyone argues with that man."

"Debts? Was he a gambler? Did he owe money?"

Pinay shook his head.

"His personal effects were brought to you and you had them shipped to his mother in Florida?"

"Through the U.S. Embassy in Port-au-Prince, that's correct."

"His mother said she expected to find a red journal among the possessions. She didn't. Did you see or hear anything about a journal or diary? Could your staff have set it aside or perhaps misplaced it?"

"No. A journal in English would mean nothing to them. … I'm assuming it was in English. I don't know. If it exists at all, I never saw it. This is the first I'm hearing of it. Do you have many more questions?"

"Yeah, who killed him? Where should I be looking?"

"He was *masisi*, you know? Maybe he brought home the wrong person. A rough person."

"On the night that he was planning to host soup joumou for a group of friends? That seems unlikely. How did you know he was gay? He didn't tell his coworkers."

"I am the boss. I saw his resume. He volunteered at an AIDS clinic. He was in his thirties and single. Always finely dressed. Always talking about how much he loved to cook. Nothing definitive. I just assumed. Now you're telling me that my assumption was correct. I would look into that part of his life."

"What should happen to the person who did this?"

JB was taught to routinely ask "the punishment question," even though it can be misunderstood or misused. The theory is that a guilty person will suggest a relatively light punishment, and an innocent person will likely prescribe a stiff punishment.

But it's also relatively easy to see through the thrust of the question, so that deceptive people often respond with what they presume the investigator expects to hear from an innocent person, something like, "Lock him up for life."

"What should happen?" JB repeated.

"Every year there are more than 1,000 homicides in Haiti," said Pinay. "The murderers should all be punished. Harshly. Is the murder of Dr. Beauvoir more important because he had U.S. citizenship? Should his killer be more harshly punished than the rest? I leave that to you and your colleagues, agent Belizaire. Now if you'll please excuse me, I have patients to attend to. I'll see you out."

Even after years on the job JB fell back on the "spy a lie" drill taught at the FBI's training and research center in Quantico, Virginia.

Spotting deception is not an exact science. But there are classic indicators of untruthfulness: the absence of a specific denial to a direct question; repeating a question to buy time to concoct an answer; pushing back with statements like, "Is this going to take much longer?"; using politeness to promote likeability; shielding the mouth or eyes to cover the telling of a lie; leaning back in a chair, shifting weight from foot to foot or a sudden tidying up, such as straightening a stack of papers or rearranging the placement of a stapler on a desk.

Thinking about Pinay as if he were a Quantico case study, JB ran through a mental checklist: the fidgeting in the swivel chair; the "not to my knowledge" modifier, the pushback to end the interview and the equivocal answer to the punishment question. No single behavior was proof positive. But as a cluster? Yeah, at the very least, Pinay seemed to know more than he was letting on.

The missing journal, Pinay's dubious denial that he knew anything about it, the discovery in plain view of a broken, heart-shaped padlock - all seemed to add up to the probable cause JB needed to ask Claud to seek a *mandat de perquisition*. With a warrant, JB thought, I can toss his office and his house, searching them thoroughly. It appeared the investigation was headed there – but not yet.

While JB was at the hospital interviewing Pinay, Corinne, Mirlande and Charlie were at *Nouri*, the feeding-center orphanage. Charlie wanted to talk with the Mother Superior, Sr. Alouette, about the possibility of doing a Sunday magazine article on the orphanage. Corinne wanted Mirlande to see how the feeding program was saving young lives.

It was admissions day at *Nouri*. Half a dozen parents with starving children on their laps sat in the shade on plastic chairs and waited to be seen. The children were mostly two- and three-year-olds. Some had rail-thin legs that dangled above the concrete floor. They sat in silence, lacking even the energy to murmur. Others, with swollen bellies, whimpered as the nuns went about filling out the admissions forms. Several looked to be less than a year old.

At first Mirlande said nothing but her eyes glistened, verging on tears.

"Come upstairs with me," said Corinne. "It's different there."

On the patio, children energized by the nutritious meals they were receiving pushed each other around on run-down tricycles. Others, arms flailing joyfully, stumbled from one end of the portico to the other like little drunken sailors. A few, looking confused, sat alone, eyes unfocused in 1,000- yard stares.

When Fabi saw Corinne, she ran to her. Corinne grabbed her up in a bear hug. The child laced her little legs as far around Corinne's waist as they would go.

"This is the girl I was telling you about," she said to Mirlande. "She's Fabilene … Fabi."

The child smiled at the mention of her name.

Corinne made a quick singsong introduction: "Fabi … Miri! Miri … Fabi!"

"If you don't mind staying here with Fabi for a few minutes," said Corinne, "I am going to the crib room to help bottle feed the babies."

Fabi started to follow Corinne but was told to stay and play with Mirlande. "I'll be back," said Corinne.

Mirlande's microbraids hung down below her shoulders. At first, Fabi was reticent. She sat beside Mirlande but didn't acknowledge her. Then Fabi tentatively took the end of one braid between a thumb and forefinger to feel its texture. Mirlande's eyes darted at her. She kept her head still but raised and lowered her eyebrows playfully. Fabi giggled.

Mirlande grabbed a handful of braids and started counting. "*En,*" she said, and handed off the first braid to Fabi. "*De,*" she said and handed off the second. "*Twa,*" she said, and handed off the third. By the time she got to the fourth braid, Fabi was counting along with her. "*Kat,*" they said together. Then, "*senk, sis, set, uit, nef, dis.*"

"That makes 10," said Mirlande. To which Fabi responded, "*Anko,*" do it "again."

They played another round. "Don't pull," Mirlande

teased.

When Fabi lost interest, Mirlande taught her *Lalin ak Soley*, the hand-clapping game. Fabi giggled with each palm strike. When that was done, she leaned in and nuzzled against Mirlande's chest. Mirlande melted.

Meanwhile, Charlie was pitching Sister Alouette on the possibility of doing a long-form story about *Nouri*, which in English means "nourished."

The Globe was one of the few regional powerhouse papers that continued to publish a Sunday magazine, he explained, which afforded the length and layout needed to tell big, important stories. The format lent itself to strong prose and powerful photography.

"*Nouri's* work is an important story," he said, turning on his story-pitch charm. "A major story in a major American newspaper could spur donations. I can't promise that, but it often happens that way with important stories."

"What we do here is by the Grace of God. He determines what's important, my son," said the Mother Superior.

Despite her warm smile, she looked stern in a plain white cotton sari with one blue stripe, the style identified with Mother Teresa.

"We survive on donations. The Lord steers caring people our way."

Charlie nodded. "Just like he sent me to you," he said, hoping that would somehow close the deal.

"I feel your heart, my son, I do. But we don't allow photography or interviews at the compound. There are too many ways that stories and photographs can be abused."

She explained that unscrupulous charities often purloin

such photos from orphanages and use them for their own fundraising. "Only the smallest fraction of our population here is ever eligible for an adoption," she said. "Much of the world doesn't understand."

Charlie said he would take pains to describe *Nouri* accurately and make the world understand.

Sister Alouette was unmoved.

"We exist to nurse these children back to health and return them to their families," she said. "Families who love them but cannot care for them. Some will go home only to be back with us within a month or two. Some go back and forth many times. All are vulnerable. We protect them. These children, in their vulnerability, have a humble openness to the message of Jesus and the gospel."

Charlie thanked her for considering the request, but inside his head he heard: "No cha--ching! No Sale," the very words that a music writer he knew used to say on the phone to nine out of 10 aspiring bands seeking coverage. "No cha-ching! No Sale." Snarky, but frank.

It had rained lightly. Now, as Charlie, Corinne and Miri departed *Nouri* there was a rainbow in the distance arcing over dripping palms.

"How'd it go with Fabi?" Corinne asked.

"She's a charmer," said Mirlande. "Sat on my lap. We played with my hair. When I had to leave, I hated putting her down."

Turning to Charlie she asked, "How'd it go with Sister Alouette?"

"No cha-ching," Charlie shrugged. "No Sale!"

CHAPTER FIFTY-NINE
Malhonnete

To show his appreciation for Kenley Claud's role in the arrest of Prantout, JB invited the Haitian lawman for a lavish lunch at Wahoo Bay, an oceanfront resort on National Route 1, 45 minutes north of Port-au-Prince.

Situated between the rugged Matheux Mountains and the turquoise expanse of Gonave Bay, the beach club offers a level of luxury rarely seen in Haiti. For their celebratory meal, JB ordered the Wahoo sampler, an over-the-top combination of rock lobsters, goat, pork, shrimp and plantain chips. At $125, it cost more than Claud earns in a month. They washed it down with Presidente, the imported beer from neighboring Dominican Republic.

"*Sante, zanmi*," said JB, lifting his glass. "Your role was crucial."

Their table wore a block-print cloth in red, blue and yellow. The chairs were straight-back, with wooden spindles and swirls of thick black wire. Gauzy, azure curtains hung from the porch rafters and were knotted at the bottom to curtail their fluttering. The breeze off the bay smelled alternately sweet and sour.

"Sitting here it's hard to believe that Cité Soleil is less than an hour away," said JB.

"Sitting in Cité Soleil," said Claud, "it's hard to believe this place exists at all."

The two talked shop as they tackled the mountain

of food.

They'd driven to Wahoo Bay in JB's borrowed Exterra and been forced to detour because a hijacked fuel truck was blocking the highway. A Port-au-Prince gang affiliated with the confederation run by Griye had thrown up a roadblock and fired semi-automatic weapons in the air to force the scared trucker to stop. Masked gunmen pistol-whipped him. Then one of the thugs took the driver's seat and commandeered the 18-wheeler. Dozens of gangbangers on motorcycles and garishing ATVs surrounded it. Like a scene from Mad Max, they whooped, hollered and popped wheelies as they inched the seized truck to an exit ramp where they held it, demanding hundreds of thousands of dollars from the company that owned it.

There were no police in sight.

"*Pa deranje tet ou* - Don't trouble yourself. None would be coming," said Claud. "The *baz* have more powerful guns, better motos, more fuel." Dependent on the resources of an increasingly depleted state, and faced with that fire-power imbalance, he said, most police interventions are untenable.

"So rule by gangs has replaced the rule of law?"

"What can I say? That's the third hijacking this week," said Claud.

"Do you ever get demoralized in this place where honest cops like you are underappreciated? Do you ever want to get out of here, like to work in the States? I could put out the word and add a strong letter of commendation. Claud put a hand on his heart and rocked forward deferentially. "I feel you," he said. "I thank you. But my place is here. Making Haiti a better place has to happen from here.

But I thank you, *zanmi*."

"Okay," said JB, holding a spicy shrimp by the tail and breaking off the plump part in his mouth. "But if that ever changes, you let me know, OK?"

"Will you and Mirlande be going home now?"

"Not yet," JB mumble-chewed. He filled Claud in about the Haitian-American doctor strangled in Hinche.

"When?"

"Pretty recently."

"Means, motive and opportunity," said Claud parroting every homicide investigator's mantra. "You got this *zanmi*?"

"Not quite. A friend of the victim is pointing me to a suspect she says has a motive."

"And what do you think?"

"Too early to say. Just getting started. I interviewed the one she suspects – a prelim - and I sensed deception."

"*Malhonnete?*"

"Not exactly dishonest. He lied about keeping me waiting. That's not a big deal. Everybody does that. But I asked him about a missing journal, and I didn't trust his answer. There was something off about his body language and the way he said he knew that Sanctis was gay."

"The murdered man was *masisi*?"

"Yes. My reporter friend Charlie tells me Sanctis complained to a gay rights group in P-a-P that he was being harassed at work. If Pinay is the only one at work who knew he was gay, that kinda throws a spotlight on him."

"Who?"

"Pinay."

"Reynard Pinay, the head of Notre Dames des

Miracles?" said Claud.

JB looked puzzled. "Yeah, that Reynard Pinay. The nurses there call it Notre Dame des Douleurs."

"We know of him," said Claud. "A bit player. The BLTS picked up intel on him as part of a Cité Soleil surveillance of a gang leader named Evans Legros. Legros is hardcore. Kidnapping for ransom, serious drug dealing; enforcement-racket violence. Pinay feeds Legros' pill-peddling hustle, but he's too small time for us to bother with."

"If he murdered a U.S. citizen to cover up the theft of U.S. medical aid to Haiti," said JB, "you can believe we're gonna bother."

CHAPTER SIXTY
Don't burn yourself

It was late one morning when the small procession passed by Charlie's apartment. It marched to the beat of a *tanbou* drum and carried a wreath of blue and white daisies. The destination of the marchers was a ceremony on Hinche's sweltering place publique. There, on a central pedestal inlaid with black tiles is the bust of Charlemagne Peralte, the Hinche-born nationalist leader who fiercely opposed the occupation of Haiti by U.S. Marines, which began in 1915 and lasted for 19 years.

"Let's follow them," said Charlie, turning from the window to face Corinne. "It'll be interesting." They threw on their shoes and rushed to catch up with the group that had grown to 20 people.

At the spot where the celebrants laid the wreath, they extolled Peralte's persistence and bravery. Charlie and Corinne stood at the back of the pack. His hands were on her sunbaked shoulders. He lifted them theatrically, touched her shoulders again, pressed his tongue to the roof of his mouth and made a sizzling sound. "*Sssss.* Ouch!" he teased.

"Don't burn yourself," she said and leaned back playfully.

The first speaker reminded the group of Peralte's life story as a career army officer during a period of intense political and social instability. Between 1911 and 1915, seven Haitian presidents were assassinated or overthrown, sparking U.S. fears that the turmoil would invite foreign rule of Haiti by its former colonizer, France, or by Germany, whose merchants had established a trading network in the country. It was a period of instability much like the uprising against Moise and threats to his life.

At 29, Peralte was Haiti's military commander in Leogane, where, in 1915, U.S. Marines disarmed the town as part of their mission to replace Haiti's army with a U.S.-controlled Gendarmerie. A defiant Peralte refused to surrender and was fired by Haitian President Phillipe Sudre Dartiguenave, a U.S. puppet.

The next speaker, a professor of political science at Universite Quisqueya in Port-au-Prince, said the Marines were sent by U.S. President Woodrow Wilson because he feared that European interests were displacing America's political and commercial influence. One of their first moves, he said, was transferring government funds from Haiti's National Bank to a bank in New York City, ostensibly for "safe keeping."

Overseen by a young assistant secretary of the Navy named Franklin Delano Roosevelt, Haiti's Constitution was rewritten to give foreigners the right to own land for the first time since the country's independence.

"Talk about a 'New Deal,'" Corinne said sarcastically. "No wonder so many here don't trust you Yanks."

Disgusted by the occupation, Peralte returned to his family's land in Hinche and organized a militia to confront the Marines. Known as the *Cacos*, that effective guerilla army forced the U.S. to commit more troops and armaments, including planes to bomb *Caco* strongholds.

In the end, Peralte was betrayed by one of his officers,

who led two white Marines disguised in black face into a rebel camp near Grand-Riviere du Nord. They shot Peralte at close range as he sat by a campfire.

"The next day," said the professor, "U.S. authorities photographed Peralte's corpse lashed to an unhinged door with Haiti's flag draped around his head. Thousands of copies of the photo were dropped over Haiti's cities and towns as a warning to others not to resist."

In 1934, then U.S. president FDR returned to Haiti to recognize the country's independence and ordered the Marines withdrawn. Peralte's remains, which had been hastily covered over by his assassins, were exhumed and reburied with honors in a state funeral as a martyr for Haiti's sovereignty. To this day, Peralte's mustachioed face appears on Haiti's five, ten and fifty centime coins.

"I knew the name, of course, but I didn't know all the gory details. What a saga," said Charlie. "It's hot as hell out here on this plaza, but I am glad we followed these wreath-layers."

Parched and hungry, Corinne and Charlie returned to the apartment. They peeled off their sweaty clothes and hung them to dry. Sitting crossed-legged in their underwear, they cut a melon and shared it. Charlie licked the juice off Corinne's lips. She slurped another bite and gave him a long, wet kiss.

"That's a proper snog," she said.

Charlie reached around and unfastened her bra. She slid off her bottoms.

"Will you help me with a bucket bath?"

"I would be honored," he said, bowing theatrically. "You get the stuff."

Bucket baths were a first-responder thing, meant for all those Godforsaken places where water is scarce and plumbing non-existent. Corinne reached under the bed for a round plastic wash tub, 15 inches deep, yellow, and about the circumference of a café tabletop.

He filled two pitchers with water. The first, with non-potable tap water for sudsing; the second, with bottled water for rinsing. He saved some for them to drink.

Corinne stepped into the center of the bucket. "Don't wet my hair. I'm not going to shampoo. I'd never get the soap out."

"Certainly, Milady" said Charlie, continuing his cartoon chivalry.

Tipping the spout of the first pitcher over Corinne's right shoulder he slowly poured out half of the water, which despite being room temperature gave her a chill. He reached over her other shoulder and dripped out the rest.

Glistening in a skim coat of water, she luxuriated as he soaped her up and down. The back of her neck, under her breasts, between her legs, over her knees, down her shins and between her toes.

Charlie had stripped naked to assist with the bath. His appreciation for Corinne was evident.

"Okay," she said. "Ready to rinse."

Charlie took the second pitcher and stepped into the tub behind her. He splayed his feet on the outside of hers, pressed against her and sent down a trickle of clean, clear water. It ran over her clavicle and sluiced into the hollow between her breasts.

"More," said Corinne.

"I know," he said. "But we've only got this one pitcher. I'm trying to make it last. Gotta go slow, get the soap off."

"Well, ducky, it's a good thing I shaved," she said, looking back flirtatiously. Charlie smiled and let loose another miserly ounce of water.

Looking down over Corinne's shoulders he watched as a rivulet of rinse water rushed through the tunnel of her cleavage, forked left and right at her belly button and disappeared between her legs.

She shook her shoulders and brushed away the remaining suds.

"This is it. Last call for alcohol," said Charlie as he poured the remainder of the pitcher over Corinne. "*No mas.*"

He put his hands on her hips and nuzzled her neck. She smelled of Palmolive and the sweet-and-sour scent of an unwashed scalp. He nibbled her earlobe and whispered, "I have to have you."

They toweled off and moved to the bed, skirting a small puddle at their feet. Charlie wanted nothing more than to crawl inside her.

But first - with his mouth on her breasts, her stomach, her thighs - he made a meal of her.

CHAPTER SIXTY-ONE
As God is my witness

Freshly showered and barefoot in a tan, linen dress, Mirlande took her breakfast coffee from the Pandiassou's room service tray. Her hair was wet and wrapped in a towel turban. She clicked on the TV and was watching CNN when a naked, sleepy JB stumbled past her to go pee and shower. He was done in a blink and came back with a towel over one shoulder, and another wrapped around his waist. He hopped from foot to foot, banging on his temples with the heels of his hands to clear water from his ears.

"The lead story while you were in the shower was about a scheme to transfer $80 million in Haitian government funds to an account controlled solely by JoMo."

JB was dressing and thinking about his next move in the Sanctis investigation when another story came on the screen.

"The number of children from outside the U.S. adopted by Americans continued its steady decline, down 66 percent from 1999, the earliest year for which comprehensive comparative data are available," the announcer said, citing a Pew Research Center report.

The study attributed the decline to a significant drop in adoptions from the five countries where most international adoptees are born: China; Russia; Guatemala; South Korea and Ethiopia.

"You don't see Haiti on that list," said JB. "Our culture

is different."

"Certainly, our orphanages are," said Mirlande. "I haven't had a chance to tell you about the day I spent at *Nouri* with Charlie and Corinne. It was amazing. There is this little girl. Her name is Fabi."

Mirlande told JB about the games she played with Fabi and the child's tragic backstory.

"Her mother was killed at a demonstration. Her father is missing and presumed dead. She's adorable and smart and spunky despite all that she has suffered. She's got no one waiting for her on the outside. She deserves to be loved. We deserve to be parents."

The weight of Mirlande's words cut through the TV's noise. "Are you talking about adoption?"

"That's what I want to talk about."

"I know adopting that little girl sounds right, like the thing we should try to do, adopting a child from Haiti. But her people are here. They're not hyphenated Haitians in the diaspora like us. We'd be taking her away from her culture and everything she knows. Besides, I thought *Nouri* does not allow adoptions."

"She's four and has no people here. She has so much to learn about the world, with or without us. We know her culture. We could nurture it while giving her opportunities she would never have here."

"She has no other family?"

"According to the Mother Superior, apparently not. Even if we are approved to go forward, Fabi's suitability for adoption would be determined by the *Institut du Bien-Etre Social et de Recherches*. They'd conduct an exhaustive search for next of kin."

"You've already looked into this?"

"I have."

"I want to talk about it as God is my witness," said JB, reaching for his shoes. "But at the moment I am late for a meeting with Kenley. I promise you, Miri. When I get back we'll give it undivided attention."

He pecked her on the cheek and made for the door. Hearing it slam, her cop's-wife brain took over and she worried about all that could happen to prevent JB from ever keeping that promise.

For their meeting this time, JB and Claud rendez-voused on the outskirts of Mirebalais near its cholera treatment center, a Lotto stand, and a line-up of skinny shacks selling *fritai* and *Pa Padap* – fried dough balls and the re-charge cards for cell phones.

"*Bonjou*, Kenley!" said JB.

"*Bonjou zanmi mwen.*"

"You already know why Pinay is our target. We need to talk about a search warrant," said JB. "The missing jour-nal, Pinay's role in the chain of custody, his deceptive an-swers when I interviewed him, the severed lock I saw on his office floor … all are probable-cause triggers."

"*Dako,*" said Claud.

"We've got two locations we want to search, his office and his house."

"When we serve the warrant, I can bring the crew we used for Prantout - the two men and the woman – you remember - all special-forces trained. Where first, office or house?"

"I've been thinking about that," said JB. "We don't want to make a public spectacle on a public street. That could draw too much attention. I'm thinking, we first go to the office. Pinay's got locked cabinets in there. That's as good a place as any to hide the journal. We may not even need to go to the house."

"Sounds good, *zanmi mwen*. But a question: If Pinay wanted to keep the journal from seeing the light of day, wouldn't he have just destroyed it?"

"Yes. But if he kept it, there would be a reason."

CHAPTER SIXTY-TWO
Voila

Having made their search plan on a Monday, Claud said he would need a day or two to get the warrant.

"So we'll greenlight the operation for Wednesday or Thursday," said JB.

"*Pa gen pwoblem,*" said Claud.

In the interim, Corinne had checked in with her colleagues at Saj Fanm and was stunned by the news from the hospital's grapevine.

The hothead porter who had argued with Sanctis had recently missed two days of work without explanation, so Pinay sent a supervisor to find out why.

The supervisor found the porter's lifeless body hanging from a tree outside his shack. Beneath the dangling feet lay an overturned stool in a puddle of urine.

This time, local police took an interest. They thoroughly searched the house and found Sanctis' red-covered journal inside a cupboard. At the back of the journal were the jagged stubs of two pages that had been torn out.

For police from the local garrison, the apparent suicide was a breakthrough that connected all the dots. The porter's noisy threat against Sanctis – "Shut your mouth or I'll shut it for you, old man" - established the bad blood between them. The suicide, police believed, was prompted either by remorse after the murder, or some unknowable trigger in the psyche of the unstable porter.

"*Ak vwala*, said the local police commander: "Case closed."

On hospital letterhead, Pinay typed up a summary of the police findings, which described the discovery of the journal and used capital letters to identify the porter as "THE KILLER OF DR. SANCTIS BEAUVOIR." Pinay ordered his secretary to deliver copies to every hospital department.

A seething Corinne called Charlie immediately.

"You won't believe this," she said, and breathlessly filled him in.

"Wow," said Charlie.

"Wow? That's it? Wow? Okay, Charlie. Certainly, you have to tell JB about this. I just hope we're all seeing through this the same way."

CHAPTER SIXTY-THREE
"You found what you found."

JB, Claud and their A-team arrived at Notre Dame des Miracles at 8:30 the next morning and found the hospital grounds plastered with dozens of copies of Pinay's summary taped and tacked on walls and trees.

"What now *zanmi*?" asked Claud.

JB looked annoyed. He tore down one of the summaries and studied it. "A little too neat, don'tcha think?" he said. "Kind of a convenient suicide scene for Pinay, isn't it? Besides, why would just two pages be torn out and who did that? The chance that the porter spoke English is slim. How would he even know what was written on them?"

If Pinay thought the announcement would remove suspicion from him, he'd miscalculated, thought JB. He instructed his plainclothes team to carry on as planned. They could expect to find Pinay in his office at 9.

Claud and the special-ops-trained trio wore an assortment of jeans and *pepe* - the ubiquitous, plain and designer-logo tee shirts, which come from the U.S. in huge bales and are stylishly refashioned into hip, contemporary styles by Haitian tailors. Despite the rising humidity, JB wore a coat and tie for the official business. All five carried concealed pistols.

On JB's signal, the men split up. One went behind Pinay's office building to keep watch on the rear exit. The other positioned himself between Pinay's office wing and the shed where the pills and supplies were stored. The woman, who would be pulled in to help with the office search, sat on a bench outside the *salle maternite*, which gave her sightlines in all directions.

JB and Claud approached the desk of Pinay's receptionist at the stroke of 9.

"He's … "

JB finished her sentence. "Yeah, not in, we know. Seems he never is. But let's just see."

He and Claud breezed past her and opened the door to Pinay's office.

Startled, Pinay turned quickly and slammed shut a filing cabinet drawer. He didn't have time to lock it.

"You again? This is ridiculous. You should know the local police have solved the murder of Dr. Beauvoir. They've closed the case. What do you want from me now? Who is this?"

"This is Kenley Claud of the Haitian National Police. He's helping me."

"Helping you with what? What do you want?"

"I'm still looking for Sanctis' journal, or maybe just two pages from it now."

"I told you I never saw it."

"Yeah, but all of Sanctis' possessions passed through you before they were sent back to his mother. You told me that. Maybe somebody grabbed the journal without your knowledge."

"And left two torn-out pages behind? Preposterous. Don't be ridiculous?"

"Maybe someone was setting you up. Stranger things have happened."

"Well, that didn't happen."

"How can you be so sure?"

"It didn't happen."

"Then you won't mind if Officer Claud and I have a look around. Can I search? Do I have your consent, your permission?"

"You most certainly do not."

"I thought you might say that, so we brought this." He handed Pinay the search warrant. While Pinay looked it over, JB and Claud snapped on surgical gloves. The first place JB searched was the filing cabinet drawer that Pinay had shut so abruptly. Nothing in there looked like torn journal pages. And because Pinay had taken pains to make his phony ledger look no different than the accurate one, nothing else stood out.

JB used a small flashlight to illuminate the corners of the dimly lit room. He saw Pinay's filthy lab coat hanging on a nail. His eyes fell on a hard-sided, foam-lined suitcase of the type used to transport musical instruments.

He released the spring-loaded latches, heard them snap, and was startled by what he saw - four life-size examples of early-stage embryos, and five of fetal development.

"Are they … real?"

Pinay was seething. "Polyurethane, you damned fool. It's a teaching tool called the Carnegie stages. Named for the U.S. institute that began classifying embryos more than 100 years ago. But I'm not here to educate you, and you are clearly wasting my time."

JB refused to be baited. In fact, as Pinay became more agitated, JB became more methodical. He swept a gloved hand under the seat cushion of a beat-up armchair. He looked inside JB's mini fridge and saw only an overripe mango, a pitcher of water and ice-cube tray. He looked in the other drawers.

"There is nothing for you to find here," said Pinay. "You need to leave."

"We'll be the ones deciding when it's time to leave," JB said calmly as he carried on. He went to the spot on the floor where he had seen the small heart-shaped padlock. It was still there, obscured by the drape's hem. He used the tip of a ballpoint pen to lift it and dropped it into an envelope marked "evidence."

"Evidence of what?" scoffed Pinay. "Evidence that someone missed the waste basket with whatever that is?"

JB turned to a bookshelf. Maybe the missing pages were tucked among its dusty volumes. As he reached for the first book, the hospital lights flickered, flared and died. Total darkness. Inside Pinay's lair, JB's flashlight cast the only light. They pulled back the heavy drapes to let in sunlight.

Claud stepped closer to Pinay, punched a number on his cell phone and called for the assistance of the female agent. She arrived, donned gloves, fitted on her headlamp and joined in the search. She started at one end of the bookshelf, peeking between its volumes. JB worked from the opposite end.

When the female agent turned to speak to Claud, the shaft of light from her headlamp played across the room and glinted off a lineup of liquid-filled specimen jars on a high shelf.

She stood on a chair for a better look.

When her beam fell upon the third jar in the line, she yelped: "*Je yo.*" *Je yo!*" – the eyes!

At the bottom of the jar were two ragged orbs. The irises were brown. The whites had turned a cloudy gray and were shot through with thin red threads.

The agent gripped the jar carefully as she came down off the chair. She placed it in the center of Pinay's desk.

"What's this?" demanded JB. "Another teaching tool?"

Pinay said nothing.

JB crouched, putting himself eye-to-eye with the seated doctor.

"What have we found here?" he demanded.

Pinay stared blankly.

"What's this? *Kisa sa ye?*" JB demanded, his voice rising.

"You found what you found," said Pinay. "You found what you found."

CHAPTER SIXTY-FOUR
Well, Bob's your uncle!

JB and Mirlande were already at Charlie's apartment that night when Corinne walked in carrying two bags of takeout from Eben-Ezer, a Hinche bar-resto near the hospital.

"Thanks," said Charlie, making room on the table. The sumptuous spread included Creole rice, tangy *pikliz*, grilled goat, red cabbage, fried plantains and the house specialty, fresh papaya juice.

JB was in mid-narration: "So he looks up at me and says, 'You found what you found.' That's it. 'You found what you found.' Unbelievable."

"Corinne," said Charlie, "you have got to hear this from the beginning. JB please start again."

JB poured himself some papaya juice, turned to face Corinne and caught her up on the story.

"We executed a search on Pinay's office this morning. … Looking for pages from Sanctis' journal, which we didn't find. But there in the open, tucked away on a shelf inside a specimen jar, we found two eyes that looked to be human."

"Eyes! Holy shit! You found eyes. Sanctis' eyes! Well, Bob's your uncle!" cried Corinne. "There you go. Journal pages or not, you've got the sodding bugger."

JB hesitated. Charlie jumped in: "But there's a problem."

"What problem? The problem that it's 100 percent

obvious that Pinay was involved in Sanctis' murder? That's your problem?" said Corinne. "You've got him. Are you daft?"

"Tell her," said Charlie.

"It's a quality-of-evidence thing," said JB. "The jar with the eyes is filled with formalin, a preservative. It breaks down DNA, preventing a clearcut analysis from the sample. How do we prove they're Sanctis' eyes?"

"Are you winding me up? Of course, they're Sanctis' eyes. Pinay's an obstetrician. What in bloody hell is he doing with eyes in a specimen jar?"

"I'm with you," said JB. "I am. Truly. But we'll have to convince a jury. Pinay's on notice now that he's our target. If we nail him on easily challenged evidence, his lawyers are going to tear us up in court, if we even get that far. Believe it or not, it's not an open-and-shut case. That doesn't mean we won't get him. In fact, Kenley Claud has an idea."

CHAPTER SIXTY-FIVE
Now or never

Having outlined the evidentiary hurdle over the take-out dinner at Charlie's apartment, JB returned to his hotel and the next morning called Claud to discuss a possible workaround involving the gang leader Evans.

"We've known about Pinay's connection to Evans for a while," said Claud. "In the grand scheme of our work on narcotics, chasing after stolen patent medicines peddled for domestic use is too *ensiyifyan* - insignificant - for us to pursue. Murder of course is a different story.

"Betraying people when it's expedient is how Evans operates. So what if we make an approach? Make it clear, with whatever assurances he needs, that he is not our target. Then he might see it as in his interest to do a favor for me, a Haitian drug agent. But only if his goose is not getting cooked."

"What sort of favor? What can he do for us? Can he lead us to Sanctis' killer?"

"He'll know what happened or make it his business to find out. We've just got to get him talking. Let him believe he is earning credit with the drug police who can do him the most harm in the long run, my unit, the BLTS. Let him think he's paying it forward. A favor for us today in exchange for leniency down the road. A corrupt bargain is the way of the world here."

"My friend Charlie works with a fixer who has good contacts with Evans. Charlie calls her Maffi Tattoo. She could set up a meeting. Might be better coming from her than if we go straight at Evans ourselves," said JB.

"Can we trust her?"

"We'll pay her for her time, same as a journalist would. She'll be working for us."

"That's no guarantee."

"Charlie says he trusts her with his life."

So JB brought in Charlie, who brought in Maffi, who set up a meeting with Evans at the Cité Soleil soccer field.

The lawmen, the journalist and the fixer were all present, and Claud took the lead. He recapped the timeline of Sanctis' murder. He said they had Pinay in their crosshairs. "What can you add," he asked Evans.

"My condolences," said Evans, playing it cute and triggering JB's anger.

"Listen, asshole. *Fout ou*! Fuck you! If it was up to me, I'd roll you up right now. I promised Sanctis' mother that I would get justice for her son, not impunity for his killers. You better provide some answers."

"To what? What do you think I know?"

"Let's start with who did it. We believe Pinay was involved. But he's basically a coward. Cold-blooded murder is something he would outsource."

"You're not coming after me for any of this, and you'll put that in writing in an immunity memo?"

"Yes. We don't think you had anything to do with it," said Claud. "But we think you know who did."

Evans stared at his shoes and said nothing, gaming out the moves of this chess match in his head.

"The one you want, the one who did it is dead," said Evans. "Pinay hired two from my crew for the hit. Two who thought they were big enough to operate on their own. I knew nothing about it," he said, weaving his alibi. "The one who strangled the doctor died in a motorcycle accident while transporting the pills."

"Isn't that convenient," said JB.

"Yeah," said Evans. "Conveniently true."

"He hired two?" said Claud.

"One was the killer," said Evans. "The other, an accomplice, who went along as backup."

"He will corroborate what you are saying?" said JB.

"He will if you grant me immunity and cut him a deal. What is he looking at? Felony murder for participating. In exchange for his testimony against Pinay, you could charge him as a lesser accessory and recommend a reduced sentence. If I can promise him short time, I can make him cooperate." Evans negotiated like a seasoned jailhouse lawyer.

JB hated the idea of cutting this thug a deal. But he knew a pair of eyes in a specimen jar, with no DNA proof, wouldn't cut it. The eyes, plus the testimony of a co-conspirator who was present at the murder, might just get the arrogant Pinay what he deserved.

"Okay. Where do we find the backup guy?" said JB. "How do we know he's not already in the wind?"

"You put his deal in writing, mine too, and I'll deliver him," said Evans, who suddenly stepped across the circle of the conversation and stood between Maffi and the lawmen. He put a hand on the back of Maffi's neck. "As a little insurance, your friend Maffi can stay with us until …"

"What the fuck?" said Maffi, twisting to escape Evans' grip.

"Hey!" Charlie blurted. "Leave her alone. She's not part of this."

"Just like me. Not part of this," Evans grinned. "And who the fuck are you?"

JB moved forcefully between Evans and Maffi.

"Enough! You're not taking her. That's not happening," he growled. "You think you have the upper hand. You don't. Touch her again, threaten her, and any prayer you have of immunity is gone. We'll charge you as the mastermind."

"But that's not true."

"Suddenly you care about the truth? Watch me make it stick."

"It doesn't have to get that far," said Claud. "Meet us here tomorrow. Same time as today. Bring the backup. We'll take his statement. Bring some proof that he's telling the truth. If it's as you say it is, we'll have enough to reel in Pinay. If you breathe a word of this to him, you're finished. You know, he will finger you for the murder, and it'll be his testimony against yours, the respected doctor versus the Cité Soleil gangbanger. You want a deal - *Li nan kounye a oswa pajanm* – it's now or never."

CHAPTER SIXTY-SIX
Help me!

The backup's story was as advertised. To prove that he was present when Sanctis was killed, he brought along the flat glass imaging filter from Sanctis' purloined telescope.

The backup told the lawmen that he had witnessed Sanctis's murder and mutilation but played no active role. He said they had grabbed the scope as an afterthought and ended up selling it for scrap. He kept the eight-inch-diameter glass disk imaging filter because it worked nicely for cutting lines of coke.

In truth, the backup was much more than an incidental eyewitness. He was a scary, motorcycle-riding co-conspirator, whose intimidating presence aided and advanced the homicide. The lawmen could hook him for that alone, and make it stick. But they chose to set that aside to take down Pinay, the central figure who they believed had bought and paid for the kill.

The plan was to have Evans lure Pinay to a lunch meeting at the Wozo Plaza Hotel near Mirebalais, telling him he wanted to talk about adjusting their pilfered-pill deal.

"If you get there first, take the table furthest from the street," Evans instructed when he called Pinay.

"I've been visited by the FBI," said the doctor.

"All the more reason we need to talk and get our stories straight. If you sense you are being followed, abort the meeting. Text my cell with that word, *avot*," said Evans.

Pinay feared Evans and was relieved that the meeting would be in a public place. The well-known, pastel-painted hotel sits halfway between Port-au-Prince and Hinche. Pinay felt safer meeting there. Alone in the woods with a thug like Evans, or in the Cité slums, anything could happen.

Still, Pinay was apprehensive. Evans did business with Pinay but usually avoided direct contact with him. Now all of a sudden he wanted a meeting. Why? Maybe he was still smarting over that load of pills that was lost when the courier's motorcycle swerved off the mountain road? How did he want to change the terms of their arrangement? Pinay's mind was racing.

A taxi driver dropped him at the hotel and parked in the shade of towering palms, where he planned to snooze on the back seat with a straw boater shading his eyes until Pinay was ready to leave.

The hotel's grounds were immaculate. Box-cut hedges lined the paved walkways, which were inlaid with randomly shaped slate tiles. The rooms, which were arranged in bungalow clusters around the central swimming pool, were mauve with pastel green trim. On his long walk from the street to the back of the hotel's outdoor restaurant, Pinay was self-conscious about how he looked, with his hobbled gait spotlighted in the sun.

As instructed, he took a table under a white awning furthest from the hotel's entrance. The tablecloth was forest green. The waitress wore a white server's dress with black buttons down the front.

"*Yon bagay pou bwe?*" she inquired.

"Just water," he said, "*Yon gwo boutey.* A big bottle. Someone is joining me."

Minutes passed. It was almost noon. The restaurant was empty except for two guests who lingered over their late breakfast. The surface of the pool shimmered aquamarine. No breeze. Brutal heat. Where was Evans?

Pinay was about to dial the gangbanger's number when he looked up and saw Claud approaching rapidly. He swiveled and saw JB coming at him from the opposite side. Panicked, he pushed back from the table and ran as best he could in the direction of his taxi driver, whom he was awkwardly trying to dial.

"*Rete! Ede mwen!*" – Stop! Help me! Pinay shouted, drawing the attention of the hotel's security staff. JB flashed his badge and the private security guards stood back.

Twisting to avoid a chaise longue that lay askew on the deck, Pinay slipped and toppled face-first into the pool. His arms flailed. He spluttered helplessly and sunk, pulled down by the weight of his heavy orthopedic boot.

JB and Claud waited for him to surface, but he did not. Pinay was drowning.

There was a life ring attached to a cord at the far end of the pool. Claud ran and got it as Pinay surfaced with a gasp and immediately sunk down again.

"We're losing him," said JB, tossing the ring repeatedly. "He's too panicky to grab it!"

The lawmen had kicked off their shoes and were ready to plunge in when JB spotted a long-handled pool skimmer hanging from two hooks. If he could just get the basket end under Pinay, he might be able to pry him to the surface. He'd have to move quickly before the hapless doctor inhaled half the pool.

Looking down into the deep end, JB saw little more than a blur. He poked with the cumbersome skimmer but couldn't make effective contact. Hand over hand he pulled the skimmer back and tried again. Precious seconds were ticking by. No luck. He retrieved it a third time and tore out its net, leaving just the metal loop.

Using the loop to snag one of Pinay's legs, he dragged his limp body to the side of the pool. He and Claud pulled him onto the deck. He looked lifeless. Hotel security called for an ambulance.

JB placed his ear near Pinay's mouth and nose. He heard gurgling. He tipped back Pinay's head to open his airway and rolled him onto his side. For what felt like an eternity there was no response.

"*Kaka!*" JB shouted. Shit!

Claud rolled him onto his back and with the heel of his hand on the middle of Pinay's breastbone began chest compressions, 100 per minute, the way he had been taught. After 30 compressions he leaned over Pinay and delivered two mouth-to-mouth breaths.

He was just about to resume the compressions when suddenly Pinay's chest heaved. His body convulsed and he vomited out a stream of chlorinated water. He retched and shot out another stream. He was dazed but starting to breathe.

JB and Claud hauled him onto a deck chair. They threw him a towel to dry his face.

JB was still barefoot when he said, "Dr. Reynard Pinay, this is Haitian National Police agent Kenley Claud. He is placing you under arrest for the contract murder of Dr. Sanctis Beauvoir. You have a right to remain silent.

Anything you say may be used against you in a U.S. court where you will be tried."

"Get on your knees. Put your hands behind your head. Lace your fingers," said Claud as he slipped on the cuffs.

Pinay muttered something indecipherable that sounded like a prayer.

CHAPTER SIXTY-SEVEN
New beginnings

JB's first call was to his office in Miami to start the ball rolling on Pinay's extradition. He told his boss that "facts on the ground" had necessitated a quick arrest, which was why he hadn't checked in with him first to get a go-ahead.

"You had told me this was an assessment," said the boss, sounding peeved. "What happened?"

"It was. Then I had a chance to take him down quickly and quietly. With a warrant. A clean arrest. I'll put it all in my after-action report."

"I'll be expecting that."

To assert "extraterritorial jurisdiction" as substantiation for its extradition request, the U.S. Justice Department would need to show that the murder was a cover-up to shield Pinay's thefts of the U.S. foreign aid. After that, DOJ's Office of International Affairs would forward the matter to the State Department. State would send the paperwork to the U.S. Embassy in Port-au-Prince, which would present it to Haitian authorities for approval or rejection. Even in a justice system not plagued by Haiti's routine dysfunction, the proceedings could take months, even years. During that time, Pinay, who refused to waive his extradition, would be imprisoned in Haiti, where jailbreaks and corruptible guards are common, and he would play the odds.

JB's next call was to Jesula Beauvoir, Sanctis' mother.

"Mrs. Beauvoir, this is Special Agent Jean Belizaire, calling you from Haiti. Please forgive the abruptness of this communication but I knew you would want to know right away. We have made an arrest for the murder of your son. The accused is a senior doctor at the hospital where Sanctis worked. The prosecution will take a while, maybe a long while, but if all goes according to plan he will be tried in the United States. None of this gives you back your son. Nothing can. But it stops his killer from getting away with it. I won't insult you by calling that justice. There is no justice when a parent loses a child. Fairness would be if Sanctis were still alive. That is beyond my ability to deliver. But there will be accountability. I can tell you that I had you in my thoughts the whole time."

"*Bondye bon*" - God is good, said the soft-spoken mother. "*Kouman poum ta remesye-w?*" - How can I ever thank you?"

"Don't thank me. We'll keep you updated on the case."

Through her tears she praised Jesus. Hanging up she said, "God bless you. *Adye.*"

Lastly, JB dialed Charlie. "C-squared, you home?"

"I am."

"I've got news."

"Wait a sec. Corinne's here. I'm putting you on speaker."

"Can you hear me?"

"Go ahead."

"We've arrested Pinay."

Corinne pumped a fist in the air.

"What happened?" said Charlie.

"Long story. I'll tell you when I see you. For the moment at least he's off the street. See you tonight."

Charlie wrapped Corinne in a bear hug. She squeezed back, hard. He was steeling himself to hear, "I told you so," but in his ear she whispered, "Finally."

Before the two couples went their separate ways, Charlie and Corinne had JB and Mirlande over to the Hinche apartment for a farewell dinner. In a tribute to the meal that Sanctis never got to serve, they pulled together a rudimentary soup joumou from ingredients they had on hand.

"It's not New Year's Day," said Charlie. "But with Pinay gone from Notre Dame des Douleurs, it is a new beginning. So, *pou sante ou* – to your health."

Corinne had picked up a bottle of bootleg *kleren*, the crystal clear, high-octane moonshine made from distilled sugar cane. She poured four more shots into the mismatched jelly jars and aimed the next toast at JB.

"There were times when I was insufferable, I know, carping about how slow I thought you moved. Sanctis was a dear friend who meant a lot to me. I should never have doubted your professionalism. Please accept my apology."

JB nodded graciously, made a fist, banged it twice on his chest above his heart and downed the *kleren* in one swig. The three others knocked back their shots too.

Charlie pointed his glass at JB. "Had this thing gone sideways, your ass and your career were on the line."

Stirred by the *kleren*, JB looked back playfully at his butt. "Still here," he joked. "I'll let you know about my career after I get back to Miami."

Even Miri laughed.

"Okay," said Charlie. "Just a couple of questions and then I promise not to speak of Pinay again. Why in the world did that bastard keep the eyes?"

"I wondered about that, too," said JB. "Apparently, it's a superstition thing. When we hauled him away, Pinay kept mumbling something indecipherable. Then I heard him say something about John the Baptist. I thought he was praying, losing his mind. Kenley connected the dots."

Claud had explained that in Haiti, June 24th, the day after the Summer Solstice - a time of change and power - is celebrated as "St. John the Baptist Day." On that day, adherents of Christianity and of Vodou offer prayers and blessings from dawn till dusk. As darkness falls, they set ablaze a massive bonfire into which they toss tangible and figurative symbols of failures, disappointments, lost causes. Believers say the bonfire's ashes have mystical powers which can be used to accomplish one's needs and desires.

"Pinay wanted to throw the eyes into the bonfire and collect the ashes. He thought they'd have magic powers. God knows what for."

"And the missing pages?"

"Never found, although likely earmarked for that bonfire, too, I'd bet."

"What a sick puppy," said Charlie. "Hard to believe he was a physician. I need another shot then to wash away his memory," he said, pouring.

"One more thing, the *bokor* Ti-Jean," said JB, reaching for his case file and putting the *bokor's* mugshot on the table. "There is a record of him entering Haiti, and no record of him leaving. He may have come here to harm Sanctis, but Pinay beat him to it. As he is wanted by the New Orleans police, I doubt he'll be going back there. I told the Nola cops what I had learned and left the case in their hands. Whether they'll pursue him to Haiti is their call."

Mirlande cut a glance at JB. "There's more that we can drink to," she said.

JB refilled the four glasses. "Go ahead," he said. "Tell them."

"JB is going back to the Bureau in Miramar. Back to work," she said. "I'm taking a leave of absence to stay on in Port-au-Prince for a while."

Charlie and Corinne looked concerned. It sounded like a breakup. Mirlande smiled at their concerned faces and went on: "The Mother Superior at *Nouri* said there is a chance, just a chance, that the little girl Fabilene will be eligible for adoption if none of her blood relatives can be located. It is highly unusual. *Nouri* is a feeding program. But the circumstance of her mother's death makes adoption a possibility. I'll stay with my cousin while the *Nouri* staff looks for Fabi's next of kin. The search will be exhaustive. I might have to be here for a few months, waiting. But then …"

"*Bon courage,*" Charlie interrupted, and "*bonne chance.*"

Tipsy and with smiles all around they downed another shot. Then Charlie noticed tears in Corinne's eyes.

She clearly loved little Fabi. Was she upset and jealous that someone else might get her? Or was she just a little bit drunk and overcome by sentiment? Corinne and Mirlande had begun as antagonists, then bonded as each in her own way had been forced to process a painful loss. Charlie watched as Corinne martialed her respect and affection for Mirlande to overcome her first rush of emotion.

"I have news too," he said. "A year ago, I had a call from an editor at Nat Geo about becoming a contributing writer. A guy I worked with at the Globe. Good guy. Great editor. Said I should let him know when I was ready to make a move. Well, I'm ready. I can do the job from anywhere. I called and said that if the offer is still good, I want to do it from Paris. My parents have a friend with an apartment on the *rue des Francs Bourgeois* that I can rent and maybe buy some day."

He reached for Corinne's hand. "I've just gotta convince this lovely lady to come with me."

Corinne smiled but kept silent.

"*Bon chans pou tout moun,*" good luck to us all, said JB, clinking glasses.

Charlie cut a lime and squeezed its juice into the soup joumou. He ladled out four portions.

"To the memory of Dr. Sanctis Beauvoir," he said. "And new beginnings."

EPILOGUE

Two weeks before New Year's Day 2022, Haiti's famous soup joumou was awarded protected, world-heritage status by UNESCO, the United Nations Educational, Scientific and Cultural Organization. The prestigious selection recognizes the velvety, bright-yellow broth as a unifying symbol of Haitian identity throughout the world, and a valuable part of humanity's cultural legacy.

Originally reserved for slaveholders because they deemed the people they enslaved as uncivilized, Haitians took ownership of the soup when they gained independence from France in 1804, "turning it into a symbol of their newly acquired freedom … dignity and resilience," reads the UNESCO citation.

Taking to Twitter to express deep pride, Haiti's former foreign minister Claude Joseph wrote that "Soup Joumou reminds us of the sacrifices our ancestors made to fight slavery and racism on earth" - and of the continuing struggle.

With a history as rich as its savory blend of pureed vegetables and meat, the meal is a "bowl of freedom" said Haiti's Ambassador to UNESCO Dominique Dupuy. "The national soup of the first free Black people in the history of humanity."

For Haitians, being included among the 140 countries already recognized by UNESCO for their unique cultural contributions is an overdue tribute for what they have long brought to the table.

"How," asked Dupuy, "can a country like Haiti, which has contributed so vitally to the history of the world, be missing on a list that showcases the diversity of the world?"

Missing no more.

While every family prepares Soup Joumou a little differently, this authentic recipe covers the basics.

MEAT SEASONING:
1 tsp fresh thyme
2 medium shallots, diced
1 tsp salt
1 tsp pepper
2 chicken bouillon cubes
1 tsp garlic powder
1 tsp onion powder
2 tsp Haitian Epis (blend of onion, garlic, fresh herbs, spices)

MAIN INGREDIENTS:
1lb of beef
½ cup olive oil Water as needed
1 large scallion, diced
½ medium cabbage, diced
1 stalk of celery, diced
Peel and roughly chop:
      2 potatoes
      2 yams
      2 malangas
      2 butternut squash
      2 turnips
      3 medium carrots
16 oz spaghetti, broken, or smaller pasta
1 tbs tomato paste
1 Scotch Bonnet pepper (or to taste)
Chopped parsley

DIRECTIONS

For the meat:

STEP 1: Marinate the meat in the olive oil and seasonings overnight or at least for one hour.

STEP 2: Place the seasoned, marinated meat in a stockpot and cover with water.

STEP 3: Add oil and let boil over high heat. Keep covered until all the water has evaporated.

STEP 4: Uncover, stir and add a few drops of water occasionally to brown the meat as it simmers.

STEP 5: Continue stirring and simmer until browned.

STEP 6: Stir in one tbsp of tomato paste and remove meat from heat.

STEP 7: Transfer meat to dish and reserve pot for vegetables.

For the vegetables:

STEP 1: In a bowl, combine the scallions and half of the cabbage.

STEP 2: In a separate pot, boil water and add the potatoes, yams, malanga, butternut squash, carrots, and turnip.

STEP 3: Cover and cook over high heat for about an hour.

STEP 4: Reduce heat and add the scotch bonnet pepper.

STEP 5: Once the vegetables are fully cooked, remove from the pot and use some of the cooking water to blend the squash into a purée.

STEP 6: Strain the purée through a fine sieve set over a bowl, pressing it through with a spoon or rubber spatula.

STEP 7: For best flavor, pour the cooked vegetables, the squash purée and cooking liquid into the pot that was used to cook the meat.

STEP 8: Add parsley, thyme, and broken spaghetti. STEP 9: Let it all cook until tender.

STEP 10: Add meat into soup.

Serve hot.

Prep time: 1 hour
Cooking time: 2 hours
Serves: 6-8

ACKNOWLEDGMENTS

Haiti, Love and Murder ... In the Season of Soup Joumou owes an enormous debt of gratitude to its generous work-in-progress readers: Philip Aaronson, Charlotte Albright, Thomas Griffin, Alissa Karp, Philip Levien, Zoe Breitstein Matza, Garry Pierre-Pierre, Greg Myre, and Stephen J. Parks. Their wise counsel contributed vast improvements to the final manuscript. A top-to-bottom developmental edit by the brilliant Chris Satullo, with whom I have been privileged to collaborate for three decades, added precision, depth and polish. Hawk-eyed proofreader Eileen Kenna provided a meticulous copy edit. I knew I was in good hands when she told me one day, "You know, I hate a split infinitive," and I thought, "Whoa. Cool. What's a split infinitive?"

For their friendship, love, support, and enduring interest in the story, my thanks to: Jessie Williams Burns of Fanlight Books, Gillian Lancaster, Marsha Aaronson, Kim Alles, Max Breitstein Matza, Daniel Barlava, Tanya Barrientos, Andrew Cassel, Darlene Craviotto, Harvey Finkle, Mark Lyons, Bonnie Prest-Thal, Amelia Powell, Daniel Powell Jr., Herb Swanson, Michael Vitez and Paul Nussbaum.

Above all: Big love and forever thanks to Linda Breitstein, who uplifted me, never lost interest, and had the stamina to read as many drafts as I had the stamina to write.

ABOUT THE AUTHOR

Michael Matza covered immigration, national, international, and metropolitan news for the Philadelphia Inquirer for three decades, serving as bureau chief in the Middle East and in New England. He is a two-time finalist for the Pulitzer Prize for Public Service and has reported from 34 countries across Europe, Asia, Africa and the Americas, including multiple assignments in Haiti. *Haiti, Love and Murder ... In the Season of Soup Joumou* is his first novel. He can be reached at michaelmatza.com

Photo Credit: David Swanson

Made in the USA
Las Vegas, NV
01 May 2023

71362817R00184